The Cat Who Wasn't There

The Cat
Who Wasn't
There

Lilian Jackson Braun

G. P. PUTNAM'S SONS
New York

G. P. Putnam's Sons
Publishers Since 1838
200 Madison Avenue
New York, NY 10016

ISBN 0–399–13780–7

Printed in the United States of America

DEDICATED TO
EARL BETTINGER, THE HUSBAND WHO . . .

The Cat Who Wasn't There

One

In late August, sixteen residents of Moose County, a remote part of the United States 400 miles north of everywhere, traveled to Scotland for a tour of the Western Isles and Highlands, lochs and moors, castles and crofts, firths and straths, burns and braes, fens and bens and glens. Only fifteen of them returned alive, and the survivors straggled home in various states of shock or confusion.

Among the travelers who signed up for the Bonnie Scots Tour were several prominent persons in Pickax City, the county seat. They included the owner of the department store, the superintendent of schools, a young doctor from a distinguished family, the publisher of the local newspaper, the administrator of the public library, and a good-looking, well-built, middle-aged man with a luxuriant pepper-and-salt moustache and drooping eyelids, who happened to be the richest bachelor in Moose County—or in fact the entire northeast central United States.

Jim Qwilleran's wealth was not the result of his own effort but a fluke inheritance. As a journalist, he had been content to pound a beat, churn out copy, and race deadlines for large metropolitan dailies Down Below. (So Pickax folk called the urban areas to the south.) Then fate brought him to Pickax City (population 3,000) and made him heir to the Klingenschoen estate. It was more money than he really wanted. The uncounted millions hung over his head like a dark cloud until he established the Klingenschoen Foundation to dispose of the fortune philanthropically, leaving him free to live in a barn, write a column for the *Moose County Something,* feed and brush his two Siamese cats, and spend pleasant weekends with Polly Duncan, head of the Pickax Public Library.

When the tour to Scotland was proposed, Qwilleran and his feline companions had just returned from a brief sojourn in some distant mountains, a vacation cut short by disturbing news from Pickax. Polly Duncan, while driving home after dark, had been followed by a man in a car without lights, narrowly escaping his clutches. When Qwilleran heard the news, he had a sickening vision of attempted kidnapping; his relationship with Polly was well known in the county, and his millions made him an easy mark for a ransom demand.

Immediately he phoned the Pickax police chief to request protection for Polly. Then, canceling his vacation arrangements, he made the long drive back to Moose County at a speed that discommoded the two yowling passengers in the backseat and alerted the highway patrols of four states. He arrived home Monday noon and dropped off the Siamese and their water dish before hurrying to the Pickax Public Library.

He went on foot, cutting through the woods and approaching the library from the rear. In the parking lot behind the building he recognized Polly's small gray two-door and an elderly friend's ancient navy blue four-door. There was also a maroon car with a Massachusetts license plate that gave him momentary qualms; he had no wish to encounter Dr. Melinda Goodwinter, who had come from Boston for her father's funeral. He mounted the steps of the stately library in unstately leaps and found the main room aflutter with small children. There was no evidence of Melinda Goodwinter. The youngsters were squealing and chattering and lugging picture books to the check-out desk, on which sat a rotund object about three feet high, like an egg with a cracked shell. The six-foot-two man pushed through the horde of knee-high tots, went up the stairs to the mezzanine three at a time, and barged through the reading room to the glass-enclosed office of the head librarian. None of the persons at the reading tables, he noted with relief, was the young doctor from Boston. Sooner or later he would have to face her, and he was unsure how to handle their reunion: with cool politesse? with lukewarm pleasure? with jocular nonchalance?

The librarian was a dignified and pleasant-faced woman of his own age, and she was eating lunch at her desk, the aroma of tuna fish adding an earthy touch to the high-minded bookishness of the office. Silently she reached out a hand across the desk and managed to smile her delight and surprise while chewing a carrot stick. A fervent and lingering handclasp was as amorous a greeting as they dared, since the office had the privacy of a fishbowl and Pickax had a penchant for gossip. Their eye contact said it all.

"You're home!" she murmured in her gentle voice after swallowing.

"Yes, I made it!" It was a dialogue unworthy of Polly's intelligence and Qwilleran's wit, but under the circumstances they could be excused. He dropped into a varnished oak chair, the keys in his back pocket clanking on the hard seat. "Is everything all right?" he asked anxiously. "Any more scares?"

"Not a thing," she said calmly.

"No more prowlers in the neighborhood?"

She shook her head.

For one uncomfortable moment his suspicious nature suggested that she might have invented the prowler episode to bring him home ahead of schedule; she was inclined to be possessive. He banished the thought, however; Polly was an honorable and loving friend. She might be jealous of women younger and thinner than she, but she had absolute integrity; of that he was sure.

"Tell me again exactly what happened," Qwilleran said. "Your voice was shaky when you talked to me on the phone."

"Well, as I told you at the time, I was returning after dark from the library banquet," she began quietly in her clear, considered manner of speaking. "When I drove into Goodwinter Boulevard—where curb parking is not allowed, as you know—I noticed a car parked the wrong way in front of the Gage mansion, and I could see someone sitting behind the wheel—a man with a beard. I thought that was strange. Mrs. Gage was still in Florida, and no one was living in the main house. I decided to notify the police as soon as I reached my apartment."

"Did you feel personally threatened at this point?"

"Not really. I turned into the side drive of the mansion and was driving back to the carriage house when I realized that the car was following me without lights! And then— *then* I was terrified! I accelerated and parked close to my doorstep with the headlights beamed on the keyhole. As I jumped out of my car, I glanced to the left. He was getting out of his car, too. I was able to rush inside and slam the door before he reached me."

Qwilleran tapped his moustache in an expression of anxiety. "Did you get a further look at him?"

"That's what the police wanted to know. I have the impression that he was of medium build, and when I first pulled up to the drive my headlights picked up a bearded face behind the wheel. That's all I can tell you."

"That narrows it down to forty percent of our male population," Qwilleran said. In Moose County beards were favored by potato farmers, hunters, sheep ranchers, fishermen, construction workers, and newspaper reporters.

"It was a bushy beard, I would say," she added.

"Did Brodie give you a police escort as I requested?"

"He offered to drive me to and from work, but honestly, Qwill, it seemed so unnecessary in daylight."

"Hmmm," he murmured, slumping in his chair in deep thought. Was it a false alarm? Or was Polly really at risk?

Rather than worry her unduly, he asked, "What's that absurd egg doing on the check-out desk?"

"Don't you recognize Humpty Dumpty? He's the focus of our summer reading program," she explained patiently. "The children are helping to put him together again by checking out books. After they've taken home a certain number, he'll be well and happy, and we'll have a party . . . You're invited," she added mischievously, knowing he avoided small children.

"How do you know the kids will read the books after they get them home? How do you know they'll even crack them?"

"Qwill, dear, you're so cynical!" she reproved him. "Your stay in the mountains hasn't mellowed you in the slightest . . . By the way, did you see our elevator installation? We're very grateful to the Klingenschoen Foundation. Now the elderly and infirm have access to the reading room."

"You should ask the K Foundation for some chairs with padded seats," he suggested, squirming uncomfortably. "Apart from Humpty Dumpty's great fall, is there any other world-shaking news in Moose County?"

"We're still grieving over the suicide of Dr. Halifax. Dr. Melinda returned for her father's funeral and has decided to stay. Everyone's pleased about that." It was a small-town custom to use the honorific when a local son or daughter had earned it.

Melinda Goodwinter had been Polly's predecessor in Qwilleran's affection—as everyone in Pickax knew—and he was careful not to react visibly. Casually he asked, "Will she take over Dr. Hal's patients?"

"Yes, she's already sent out announcements." Polly spoke of Melinda with studied detachment.

"How about dinner tonight at the Old Stone Mill?" he asked, changing the subject to conceal his personal concern about Melinda redux.

"I was hoping you'd suggest it. I have something exciting to discuss."

"About what?"

She smiled mysteriously. "I can't tell you right now. It's a wonderful surprise!"

"Where shall I pick you up? And at what time?"

"Shall we say seven o'clock?" Polly suggested. "I'd like to go home to change clothes and feed Bootsie."

"Seven o'clock it is."

"Are you sure you aren't too tired after all that driving?"

"All I need is a strong cup of coffee, and I'll be swinging from the chandeliers."

"I've missed you, dear. I'm so glad you're home," she said softly.

"I've missed you, too, Polly." He started to leave her office and paused on the threshold, from which he could see the reading tables. A white-haired woman sat knitting laboriously with arthritic hands; an elderly man was bent over a stack of books; a younger man with an unruly beard was leafing idly through a magazine. "Who's the fellow with the beard?" Qwilleran mumbled behind his hand as he stroked his moustache.

"I don't know. The woman is Mrs. Crawbanks; her granddaughter always drops her off here while she does errands. Now that we have an elevator we've become a day-care center for grandparents. Homer Tibbitt—you know him, of course—is doing research for the Historical Society. The younger man, I don't know."

Qwilleran strode through the reading room to speak to the thin and angular Mr. Tibbitt, who was in his nineties and still active, despite creaking joints. "I hear you're digging into Moose County's lurid past, Homer."

The retired school principal straightened up, his bony frame clicking in several places. "Got to keep the old brain cells functioning," he said in a cracked voice. "No one's ever recorded the history of the Goodwinters, although they founded Pickax one hundred fifty years ago. There were four branches of the family, some with good blood and some with bad blood, sorry to say. But the clan's dying out in these parts. Amanda's the last of the drinking Goodwinters. Dr. Halifax had two children, but the boy was killed in an accident a few years ago, and if Dr. Melinda marries and produces sons, they won't continue the family name. Of course," he continued after a moment's reflection, "she could do something unconventional; you never know what the young ones will do these days. But at present, Junior Goodwinter is the only hope. He's produced one son so far . . ."

Mr. Tibbitt would have rambled on, but Qwilleran noticed that the bearded man had left the reading room, and he wanted to follow him. Excusing himself, he bolted down the stairs and out of the building, dodging preschoolers, but the car with the Massachusetts plate was pulling out of the parking lot.

From the library he took the back street to the police station, hoping to avoid acquaintances who would question his premature return from the mountains. He found Andrew Brodie, the big, broad-shouldered chief of police, hunched over a computer, distrustfully poking the keys.

"Who invented these damn things?" Brodie growled. "More trouble than they're worth!" He leaned back in his chair. "Well, my friend, you hightailed it back to Pickax pretty fast! How'd you do it?"

"By flying low, bribing cops, and not giving my right name," Qwilleran retorted in the familiar bantering style that Brodie liked. "How's it going, Andy? Have you logged any more reports of prowlers?"

"Nary a one! The incident on Goodwinter Boulevard is hard to figure. Can't say that I buy your theory, Qwill. Kidnapping is something we've never had around here, except once when a father snatched his kid after a custody battle."

"There was a stranger loitering in the reading room outside Polly's office a few minutes ago, a youngish man with a bushy beard and a gray sweatshirt. He was driving a car with a Massachusetts license plate, but he pulled out of the lot before I could catch the number."

"Could it be Dr. Melinda's car? She's back in town."

"This was an old model, and muddy. I'm sure she drives something new and antiseptic-looking."

"If you see it again, get the number and we'll run a check on the registration just for the hell of it. Did you get a description?"

"All I can tell you is that it's a medium-sized car in dull maroon, and it looks as if it's been on dirt roads lately."

"Not hard to do in this neck o' the woods."

Qwilleran looked over Brodie's shoulder toward the coffeemaker. "Could the taxpayers afford a cup for a weary traveler?"

"Help yourself, but don't expect anything like that liquid tar that you brew!"

Qwilleran pushed open the gate into the enclosure, poured a cup of weak coffee, and sat down in another hard institutional oak chair. "Did you play your bagpipe at Dr. Hal's funeral, Andy?"

The chief nodded soberly. "Everybody broke up! Men, women, and children—all in tears! There's nothing sadder than a dirge on a bagpipe. Dr. Melinda requested it. She said her dad liked the pipes." Switching to a confidential tone, he went on. "She thinks she's gonna take over his patients, but the guys around here won't warm up to the idea of stripping and being examined by a woman doctor. I'm squeamish about it myself. I'll find me a male doctor even if I have to go down to Lockmaster. How about you?"

"I'll cross that bridge when I come to it," Qwilleran said carelessly, although he knew the situation would be awkward in his own case. "Our health-care setup will improve when the Klingenschoen Professional Building is finished. We'll be able to lure some specialists up here from Down Below. After all, it's a good place to raise a family; you said so yourself." His effort to divert attention from Melinda was unsuccessful.

Brodie regarded him sharply. "You and her were pretty thick, I understand, when she was here before."

"She was the first woman I met when I came to Moose County, Andy, but that's ancient history."

"I don't know why you and Polly don't get hitched. It's the only way to live, to my way of thinking."

"That's because you're a dedicated family man. Try to get it through your skull that some of us make rotten husbands. I found it out the hard way, to my sorrow. I lost several years of my life—and ruined another life in the process."

"But Polly's a good woman. Damn shame to see her wasted."

"Wasted! If she knew you called her life wasted, she'd tear up your library card! Polly is living a useful and rewarding life. She's the lifeblood of the library. And she chooses to be independent. She has her women friends and her bird-watching and a comfortable apartment filled with family heirlooms . . ."

And she has Bootsie, Qwilleran said to himself as he walked from the police station to the newspaper office. He huffed into his moustache. It was his impression that Polly lavished too much maudlin affection on the two-year-old Siamese. When Bootsie was a kitten, she babied him unconscionably, but now he had outgrown kittenish ways and she still babbled precious nonsense in his ear. In Qwilleran's household, the Siamese were sophisticated companions whom he treated as equals, and they treated him the same way. He addressed them intelligently, and they replied with expressive yips and yowls. When he discussed problems in their presence, he felt their sympathy. He regularly read aloud to them from worthwhile books, news magazines, and—on Sundays—the *New York Times*.

Kao K'o Kung, the male (called Koko as a handy everyday diminutive), was a gifted animal endowed with highly developed senses quite beyond those of humans and other cats. Yum Yum was a female who hid her catly wiles under a guise of affectionate cuddling, purring and nuzzling, often extending a paw to touch Qwilleran's moustache.

From the police station it was a short walk to the office of the *Moose County Something,* as the local newspaper was named. (Everything in mile-square Pickax was a short walk.) The publication occupied a new building made possible by financial assistance from the Klingenschoen Foundation, and the editor-and-publisher was Qwilleran's longtime friend from Down Below, Arch Riker. In the lobby there were no security guards or hidden cameras such as those employed by the large metropolitan dailies for which Qwilleran had worked. He walked down the hall to Riker's office and found the door open, the desk unoccupied.

From the managing editor's office across the hall Junior Goodwinter hailed him. "Arch went to Minneapolis for a publishers' conference. He'll be back tomorrow. Come on in! Have a chair. Put your feet up. I don't suppose you want a cup of coffee."

Recalling the anemic brew he had just swallowed, Qwilleran replied, "I majored in journalism and graduated with a degree in caffeine. Make it black and hot."

Junior's boyish build, boyish countenance, and boyish enthusiasm were now tempered by a newly grown beard. "How do you like it?" he asked as he stroked his chin. "Does it make me look older?"

"It makes you look like a young potato farmer. What's your wife's reaction?"

"She likes it. She says it makes me look like a jolly elf. What brings you home so soon?" he asked as he handed over a steaming cup.

"Polly was frightened by a prowler on Goodwinter Boulevard. I didn't like the sound of it."

"How come we didn't hear about it?"

"She reported it, but there's been no further incident, so far as anyone knows."

"They've got to do something about Goodwinter Boulevard, no kidding," said Junior. "It used to be the best street in town. Now it's getting positively hairy with all those vacant mansions looking like haunted houses. The one

where Alex and Penelope lived has been up for sale for
years! The one that VanBrook rented is empty again, and
it's going begging. Who wants fifteen or twenty rooms
nowadays?"

"Rezoning, that's what it needs," Qwilleran said. "It
should be rezoned for apartments, offices, good restaurants, high-class nursing homes, and so forth. Why don't
you write an editorial?"

"I'd be accused of special interest," Junior said.

"How do you figure that?"

"Grandma Gage has bought a condo in Florida and wants
to deed the mansion to me while she's still living. What
would I do with fifteen rooms? Think of the heating bills
and the taxes and all those windows to wash! I'll own just
another white elephant on Goodwinter Boulevard."

Qwilleran's eyes, known for their doleful expression and
drooping lids, roamed over the clutter on the editor's desk,
the crumpled paper that had missed the wastebasket, the
half-open file drawers, the stacks of out-of-town newspapers. But he wasn't looking; he was thinking. He was
thinking that the Gage mansion occupied the property in
front of Polly's carriage house. If he lived there, he could
keep a watchful eye on her. Also, it would be convenient
for other purposes, like dropping in for dinner frequently.
He smoothed his moustache with satisfaction and said to
Junior, "I could use a winter house in town. My barn is
hard to heat and there's too much snow to plow. Why
don't I rent your house?"

"Wow! That would be great!" the young editor yelled.

"But I still think you should run that editorial."

"The city will never do anything about rezoning. Tradition dies hard in Pickax."

"How about Stephanie's Restaurant in the old Lanspeak
house? It was opened a couple of years when I first came
here."

"That was the first house on the boulevard," Junior explained. "It faced Main Street and could be legally used for

commercial purposes. Too bad it closed; the building's still empty . . . No, Qwill, there are still influential families on the boulevard who'll fight rezoning like tigers. We'll have to wait for some more of them to die off. Dr. Hal lived on the boulevard, you know."

"Do you think Melinda will keep the house?"

"No way! She has an apartment and intends to sell the house and furnishings. Off the record, her dad didn't leave much of an estate. He was an old-fashioned country doctor, never charging patients who couldn't pay and never taking advantage of the insurance setup. And don't forget the expense of round-the-clock nurses for his wife for all those years! Melinda has inherited more problems than property . . . Have you seen her?" Junior asked with a searching look. He knew about Melinda's former pursuit of the county's most eligible bachelor. She was Junior's cousin. All Goodwinters were cousins to a degree. "She's changed somehow," he said. "I don't know how to pinpoint it."

"Three years on the staff of a Boston hospital can do that," Qwilleran said.

"Yeah, they worked her pretty hard, I guess. Well, anyway, can we expect some copy from you this week? Or are you too bushed?"

"I'll see what I can do."

Walking home, Qwilleran recalled his earlier association with Dr. Melinda Goodwinter. He had been a stranger in Moose County at the time, suffering from a fierce case of ivy poisoning. After treating his condition successfully, she offered friendship, flip conversation, and youth. She was twenty years his junior, with green eyes and long lashes and the frank sexuality of her generation. As a doctor, she had convinced him to give up smoking and take more exercise. As a woman, she had been overly aggressive for Qwilleran's taste, and her campaign to bulldoze him into matrimony resulted in embarrassment for both of them. She moved to Boston after that, telling everyone she had no desire to be a country doctor.

When he met Polly, it was he who did the pursuing—an arrangement more to his liking. She was not so thin as Melinda, nor were her lashes so long, but she was a congenial companion and a good cook, who shared his literary interests. They liked to get together and read Shakespeare, for one thing. She made no unacceptable demands, and, more and more, Qwilleran found Polly occupying his thoughts.

On the way home he stopped at Toodles' Market to buy the Siamese something to eat—always a problem because they had fickle palates. Their preferences changed just often enough to keep him perpetually on his toes. There was only one constant: no cat food! As if they could read labels, they disdained any product intended for the four-legged trade. Sometimes they were satisfied with a can of red salmon garnished with a smoked oyster or a dab of caviar, preferably sturgeon. At other times, they would kill for turkey, but he could never be sure. At Toodles' he considered a slice of roast beef from the deli or some chicken liver pâté. Better yet would be a few ounces of tenderloin from the butcher, to serve *au tartare,* but he would have to hand-mince it; ground meat was somehow objectionable. He settled for the pâté.

From there he followed the long way home, just for the exercise, trudging along a back road, then up a gravel trail through an old orchard. He was a hundred feet from the apple barn when he heard clarion voices yowling a welcome. The nineteenth-century barn was an octagonal structure four stories high, with large windows cut into the walls at various levels, and he could see two furry bodies darting about indoors, observing him first from one window and then another. They met him at the door, prancing and waving their tails like flags. It was a ritual that gave him a leap of inner joy in spite of his unsentimental greeting. "What have you young turks been doing since you got home?"

They sensed the liver pâté with quivering whiskers. In spasms of anticipation they dashed up the ramp that spiraled around the interior of the building, connecting the three balconies and ending in narrow catwalks under the roof. Then they pounded pell-mell down the slope to the first balcony, from which they flew like squirrels, landing in the cushioned seating on the main floor. There they washed their paws and whiskers before dinner.

When Qwilleran spread the pâté on a plate and placed it on the floor, he watched them with fascination as they devoured it. They were masterpieces of design: sleek fawn bodies on long brown legs; incredibly blue eyes in seal-brown masks; expressive brown tails tapered like rapiers. To Qwilleran they seemed to have more elegance than Bootsie, who was being overfed to compensate for the loneliness of his solitary life.

At seven o'clock he called for Polly at her carriage-house apartment behind the Gage mansion, and as he climbed the narrow staircase, Bootsie was waiting at the top with ears back and fangs bared.

"Greetings, thou paragon of animals," Qwilleran said, thinking a phrase from Shakespeare would please Polly.

Bootsie hissed.

"You must forgive him," she apologized. "He sensed danger when the prowler was outside, and he's been edgy ever since."

After a warm, silent, meaningful embrace that would have astonished the library patrons and started the Pickax grapevine sizzling, Qwilleran presented Polly with a tissue-wrapped bundle. "Sorry it isn't gift-wrapped," he said. "I brought it from the mountains. It looked like your shade of blue."

Polly was thrilled. "It's a batwing cape! It's handwoven! Who did it?"

"One of the mountaineers," he said, shrugging off the question. "They're all weavers and potters and woodworkers in the mountains." He avoided mentioning that the weaver was an interesting young woman whom he had taken to dinner and who had rescued him twice when he was in trouble on mountain passes.

Polly had shed the drab suit she wore at the library and was looking festive in a summer dress of mixed polka dots, red-on-white and white-on-red. "You're sure it isn't too bold for me?" she asked when Qwilleran complimented her. "Irma Hasselrich helped me choose it."

They drove to the restaurant in the rental car that had brought him from the mountains. "My own car broke down," he explained, "and I left it there." The tale was loosely true; the car had bogged down in mud, and he had given it to the young mountain woman, who would be able to haul it out with her swamp buggy.

The restaurant called the Old Stone Mill occupied a historic gristmill. There was enough affluence in Pickax—and there were enough educated palates—to support one good eatery, and it was owned by a syndicate of businessmen who needed an unprofitable venture for tax purposes. It paid its chefs handsomely and offered a menu worldly enough for local residents who had dined in San Francisco, New Orleans, and Paris.

After Qwilleran and Polly were greeted and seated at their usual table, a six-foot-seven busboy, who towered above customers and staff alike, shuffled up to the table with a water pitcher and basket of garlic toast. His name was Derek Cuttlebrink. "Hi, Mr. Q," he said in friendly fashion. "I thought you were going away for the summer."

"I came back," Qwilleran explained succinctly.

"I'm taking two weeks in August to go camping."

"Good for you!"

"Yeah, I met this girl, and she has a tent. Blue nylon, seven-by-eight, with aluminum frame. Sets up in five minutes."

"Take plenty of mosquito repellent," Qwilleran advised. "Stay away from poison ivy. Watch out for ticks."

Polly asked, "Have you given any more thought to college, Derek?"

"Well, you know, it's like this, Mrs. Duncan. I've decided to stay in the food business. I'm getting promoted to the kitchen, end of the month—in charge of French fries and garlic toast."

"Congratulations!" said Qwilleran.

When the busboy had sauntered away, Polly wondered, "Do you think Derek will ever amount to anything?"

"Don't give up hope," Qwilleran said. "One of these days he'll meet the right girl, and he'll become a famous brain surgeon. I've seen it happen."

He ordered dry sherry for Polly and, for himself, a local product called Squunk water—from a flowing well in Squunk Corners. He always drank it on the rocks with a twist.

Polly raised her glass. *"Slainte!"*

"Ditto," Qwilleran said. "What does it mean?"

"I don't know exactly. It's a toast in Gaelic that Irma Hasselrich always uses." Polly often quoted her new friend.

Personally, Qwilleran had his doubts about Irma Hasselrich. In her forties, she still lived at home with her parents, her father being senior partner in the law firm of Hasselrich, Bennett & Barter. She was the chief volunteer at the Senior Care Facility, and Qwilleran had met her while interviewing an aged patient. At that time, he thought her a handsome woman. She had a Junoesque figure, a polished appearance, and a charming manner. Since Polly was spending the summer in England, he tried to take Irma to dinner, but his invitation was pointedly avoided. He was not accustomed to being rejected, and his reaction was distinctly negative.

Recently the two women had discovered a mutual interest: They often went bird-watching with binoculars and notebooks on the banks of the Ittibittiwassee River or in the wetlands near Purple Point. Furthermore, the well-groomed, well-dressed Irma was influencing Polly to wear brighter colors and touch up her graying hair.

"You're looking especially young and attractive tonight," he remarked as they sipped their aperitifs. "Soon you'll be joining the Theatre Club and playing ingenue roles."

"Not likely," she said with her musical laugh. "But did you hear that the club is doing *Macbeth* in September?"

"That's a surprise!"

"Why? It's a highly dramatic play with witches, ghosts, swordplay, a sleepwalker, and some ghastly murders, and it has plenty to say about temptation, human failure, spiritual evil, and compulsive ambition."

"But according to superstition, it brings bad luck to the company that stages it."

"No one around here is aware of that, so don't enlighten them," Polly advised. "Of course, it's almost certain that Larry will play the title role."

"He'll have to grow a beard again. He won't like that. Who's directing?"

"A new man in town, Dwight Somers, who's taken a position with XYZ Enterprises. He's had theatre experience and is said to be very nice. Auditions have been announced, and it's rumored that Dr. Melinda is going to read for Lady Macbeth." The Pickax library was a major listening post in the local grapevine.

Qwilleran wanted to ask: Have you seen Melinda? . . . How does she look? . . . They say she's changed a lot. He deemed it wise, however, not to exhibit that much interest, so he asked casually, "Would she be any good in that role?"

"Quite possibly. I saw her at Dr. Hal's funeral and thought she was looking . . . much *older*. The Goodwinter face—long and narrow, you know—has a tendency to look haggard. It doesn't age well."

They ordered jellied watercress consommé and grilled swordfish with pineapple-jalapeño salsa, and Qwilleran asked, "What's the surprise you have for me tonight?"

"Well!" she began with evident relish. "Irma and I had dinner one night while you were away, and we were talking about Scotland. She went to art school there and still has connections, whom she visits frequently. I mentioned that I've always wanted to see Macbeth country, and that started a train of thought. Why not organize a group tour of Scottish Isles and Highlands, with a percentage of the tour cost going to the Senior Care Facility, tax deductible?"

"Sounds okay. Who'd manage it?"

"Irma is plotting the itinerary, and she'll make the reservations and act as tour guide."

"Is she experienced at handling group tours?"

"No. But she's in charge of the volunteer program at the facility, and she's a natural leader, well organized, and certainly knowledgeable about Scotland, especially the Western Isles and Highlands.

"How will you travel in Scotland?"

"By chartered minibus. The Lanspeaks and the Comptons have signed up, and Irma and I will share a room. The price of the tour is based on double occupancy, but singles are available."

Qwilleran said to himself, It's a good idea for Polly to leave the country until the prowler threat blows over. "You'll like the Highlands. I spent my honeymoon there. As I recall, the food wasn't very good, but that was quite a long time ago, and when you're a newlywed, who cares? . . . Would you like me to feed Bootsie while you're away?"

She regarded him hopefully. "We were thinking . . . that you might . . . join the tour."

The suggestion caught him off-guard, and he stared into space for a few moments before answering. "How long is the trip? I've never left the cats for more than a couple of days. Who'd take care of them?"

"Is there someone you could trust to move into your barn for two weeks? My sister-in-law is going to stay with Bootsie."

Qwilleran stroked his moustache with uncertainty. "I don't know. I'll have to think about it. But whatever I decide, the K Foundation will match whatever you raise for the Senior Facility. Will it be advertised?"

"Irma says it's better to make it invitational to ensure a compatible group. We'll go in late August when the heather is in bloom. The tour will start in Glasgow and end in Edinburgh."

"Glasgow?" Qwilleran echoed with interest. "I've been reading about the Charles Rennie Mackintosh revival in Glasgow. My mother was a Mackintosh, you know."

Polly knew, having heard it a hundred times, but she asked sweetly, "Do you think you might be related to him?"

"I know nothing about my maternal ancestors except that one of them was either a stagecoach driver who was killed by a highwayman, or a highwayman who was hanged for murdering a stagecoach driver. As for Charles Rennie Mackintosh, I know only that he pioneered modern design a hundred years ago, and he sounds like an interesting character."

"If you wish to extend your time in Glasgow, you can do that," Polly said encouragingly. "Carol and Larry will go early and see a few plays in London."

"Okay, sign me up for a single," he said. "I'll find a cat-sitter. Lori Bamba would be perfect, but she has kids, and they'd fall off the balconies. The barn was designed for cats and adults."

The soup course arrived, and they savored it in silence as they thought about the forthcoming adventure. When the swordfish was served, Qwilleran said, "I've heard a rumor about Irma Hasselrich, although not from a reliable source. Perhaps you could set me straight."

Polly stiffened noticeably. "What have you heard? And from whom?"

"I protect my sources," he said, "but the story is that she shot a man twenty-odd years ago and was charged with murder, but the Hasselriches bribed the judge to let her off without a sentence."

Drawing a deep breath of exasperation, Polly replied, "Like most gossip in Pickax, it's only ten percent accurate. The motive for the shooting was what we now call date rape. In court, Hasselrich defended his daughter brilliantly. The jury found her guilty of manslaughter but recommended leniency, and the judge was more understanding than most jurists at that time; he gave her probation, plus an order to do three years of community service . . . Does that answer your question?"

Detecting annoyance in the curt explanation, he said, "I'm sorry. I simply repeated what I had heard."

More softly Polly said, "After completing her community service, Irma went on to devote her life to volunteer work. She'll do *anything* for charity! She's raised tons of money for good causes."

"Quite admirable," Qwilleran murmured, but it crossed his mind that "anything" was a strong and suspect word.

He ordered strawberry pie for dessert, and Polly toyed with a small dish of lime sorbet. She had eaten only half of everything that was served. "I'm watching my diet," she explained. "I've lost a few pounds. Does it show?"

"You're looking healthy and beautiful," he replied. "Don't get too skinny."

After dessert they went to her apartment for coffee, and then did some reading aloud. They read two acts of *Macbeth* while Bootsie sniffed Qwilleran's trouser legs with distaste.

It was late when Qwilleran returned to the apple barn, and two indignant Siamese met him at the door. Sensing that he had been associating with another cat, they walked away with a lofty display of superiority.

"Come off it, you guys!" he rebuked them. "I have news for you. I'm taking a trip to Scotland, and *you're not going!*"

"Yow!" Koko scolded him.

"That's right. You're staying here!"

"N-n-now!" shrieked Yum Yum.

"And you're not going, either!"

TWO

The day following his evening with Polly, Qwilleran regretted his impulsive decision to go to Scotland and leave the Siamese for two weeks. As he brushed their silky coats—Yum Yum with hindlegs splayed like a Duncan Phyfe table, and Koko with tail in a stiff Hogarth curve—he thought of canceling his reservation, but an inner voice deterred him, saying: *You're a two-hundred-pound man, and you're allowing yourself to be enslaved by eighteen pounds of cat!*

That evening he was reading aloud with the female cuddling contentedly on his lap and the male perched on the arm of his chair, when the telephone rang. "Excuse me, sweetheart," he said, lifting Yum Yum gently and placing her on the warm seat cushion he had just vacated.

It was Irma Hasselrich on the line, speaking with the syrupy, formal charm that was her style. She said, "Mr. Qwilleran, I learn with a great deal of pleasure that you wish to join the Bonnie Scots Tour."

"Yes, it strikes me as an interesting adventure. My mother was a Mackintosh. And by the way, please call me Qwill."

"Needless to say, Mr. Qwilleran," she continued as if she had not heard, "we're delighted that the Klingenschoen Foundation is offering a matching grant. We want to create a park for the patients at the facility, with flower beds, winding paths for wheelchairs, and a pavilion with tables for picnic lunches and games."

"Very commendable," Qwilleran murmured. "How many persons do you expect to enlist for the tour?"

"Our goal is sixteen. That number will fill a minibus."

"Did Polly tell you I want to spend some time in Glasgow?"

"Yes. Several participants want to extend their stay abroad, so I suggest that we all make our own flight arrangements and meet on Day One at a prescribed location in Glasgow."

"How many have signed up so far?"

"Eleven. Perhaps you can suggest other compatible travelers that we might contact."

Qwilleran thought for a few seconds. "How about John and Vicki Bushland? They have a summer place in Mooseville, although they're residents of Lockmaster, where he has a commercial photography studio."

"We would love to have a professional photographer along! May I call them and use your name?"

"By all means."

"As soon as it was known that you were joining the tour, Mr. Qwilleran, I was able to sign up three others: Mr. and Mrs. MacWhannell—he's the CPA, you know— and Dr. Melinda Goodwinter. Aren't we fortunate to have a doctor with us?"

Qwilleran cringed inwardly and combed his moustache with his fingertips. He had visions of the importunate Melinda tapping on his hotel door at a late hour and inviting herself in for a chat. She was a persistent young woman, and, according to Arch Riker, who had met her after her father's funeral, she was still carrying the torch for him, Polly or no Polly.

Qwilleran veiled his distress by inquiring about the weather in Scotland, and Irma assured him that she would send all pertinent travel information in the mail.

When the conversation ended, he immediately phoned

Arch Riker at the office of the *Moose County Something*. The two men had grown up together in Chicago and had pursued separate careers in journalism Down Below. Now they were reunited in Pickax, where Riker was realizing his dream of publishing a small-town newspaper.

"Arch, how would you like to knock off for a couple of weeks and go to Scotland with a local group?" Qwilleran proposed. "We could save a few bucks by sharing accommodations." He added a few details and dropped some important names: Hasselrich, Lanspeak, Compton, Goodwinter, MacWhannell.

Riker liked the idea, saying that he'd always wanted to play the seventeenth hole at St. Andrews.

"And now the bad news," Qwilleran said. "Melinda Goodwinter is going."

"The plot thickens," said Riker with a chuckle. He was amused by his friend's problems with women. "Does Polly know?"

"If she doesn't, she'll soon find out!"

Complimenting himself on a successful maneuver, Qwilleran called Irma Hasselrich and changed his reservation to double occupancy. The next day it was his turn to chuckle when Riker telephoned.

"Hey, listen to this, Qwill," he said. "I took Amanda to dinner last night and told her about the Scottish tour, and *she wants to join!* How do you like that kettle of fish?"

"She'll have to pay the single supplement. No one will be willing to room with Amanda—not even her cousin Melinda."

Amanda Goodwinter was a cranky, outspoken woman of indefinite age who "drank a little," as Pickax natives liked to say. Yet, she operated a successful studio of interior design and was repeatedly elected to the city council, where she minced no words, spared no feelings, played no politics.

Riker, with a journalist's taste for oddballs, found her entertaining, and for a while the Pickax grapevine linked them as potential mates, but Amanda's prickly personality guaranteed that she would remain single for life. Now he was enjoying the prospect of Amanda disrupting the harmony of a group tour. "I hope everyone has a sense of humor," he said to Qwilleran on the phone. "What's so absurd is that she hates bagpipes, mountains, bus travel, and Irma Hasselrich."

"Then why is she going? Surely not only to be with you, old chum!"

"No, I can't take the credit. She's excited about visiting whiskey distilleries. She's heard they give free samples."

While Qwilleran was relishing this news, Chief Brodie phoned to report that state troopers had spotted a Massachusetts license plate on a maroon car headed south near the county line. "Probably leaving the area," he said. "We ran a check, and it's registered to one Charles Edward Martin of Charlestown, Massachusetts."

"What was he doing here?" Qwilleran asked sharply, a rhetorical question. "In five years I've never seen a Massachusetts car in Moose County. Those New Englanders don't even know it exists!"

"Could be a friend of Dr. Melinda's. Could be he came for her dad's funeral. There were lots of beards there," Brodie said. "Tell you what, Qwill: If he shows up again and we get a complaint, we'll know who he is, at least. For now, we're stepping up the night patrols on Goodwinter Boulevard, and you tell Polly not to go out alone after dark."

Qwilleran's moustache bristled. Whenever he thought of that maroon car, he felt a distinct tremor on his upper lip. His luxuriant moustache was more than a prominent facial feature; it had long been the source of his hunches and suspicions, bristling and tingling to get his attention, and experience had taught him to trust the signals. This peculiar sensitivity was a matter he was loath to discuss with any but his intimate friends, and even they were disinclined to believe it. Nevertheless, it was a fact.

He was not alone in his ability to sense trouble. Kao K'o Kung possessed a unique faculty for exposing evil deeds and evildoers, in the same way that he sniffed a microscopic spot on the rug, or detected a stereo control turned to "on" when the power should be off. When Koko's ears pointed and his whiskers twitched, when he scratched industriously and sniffed juicily, he was on the scent of something that was—not—as—it—should—be!

After the phone conversation with Brodie, Qwilleran turned to Koko, who always perched nearby to monitor calls. "Well, old boy," he said, "the Boulevard Prowler seems to have left town."

"Yow," said Koko, scratching his ear.

"So far, so good. Now, how do we find you a suitable cat-sitter?"

Koko jumped to the floor with a grunt and trotted to the pantry, where he stared pointedly at his empty plate. Yum Yum was not far behind. It was time for their mid-day snack.

Qwilleran gave them a handful of crunchy cereal concocted by the food writer of the *Moose County Something*, Mildred Hanstable. It was the only dry food the Siamese would deign to eat. As he watched them munching and waving their tails in rapture, an idea struck him.

"I've got it!" he said aloud. "Mildred Hanstable!"

Besides writing the food column for the newspaper, she taught home economics in the Pickax schools, and she enjoyed cooking for cats, dogs, and humans. Widowed, she lived alone. Plump and pretty, she had a kind heart, a lively imagination, and an ample lap.

"Perfect!" Qwilleran yelped, so loudly that the Siamese turned to look at him in alarm before finishing the last morsel on the plate.

Mildred Hanstable was the mother-in-law of his friend Roger MacGillivray, and he tracked down the young reporter at Lois's Luncheonette. "What do you think of the idea, Roger? She likes the cats, and they like her."

"It would do her a lot of good—help get her mind off the past," said Roger. "She thinks your barn is sensational, and the chance to live there for a couple of weeks would be like halfway to heaven!"

"One thing I must ask: Is she still drinking heavily?"

"Well, she went through a twisted kind of alcoholic mourning for that no-good husband of hers, but she snapped out of it. Now she's overeating instead. Basically she's lonely. I wish she could meet a decent guy."

"We'll have to work on that, Roger . . . Where are you headed now?"

"I have an assignment in Kennebeck. The Tuesday Afternoon Women's Club is planting a tree in the village park."

It so happened that Qwilleran had brought several handwoven batwing capes from the mountains, and he presented one to Mildred after a staff meeting at the newspaper. It was the kind of voluminous garment that she liked for camouflaging her excess poundage, and the invitation to cat-sit and barn-sit for two weeks thrilled her beyond words.

With that worrisome matter concluded, he now applied himself to other matters. He gave batwing capes to his part-time secretary, the young interior designer who had helped him furnish the barn, and the advertising manager of the *Moose County Something,* making three women deliriously happy. Next, to replace the car that was left mired in the mountains, he found a white four-door on the used-car lot; he never wasted money on new models. All the while, he was cleverly managing to avoid Dr. Melinda Goodwinter, ignoring the reminder that he was due for his annual checkup according to the records of the late Halifax Goodwinter, M.D.

Irma Hasselrich was prompt in mailing tour participants a detailed itinerary as well as information on Scottish weather and appropriate clothing: "Sweaters and jackets are a must, because evenings can be cool, and we'll be traveling to windswept islands and mountaintops. Be sure to include a light raincoat, umbrella, and waterproof shoes or boots." The last was underlined in red. Then: "For special evenings, men are requested to pack a blazer or sports coat with shirt and tie, and women are advised to have a dress and heels for such occasions. Luggage must be limited to *one bag per person,* plus a small carry-on. There will be no smoking on the bus or in restaurants as a matter of courtesy, and no smoking in country inns because of the fire hazard." Enclosed was a brief glossary of Highland and Lowland terms:

> *loch* . . . lake
> *moor* . . . treeless hill
> *glen* . . . secluded valley
> *fen* . . . marsh
> *ben* . . . mountain
> *firth* . . . arm of the sea
> *burn* . . . creek
> *strath* . . . wide river valley
> *kyle* . . . strait
> *croft* . . . farmhouse
> *crofter* . . . farmer
> *bothy* . . . farmhands' barracks
> *neeps* . . . turnips
> *tatties* . . . potatoes
> *haggis* . . . meat pudding
> *toilet* . . . restroom
> *usquebaugh* . . . whiskey
> (spelled "whisky" in Scotland)

Included was a suggested reading list: Boswell, Dr. Johnson, Sir Walter Scott, and the like, most of which were in Qwilleran's growing collection of secondhand books.

Nevertheless, he went to Eddington Smith's used-book store and picked up an old travel book with a yellowed fold-out map of Scotland. The bookseller also suggested *Memoirs of an Eighteenth Century Footman.* He said, "It's about Scotland. It was published in 1790 and reprinted in 1927. It's not in bad condition for a sixty-year-old book."

Qwilleran bought it and was on his way out of the store when Eddington mentioned, "Dr. Melinda came in yesterday. She wants me to buy Dr. Hal's library, but she's asking too much money."

That evening, as Qwilleran sat in his favorite lounge chair with *Memoirs,* the cats arranged themselves for a read: Koko on the wide upholstered arm of the chair and Yum Yum on his lap with forelegs extended and paws crossed prettily. Sixty years of assorted household odors made the book fascinating to the Siamese. Qwilleran was enthralled by the incredible account of four motherless children—ages two, four, seven, and fourteen—setting out to find their father, who had left to fight for Prince Charlie. After walking 150 miles, being on the road for three months, begging for food and shelter, they learned that he had fallen in battle at Culloden.

Absorbed in their predicament, Qwilleran was almost too stunned to answer when the telephone rang, until Koko yowled in his ear.

"Uh . . . hello," he said vaguely.

"Hello, lover. Is that you? You sound far away. Do you recognize a voice from your high-flying past?"

"Who is this?" he asked in a flat voice, although he knew.

"Melinda!"

"Oh . . . hello."

"Am I interrupting something important?"

"No. I was reading a book."

"It must be pretty good. What's the title?"

"It's . . . uh . . . *Memoirs of an Eighteenth Century Footman* by John Macdonald."

"Sounds like hot stuff. Someone told me you're collecting old books now."

"I have a few." He was trying to sound like a poor prospect, not to mention a dull and uninteresting person.

"I'm selling my father's library. Are you interested?"

"I'm afraid not. I pick up one book at a time, here and there."

"Why don't you meet me at the house for a look at Dad's library. You might see—something—you like. I'm living at Indian Village, but I could run into town."

"That's a good idea," he said with misleading enthusiasm. "I'll see when Polly Duncan's available, and we'll make an appointment with you. She's my guru when it comes to old books."

There was a pause on the other end of the line. "Okay. I'll get in touch with you later, if the books are still available . . . I hear we're going to Scotland on the same tour, lover."

"Yes, Polly talked me into it."

"Well, don't let me keep you away from your exciting book."

"Thanks for calling," he said in a routine voice.

"Nighty-night."

Melinda never called back about the books, for which Qwilleran was thankful, but her name was frequently mentioned around town. One afternoon he dropped into Amanda's Studio of Interior Design to scrounge a cup of coffee and use the telephone, as he often did when Fran Brodie was in-house. Fran was assistant to Amanda Goodwinter but younger, more glamorous, and better-dispositioned. As a member of the Theatre Club and daughter of the police chief, she had still another attraction: She could always be relied upon for the latest gossip—or local information, as Qwilleran preferred to call it.

Fran greeted him with welcome news: "You've just missed Melinda! She came in to try to sell us her father's books. I don't know what she thought we could do with them . . . Cup of coffee?" She served it in a mug stenciled with the letter Q, a mischievous reference to his habitual freeloading. "I'm glad you dropped in, Qwill. I've found something that you simply must have! It's *you!*"

"I should know the free coffee is never free," he said. "What is it?"

She opened a flat box with exaggerated care. "This is an acid-free box, and this is acid-free tissue," she explained, as she unwrapped a drab fragment of cloth.

"What the devil is that?"

"It's a Scottish relic—a fragment of a Mackintosh kilt that was worn by a Jacobite rebel at the Battle of Culloden in 1746!"

"How do you know it is? It looks like a reject from a trash can."

"It's documented. It belonged to an old family in Lockmaster, who came here from Canada. Their ancestors were exiled to the New World during the Scottish Clearances."

"And what am I supposed to do with this faded rag? It wouldn't even be good enough to wash the car!"

"We'd preserve it in a protective frame for you, as they do in museums, and you could put it on display. Of course, we'd have to pick a location without much daylight or artificial light."

"That limits us to the broom closet and the cats' bathroom," he said. "How much is it worth?"

"It's expensive, but you can afford it, considering all the money you save on coffee and phone calls."

"I'll kick it around."

"Do that," Fran said, refilling his coffee mug. "So you're going to Scotland with my boss! I hear they're having trouble filling all the seats. Is that because Amanda is one of the passengers? Or because Irma Hasselrich is the tour director?"

"Doesn't Irma have much of a fan club?" Qwilleran asked.

"I'm afraid people think she's snobbish and bossy, and her perfect grooming frightens some of the casual types around town. Amanda says she looks like a peeled egg . . . One thing I'd like to know: Why did Irma schedule the tour to overlap our rehearsals of *Macbeth*? Our three most important people are taking the trip: the two leads and the director!"

"Is Melinda playing Lady Macbeth?"

Fran nodded with disapproval. "Several women read for it, and Carol was my choice, but Dwight Somers wanted Melinda. He's sort of goggle-eyed about Melinda. She's probably the reason he signed up for the Scottish tour."

Qwilleran thought, Good! I hope he monopolizes her and keeps her out of my hair.

One evening shortly after that, when he and Polly were dining at Tipsy's Tavern in North Kennebeck, Melinda was seated at a table in the same room. He avoided looking in her direction but was aware that her escort was a man with a neat beard.

Polly said it was Dwight Somers. "They're both going on the Bonnie Scots Tour. Melinda is a longtime friend of Irma, you know."

"Is that so?" Qwilleran remarked inanely, wincing at the prick of his vanity; he thought that he himself was Melinda's reason for signing up.

Polly was saying, "I had a physical at her office today. I remember her fifteen years ago when she brought her high-school assignments to the library, and it's difficult to relate to her as a doctor, but Irma says we women must be supportive. My sister-in-law works in the office at the Goodwinter clinic, and I've learned that Dr. Hal's male patients are transferring their records to a man in Lockmaster, an internist and urologist."

Qwilleran said, "If you want my guess, it's their wives who don't want them going to a young . . . *woman* doctor." He was going to say "young attractive woman doctor" but edited his own dialogue.

As if on cue, Melinda passed their table on the way to the restroom. "Hi, lover," she said breezily, pausing for a moment that seemed too long.

Qwilleran rose from his chair and said something trite. "Dr. Goodwinter, I presume." He rose courteously, but he kept one hand on the back of his chair and stood in a semicrouch, ready to sit down again when she moved on, which he hoped would be soon.

"Are you all excited about our trip together?" she asked with a sly glance, addressing him directly.

"Polly and I are both looking forward to it." He nodded graciously to his guest.

"Then I'll see you on the bonnie banks of Loch Lomond, lover," Melinda said as she sauntered away, drawing a manicured hand suggestively across their tabletop. The whiff of fragrance that she left behind was the same she had worn three years before.

"Indeed!" Polly said with raised eyebrows. "What was the significance of that pretty performance?"

"She's half-bombed," Qwilleran said with a sense of relief. He had feared he might find Melinda as appealing as before, but the impudent manner that formerly enchanted him now annoyed him; her hair was done in a trendy style he disliked; and she was too thin. His taste had changed. Lest his silence be misconstrued, he quickly said to Polly, "I don't know about you, but I've never traveled with a group, except for a bunch of hyper reporters on a press junket, so I'm hoping for the best and expecting the worst on this excursion."

"We'll enjoy it," she assured him and then said, "Do you remember the bronchitis I had when I spent the summer in England? On this trip I'm taking vitamin C as a preventive. The pharmacist told me about a high-potency capsule, and I respect his advice."

"Did you discuss it with—your doctor?" Qwilleran was dubious of vitamins, broccoli, and anything else said to be salubrious.

"I mentioned it to Melinda, and she said it wouldn't do any harm but probably wouldn't do any good, either. Nevertheless, I intend to try it . . . Have you made your packing list, Qwill?"

"I never make a list. I just throw stuff into my suitcase."

THE CAT WHO WASN'T THERE   43

"You're singularly offhand, dear! I make a list and take only basic colors, double-duty garments, minimal accessories, and just enough toothpaste, face cream, and shampoo for fourteen days."

"You're singularly efficient," he retorted dryly. "No wonder the library operates so smoothly."

"Have you done any of Irma's suggested reading?"

"No, but Edd Smith sold me a book with a fold-out map of Scotland. As soon as I opened the map, both cats came running and pounced in the middle of it, tearing it along the old yellowed creases and making a horrible muddle, as Old Possum would say. I hope it was not a prediction that our trip is going to be a horrible muddle."

"With Irma in charge, have no fear!" Polly assured him.

During the summer, following that accidental meeting with Melinda at Tipsy's Tavern, Qwilleran received several phone calls from her, making unacceptable suggestions that he found annoying. He solved that problem by screening calls through his answering machine, but the proximity of two weeks in a minibus could lead to murder, he reflected with testy humor.

Eventually the final orders came from Sergeant Hasselrich, as Lyle Compton called her: "The evening before Day One we shall gather in a private parlor at our Glasgow hotel (see itinerary) for a Happy Hour from six to seven o'clock, after which you will be on your own for dinner. The tour will depart the next morning after a lavish Scottish breakfast (included in your tour package)." There followed a list of participants in alphabetical order:

John Bushland
Ms. Zella Chisholm
Mr. and Mrs. Lyle Compton (Lisa)
Mrs. Polly Duncan
Ms. Amanda Goodwinter
Dr. Melinda Goodwinter

Ms. Irma Hasselrich
Mr. and Mrs. Lawrence Lanspeak (Carol)
Mr. and Mrs. Whannell MacWhannell (Glenda)
James Qwilleran
Archibald Riker
Dwight Somers
Mrs. Grace Chisholm Utley

Qwilleran showed the list to Mildred Hanstable when she arrived at the barn for her briefing prior to cat-sitting with their Royal Highnesses. She arrived in a cloud of fluttering gauze garments that did nothing to minimize her corpulence but gave her the majesty of a clipper ship in full sail. The Siamese greeted her with enthusiasm, knowing her as the source of their crunchy treats.

Mildred perused the list of names and predicted, "Interesting group! Lyle is a certified sourpuss, but nice . . . Amanda has foot-in-mouth disease, which can be very funny at times . . . Irma is so fastidious, she'll probably inspect everyone's fingernails before breakfast . . . Let me know how you like the Chisholm sisters."

"Do they sing?"

"You don't know them, Qwill, because you don't belong to the country club. Grace is a rich widow, and her unmarried sister lives with her on Goodwinter Boulevard. They collect teddy bears."

"May I offer you a drink, Mildred?"

"Make it coffee," she said. "I've brought some cookies. But first show me the ropes."

As he conducted her up the ramp to the three balconies, they were followed by two inquisitive cats with stiffly vertical tails and stiffly horizontal whiskers. He explained, "My bedroom and studio are on the first balcony. The door is closed to keep the cats out, because Koko licks postage stamps and gummed envelopes . . . The guestroom is on the second balcony. I suggest you lock up your toothbrush. Yum Yum has a brush fetish; she'd steal my moustache if it weren't firmly attached . . . I regret that the only television is in the cats' loft on the top balcony."

"Don't apologize. I'll just set up my quilting frame on the main floor and listen to radio," she said. "How often are the cats fed?"

"Morning and evening, plus a handful of your crunchy cereal at noon and bedtime. You'll find canned and frozen delicacies for them in the kitchen."

"To tell the truth, I'd rather cook for them," Mildred said. "I really would! I miss having someone to cook for. What other care do they require?"

"They appreciate brushing once a day, and intelligent conversation, and a little entertainment. Koko prefers activities that challenge his intellect; he's a very cerebral animal." As they both turned to look at him in admiration, Kao K'o Kung rolled over and groomed the base of his tail. "Forget I said that," Qwilleran added. "That scoundrel likes to make a fool of me."

Mildred picked up the female cat, who was now rubbing against her ankles. They were slender and shapely, he noted, for a woman of her weight. "Yum Yum is so huggable," she said.

"Yes, propinquity is her middle name . . . And now let me demonstrate the fine art of policing their commode."

After the briefing they sat in the lounge area with coffee and Mildred's date-nut bars. Massive, square-cut, deep-cushioned chairs and sofas were arranged around a large square coffee table, facing the fireplace cube—a large white monolith with fireplaces on two sides and bookshelves on a third. It was high enough for two Siamese cats to perch like Olympian deities, looking down on the mere mortals below.

"Now, is there anything else I should know?" Mildred asked.

"Mrs. Fulgrove comes in once a week for light cleaning. Mr. O'Dell is our handyman. We have a colony of fruit flies that came with the apple barn, and they come out of hibernation at this time of year. Koko catches them on the wing and munches them as hors d'oeuvres. . . . I guess that's about all."

"And tell me what you're going to do in Scotland."

"Listen to bagpipes, stay in country inns, visit castles, eat haggis—all the usual, I imagine."

"Ugh! Haggis is the innards of sheep, boiled and cut up and mixed with oatmeal and spices, then sewn into a sheep's stomach."

"Sounds delicious."

Mildred's attitude turned suddenly sober. "Before coming over here," she said, "I read the tarot cards for you, and I think you ought to know what they revealed."

"It doesn't sound propitious, but let's hear it." Qwilleran was skeptical about card reading, palmistry, and all the occult sciences that interested his plump friend, but she was sincere, and he always humored her. "Do you mind if I tape this, Mildred?"

"Not at all. I wish you would."

He had already turned on his pocket-size recorder. "What did you learn?"

"Strangely, when I asked the cards about you," she began, "the answers concerned someone else—someone in danger."

"Man or woman?"

"A mature woman. A woman with strict habits and upright values."

That's Polly, Qwilleran thought; someone has told Mildred about the prowler. "What kind of danger?" he asked.

"Well, the cards were rather vague, so I brought the pack with me, and I'd like to do another reading—in your presence."

With mental reservations, he agreed, and they moved to the card table, Qwilleran politely averting his eyes as Mildred struggled to get out of the deep-seated lounge chair. When she asked him to shuffle the pack, Koko hopped to the table with an excited "Yow!"

"Want me to lock him up, Mildred?" Qwilleran suggested.

"No, let him watch." She was laying out a certain number of cards in a certain pattern. "I'm using the Celtic pattern for this reading. This card is the significator." They were colorful cards in fanciful designs, and as she manipulated them she mumbled to herself. There was a thoughtful pause. Then she said, "I see a journey . . . a journey across water . . . with stormy weather ahead."

"Glad I packed my raincoat," he said lightly.

"Stormy weather could stand for dissension, mistakes, accidents, or whatever."

"Too bad I didn't know before I paid my money."

"You're not taking this seriously, Qwill."

"Sorry. I didn't mean to sound flippant."

"This final card . . . is not auspicious . . . You might consider it a warning."

The card showed a scene in a grape arbor, with a woman in flowing robes, a bird perched on her wrist, and a scattering of gold coins. "Looks like a happy card to me," Qwilleran observed.

"But it's reversed."

"Meaning . . ."

"Some kind of fraud . . . or treachery."

"Yow!" said Koko.

"In conclusion . . . I urge you to be prepared . . . for the unexpected." Mildred always became short of breath toward the end of a reading, and her energy flagged, so Qwilleran thought it best not to pursue the subject.

"Very interesting. Thank you," he said as he turned off the tape recorder.

Mildred walked away from the table and took a few deep breaths. When she recovered, she said, "I'll look forward to hearing the outcome."

"So will I!" Qwilleran admitted.

"When do you leave?"

"I catch the shuttle to Chicago tomorrow noon, and the international flight leaves at six P.M. After changing planes at Heathrow and going through the formalities, I should arrive in Glasgow at ten A.M., their time. I'm leaving a list of telephone numbers where we can be reached, and don't hesitate to call if there's an emergency. Mildred, you don't realize how much this is appreciated by all three of us."

"The pleasure is all mine. We'll have a ball, won't we, cats?"

"Yow!" said Koko, squeezing his eyes as if visions of shrimp Newburgh danced in his head.

The next morning Qwilleran said a regretful goodbye to the cats and looked back as he walked out the door to see two pairs of large blue eyes filled with concern. He would have wished for a more cheerful send-off. And when he drove away he was aware of two tiny creatures watching him from an upper level of the huge barn.

At the Moose County Airport he parked his car in the new indoor facility, and the shuttle plane departed without requiring the usual last-minute repairs. The connection in Chicago went smoothly, perhaps too smoothly. Three meals and several magazines later, he arrived in Glasgow on schedule. His luggage was flown, unfortunately, to another city in Western Europe. So began the Bonnie Scots Tour.

Three

By the time the participants in the Bonnie Scots Tour gathered for the Happy Hour on the eve of Day One, Qwilleran had recovered from jet lag, retrieved his luggage, and paid homage to Charles Rennie Mackintosh. Throughout the day other travelers from Moose County had been straggling wearily into the centrally located hotel selected for the jumping-off place.

At six o'clock Qwilleran—dressed in blazer, shirt, and tie according to instructions from Sergeant Hasselrich—reported to the hotel lobby and found it bright with kilts worn by males of all ages; there was a wedding reception in the banquet hall. The Bonnie Scots party was scheduled for the Robert Burns parlor, which was no different from the Sir Walter Scott Parlor or the Bonnie Prince Charlie Parlor or the Robert Louis Stevenson Parlor, except for a portrait of the poet hanging above the bar. When Qwilleran entered, a white-coated young man with red hair was circulating with a tray of champagne and orange juice.

Among the guests already on hand were Larry and Carol Lanspeak, the most likable couple in Pickax. They were civic leaders, owners of the Lanspeak Department Store, and mainstays in the Theatre Club. Qwilleran approached them, saying, "All hail, Macbeth! Hail to thee, Thane of Cawdor!"

"Dammit! It means growing a beard again," said the actor ruefully, rubbing his chin. "First it's Henry VIII, then Abe Lincoln, and now this. How come I never get a chance to play Peter Pan?" He was a mild-mannered man, difficult to imagine as the murderous Macbeth.

Carol said, "Qwill, this is Dwight Somers, who's directing *Macbeth.* I don't think you two have met . . . Dwight, Jim Qwilleran is better known as Qwill. You've seen his column, 'Straight from the Qwill Pen,' in the paper."

"I've heard a lot about you," said the man with the neatly clipped beard, "and I enjoy your column. It's always right on."

"Thanks. You're new in Moose County. Where do you hail from?"

"Most recently, from Iowa. Should I read that line with pride or apology?"

"There's nothing wrong with Iowa that couldn't be fixed with a few Wisconsin lakes and Pennsylvania mountains," Qwilleran said encouragingly. He liked Dwight Somers on sight; the man exuded an inner energy characteristic of theatre people. And his compliments did not go unnoticed; Qwilleran was vain about his writing.

The foursome was joined by the other couple, the Comptons. Lyle was the tall, lanky, saturnine superintendent of schools; Lisa, who worked for Social Services, had dancing eyes and a sense of humor that contrasted with her husband's dour demeanor. She asked, "Who's taking care of your cats, Qwill?"

"Mildred Hanstable. I hope she doesn't overfeed them. They're con artists when it comes to food . . . Are you two ready for a happy adventure in the Highlands?"

With his usual scowl Lyle said, "I'm going to be happy if it kills me!"

A young man with thinning hair walked into the parlor, a camera slung over his shoulder, and Qwilleran introduced him as the photographer from Lockmaster, John Bushland.

"Call me Bushy," he said congenially, stroking his nearly bald head.

"How come you brought your camera and not your wife, Bushy?"

"Well, you see, Vicki started a catering service this summer, and she has bookings she can't cancel. What did you do about the cats, Qwill?"

"They're holding the fort in Pickax, with a live-in cook to cater their meals. I hated to leave them. I left some of my old sweaters lying around, so they can sit on them and not feel abandoned."

"That's thoughtful of you," said Carol Lanspeak, "but I suspect you'll miss the cats more than they'll miss you."

"You don't need to tell me that, Carol. I've been bluffed and bullied by those two opportunists long enough to know."

Gradually the others arrived—the women in skirts and heels, the men in coats and ties. Mr. and Mrs. Mac-Whannell were a quiet couple, stiffly formal—a tall, portly man and a tiny birdlike woman. Arch Riker and Amanda Goodwinter had obviously had a headstart at a pub. Irma and Polly arrived with a large map of Scotland, which the red-haired waiter hung on the wall. Irma was, indeed, meticulously dressed and groomed, and her statuesque figure had a polished perfection that put the other women at a disadvantage.

The map was an instant attraction, especially the west coast, fringed with firths, lochs, kyles, and isles. "Caused by glacial movement in the Ice Age," the leader explained with authority.

Someone asked, "How big is Scotland?"

Before Irma could answer, a man's voice came from the rear of the group—the chesty voice that goes with a portly figure. "The country is 30,414 square miles, smaller than South Carolina."

Everyone turned to gaze in speechless wonder at Whannell MacWhannell, accountant.

In a small, fearful voice his wife asked him, "Do we have to drive over any mountains, Daddy?"

"Not big ones, Mother," he assured her.

Amanda whispered, "Aren't they a sweet couple? I may throw up!"

The map brought forth a variety of comments:

"Look! There's the famous Loch Lomond!"

"Hope we see the Loch Ness monster."

"Where are the distilleries?"

The deep voice in the rear said, "There's a famous railway bridge over the Firth of Forth, with two spans of 1,710 feet each and two of 690 feet. The tracks are 157 feet above the water."

Amanda groaned. "Big Mac is going to be the official bore on this trip."

Someone said quietly, "Put on your sunglasses, everybody. Here come the Chisholm sisters."

The two women who entered the parlor were older than the others in the group, both having white hair. One walked a few steps behind the other. In the lead was a short, stocky woman wearing a dazzling array of jewelry, her bosomy figure displaying it like a jeweler's velvet tray.

Carol confided to Qwilleran in a whisper, "It's all the real thing! You should see her on Saturday night at the country club! She and Zella also collect teddy bears on a large scale."

He was no connoisseur of jewelry, but he was impressed by the strands of pearls twisted with chunky gold chains and clasped at the left collarbone with a spray of diamonds. Her sister—taller and thinner and plainer—wore a small gold teddy bear with ruby eyes.

The pair headed directly toward him, and the bejeweled sister said in a raspy voice, "You're Mr. Qwilleran! I recognized the moustache from your picture in the paper. We always read your column." She looked up at him brightly. "I'm Grace Utley, and this is my sister, Zella. We're Chisholms. You must have heard of the Chisholms. Our grandfather built the Moose County courthouse . . . yes!"

"How do you do," he said with a gracious bow. "My mother was a Mackintosh."

"We collect teddy bears!" she said, eagerly awaiting a newsman's reaction to this newsworthy credential.

"Very interesting," he said stolidly.

"Yes . . . We have a button-in-ear Steiff that's very rare."

At that moment he was aware that Melinda Goodwinter was entering the parlor; he caught a whiff of her familiar perfume. As a doctor and a Goodwinter she was being greeted with suitable respect, but her eyes wandered around the room until she spotted Qwilleran. Within seconds she was at his side.

"Hello, lover," she said coolly.

"Melinda, have you met Grace Utley and Zella Chisholm?" he asked. "Ladies, do you know Dr. Melinda Goodwinter?"

"We do indeed . . . yes!" said Mrs. Utley. "How are you, dear heart? We were distressed to hear about your father. You have our deepest sympathy."

The waiter reappeared with his tray of champagne and orange juice, and while the older women were momentarily distracted, Melinda managed to draw Qwilleran aside, saying, "Alone at last! You're looking great, lover!"

"How did you like Boston?" he asked, avoiding any lingering eye contact. "It's good of you to come back and take over your father's clinic."

"Boston served its purpose, but I'm glad to be home. I heard you've converted the Klingenschoen barn, and you're living in it."

"For a while, at any rate."

"Do you still have the cats?"

"I provide their bed and board." Koko, he recalled, had not cared for Melinda, always telling her to go home in his subtle, catly way. Trying to keep the conversation impersonal, Qwilleran asked, "How do you like Moose County's new newspaper?"

"Big improvement." Melinda gulped the rest of her champagne. "Aren't you the one who's financing it?"

"The Klingenschoen Foundation is behind it," he cor-

rected her. "Arch Riker is editor-and-publisher. Have you
met him? He and I are old friends, and we're sharing accommodations on this tour . . . Arch! Come over here!"

The publisher caught the significance of the situation and
rose to the occasion. "We met at the funeral," he said when
Qwilleran introduced him. "I'm glad you're taking over
your father's practice, Melinda. We need all the doctors we
can get. They keep inventing new diseases. I hope you
brought your little black bag on this trip, in case anyone
chokes on the porridge or gets bitten by a haggis . . ."

Good old Arch! Qwilleran thought. "May I bring you
some champagne, Melinda?" he asked. Without waiting for
an answer, he slipped away toward the bar and before he
could complete his mission, Irma clapped hands for attention, and the group gathered around the map.

"Welcome to Scotland," she said. "I hope you will have
a joyous time on the Bonnie Scots Tour. We'll be traveling
in Bonnie Prince Charlie country, a region brimming with
history and romance."

Qwilleran heard a veiled grunt of protest from Lyle
Compton.

"Some of the places we'll visit," Irma went on, "are not
open to the average tourist, and most of the inns are off
the beaten path, but because of my connections we'll be
made welcome. I would like to make one suggestion at this
time. For two weeks we'll be traveling as one big happy
family, and it would be friendly to alternate seats in the
bus and at the table when we stop for meals. Is that
agreed?"

There was a vague murmur among the group.

"Day One starts tomorrow morning at seven o'clock
when we meet in the hotel coffee shop for breakfast. Your
bags should be packed and outside the door of your room
not later than six-thirty. I suggest you request wake-up calls
for five-thirty to give you ample time."

Five-thirty! Qwilleran huffed into his moustache.

Irma concluded her speech to polite applause, and Qwilleran grabbed Riker's arm. "Round up Amanda and Polly,

THE CAT WHO WASN'T THERE

and let's go to dinner," he said. "I've found a good Indian restaurant. I'll meet you in a taxi in front of the hotel." He made a quick escape.

The restaurant, in true Anglo-Indian style, had white tile floors, tinkling fountains, hanging brass lamps, an assertive aroma of curry, and a background of raga music played on the sarod, tabla, and tamboura. The plucked strings, rhythmic percussion, and hypnotic drone of the instruments provided a soothing background for conversation.

Polly was looking handsome in her blue batwing cape, but Amanda—no matter how carefully she tried to dress—always looked as if she had just washed the car or cleaned the basement. Riker, with his bent sense of humor, thought it was part of her attraction.

"What would it take," she grumbled, "to get them to turn off the music and the fountains?"

"Quiet, Amanda," he said with amusement suffusing his ruddy face. "When in Glasgow, do as the Glaswegians do."

Qwilleran suggested ordering samosas with the drinks, saying they were meat-filled pastries. Then he recommended mulligatawny soup and a main course of tandoori murghi and pulao, with a side order of dal. "All spicy dishes, I don't need to tell you," he warned.

"Why, this is nothing but roast chicken with rice and lentils," Amanda announced when the entrée was served.

Riker nudged her. "Just enjoy it, and don't editorialize." As conversation focused on the forthcoming tour, he remarked, "Compton really knows his Scottish history. He gave a talk at the Boosters Club last month."

"I hope he won't be too argumentative," Polly said with concern. "Irma accepts the romantic version of Scots history, but Lyle is a militant revisionist."

"I like the idea of having a historian on board," Riker said. "Not to mention a professional photographer and a physician."

"Don't you think Melinda is looking rather world-weary?" Polly asked. "Her eyes look strange."

"She's stopped wearing green contacts and three sets

of false eyelashes," said her cousin Amanda with 'tart authority.

"Will someone explain the Chisholm sisters?" Qwilleran asked.

Amanda had the whole story. The Chisholms and the Utleys represented "old money" in Moose County, the former having rebuilt most of Pickax following the fire of 1869. The Utleys, as owners of fisheries, were several rungs down the social ladder but grew rich on trout and whitefish. Grace's late husband invested the family fortune cleverly and, it was rumored, illegally, returning from mysterious business trips with lavish gifts of jewelry for his wife.

Amanda grumbled, "You could buy a fifty-foot yacht with what she's wearing around her neck, but she's slow in paying her decorating bills . . . *Yes!*" she added mockingly.

Over a dessert of gajar halva, which Amanda insisted was nothing but carrot pudding, the conversation turned to Charles Rennie Mackintosh.

"He wore flowing silk ties and had a prominent moustache," Qwilleran reported, preening his own, "and he liked cats."

"How do you know?"

"There was one small clue in the Mackintosh house, which has been reconstructed by the university. The designer and his wife lived there in the early 1900s, and he had the guts to transform a Victorian townhouse into light, airy living spaces! In the drawing room everything is white—walls, carpet, fireplace, furniture, everything—except for two gray cushions on the hearth, for their two Persian cats."

"How charming!" Polly said. "Irma attended the art school he designed."

"I think his most daring innovation was a narrow chair with an extremely high back. He liked to use a grid pattern in wallpaper and furniture—also a small oval shape said to represent the eye of a peacock feather."

Amanda said, "Peacock feathers are bad luck. I wouldn't have one in the house!"

Too bad about that, Qwilleran thought. He had bought several silver brooches based on the Mackintosh peacock feather, to take home as gifts.

The evening ended early; Day One would start at five-thirty.

When the telephones jangled in certain hotel rooms at that hour, disgruntled travelers from Moose County got out of bed and stumbled about their rooms, making tea with their tea-makers. They dressed, packed, put their luggage out in the hall, and reported for breakfast at seven o'clock. No one was really hungry, and they were dismayed by the array of oatmeal, eggs, meat, fish, fruit, pancakes, scones, currant buns, oatcakes, bannocks, jams, marmalade, and more.

"No waffles?" Amanda was heard to complain.

Irma assured them that a full Scottish breakfast would be included with all their overnights. "So take advantage of it," she advised. "For lunch we'll just have a bowl of soup in a pub."

Amanda's grim expression brightened.

At eight o'clock the minibus was waiting in front of the hotel, with the luggage partly loaded in the baggage bins underneath. A red-haired man in a chauffeur's cap was speaking angrily to Irma in a tongue that appeared to be Gaelic, the gist of his argument being that there was too much luggage to fit in the bins. A reassessment of the load indicated that Grace Utley, ignoring the limit on personal luggage, was traveling with three alligator bags plus an alligator carry-on. To make matters worse, she was half an hour late, a fact resented by passengers who had been up since five-thirty.

"There's one on every tour," said Carol Lanspeak philosophically.

Space was found in the passenger compartment for the

surplus cases at the expense of rider comfort, and the culprit finally arrived, saying a blithe good-morning to everyone. She was wearing, with her sweater and slacks, some ropes of twisted gold from which dangled a fringe of gold and enamel baubles.

The driver, a sullen man of about forty, was introduced as Bruce, and the bus pulled away from the hotel with Irma sitting on a cramped jumpseat at the front. Using a microphone, she described points of interest as they drove out of the city and into the countryside, while the passengers looked dutifully to right and to left until their necks ached. "In the distance is Ben Nevis, Britain's highest mountain," she would say, and Big Mac's voice would come from the back of the bus: "Elevation 4,406 feet." By the time they stopped for their bowl of soup, they were stunned into silence by the abundance of scenery and commentary.

After lunch, their leader clapped hands for attention. "We shall soon be in Bonnie Prince Charlie country," she told them. "For six months the handsome young prince was trapped like a fox pursued by hounds. After the defeat at Culloden he fled for his life, sometimes betrayed by treacherous friends and sometimes harbored by unexpected supporters attracted by his charisma."

"Charisma? Bunk!" Lyle Compton muttered to Qwilleran. "It was all politics!"

"With a price on his head," Irma went on, "he was trying desperately to escape to France. He slept in the bracken by day and traveled by night, stumbling across moors and through glens. Weary, tattered, and obviously defeated, he kept up his good spirits. After all, he was a prince, and the lovely Flora Macdonald fell in love with him and risked her life to smuggle him out of enemy territory."

Lyle spoke up, his voice crisp with exasperation. "Irma, you've been reading romantic novels and watching old movies! Charles was a liar, an alcoholic, and a fool! He made all kinds of tactical mistakes and had a talent for trusting the wrong aides and taking the advice of idiots.

Flora Macdonald had no use for him, but she was pressured into the plot to rescue him—" He stopped abruptly and threw a sharp glance at his wife as if she had kicked him under the table.

Irma's face flushed and her eyes flashed, and Polly rushed in to fill the awkward silence. "What was the date of Culloden?" she asked, although she knew.

"April 16, 1746," Irma said, and big Mac rattled off some statistics.

Later, Amanda said to Qwilleran, "Lyle had better watch his step. She's already shot one man."

On that day, and the next, and the next, Irma herded the group through fishing villages, among ruins, aboard ferries, around rocky islands, across moors covered with purple heather, past granite quarries and peat bogs.

"Where are the people? Where are the farmhouses?" Carol complained. "All we see is sheep!" Flocks of them grazed on the hillsides or crossed the road in front of the bus.

Compton snorted and said to Qwilleran, "I could tell you what happened to the people, but Irma wouldn't like it, and my wife would give me hell again."

At each rest stop the driver assisted women passengers off the bus in solemn silence, then wandered away for a cigarette while the travelers used the facilities and explored the gift shops. Qwilleran bought a tie in the Mackintosh tartan; Larry bought a staghorn cane that he said he might use in the play; Dwight Somers bought a tin whistle.

The family-type seating on the bus and at meals, as suggested by Irma, became a discordant game of musical chairs. Qwilleran avoided sitting with Melinda. No one wanted to sit with Grace Utley or Glenda MacWhannell. Arch Riker was always getting stuck with Zella Chisholm. Both Dwight and Bushy had a desire to sit with Melinda. Melinda kept trying to sit with Qwilleran. And Amanda often ended up with Big Mac.

The bus traveled on single-track roads most of the time,

so passengers worried about meeting another vehicle head-on, but Bruce wheeled the bus up and down hills and around endless curves with reckless abandon, causing Glenda MacWhannell to scream at the roller-coaster effect and Zella Chisholm to complain of car sickness.

Hour after hour Irma talked into the microphone, and the monotony of her voice put the riders to sleep, especially after lunch. In the afternoon they would wake up for tea and shortbread at some modest cottage that advertised "Teas" on a modest signboard. Then, at the end of the day, everyone would stumble off the bus, stiff and sore, to check into a quaint inn tucked into a glen or overlooking a loch. In this way Day One, Day Two, and Day Three became a blur.

Qwilleran said to Riker, "I can't remember what we saw yesterday or what we had for dinner last night. If I weren't recording some of this on tape, I'd get home and never know I'd been here."

"I'm not even sure where we are," said his roommate.

The inns, adapted from old stone stables and ruined abbeys, were cozy and rustic, and since there were no room keys—only bolts inside the bedroom doors—Grace Utley had to entrust her jewel cases to the innkeeper's safe. Amanda complained that there were no ice machines, no telephones or TV in the bedrooms, and no washcloths in the bathrooms. Glenda MacWhannell worried about fire.

At the dinner hour, the women reported in skirts and heels, the men in coats and ties, while Mrs. Utley outshone them all with four strands of sapphire beads accented with a chunk of carved white jade, or a necklace of black onyx and gold, clasped at the collarbone with lapis lazuli. Thus arrayed, they dined on fresh salmon or roast lamb with neeps and tatties, served by the jovial innkeeper and his rosy-cheeked daughters.

Come morning, the group would be herded aboard the bus once again, only to wait for the late Grace Utley. There was usually a misty rain at the start of each day, but the

afternoon sun made the waters of the lochs and kyles spar-
kle like acres of diamonds.

On one wet morning they visited a damp and chilly castle
with a moat and a drawbridge, a massive gate and a stone
courtyard, and a Great Hall hung with armor and ancestral
portraits. Here a guide recited a catalogue of battles, con-
quering heroes, scandals, ghosts, and assassinations, after
which the visitors were free to explore regal apartments,
dungeons, and staircases carved out of solid rock. Windows were small, passages were narrow, and doorways
were low.

"The early Scots must have been pygmies," Qwilleran
said as he stooped to maneuver his six-feet-two through a
low doorway.

"Look out!" someone yelled.

Turning to check the danger, Qwilleran straightened up
and struck his head on the stone lintel above. The blow
knocked him to his knees, and he saw blinding flashes of
light and heard distant screams and calls for help. Next he
was being seated on a bench, and Melinda was checking
his pulse and lifting his eyelids, all the while asking questions: "Do you know your name? . . . What day is it? . . .
Do you know where you are?"

At this point, Qwilleran was feeling more anger than
pain, and he snapped, "Shakespeare wrote *Macbeth*. Moose
County is north of the equator. Eli Whitney invented the
cotton gin. And if you don't mind, I'd like to go outside
and sit in the bus while you people finish your sightseeing
and buy your postcards."

Dwight Somers volunteered to go with him.

"I've had enough castle for one day," Qwilleran told him.

"Same here. How did they exist in that damp, gloomy
environment?"

"They didn't. If they weren't murdered in their twenties,
they died of pneumonia in their thirties."

"I've been wanting to ask you, Qwill: Have you done
any theatre?"

"Only in college. At one time I was planning to be an actor, until a wise professor steered me into journalism, and I must admit that a little acting experience doesn't hurt in my profession."

"I was sure you had training. You have a very good voice. I wish you'd take a role in *Macbeth*."

"What did you have in mind for me?" Qwilleran asked. "Banquo's ghost? One of the three witches? Lady Macbeth?"

"You're not too far off base. In Shakespeare's time she was played by an actor in drag, but he didn't have a moustache. How about doing Macduff? He has a couple of great scenes, and I don't think the guy we've cast is going to work out."

"That's a sizable part," Qwilleran objected. "It would be tough to learn lines after so many years away from the stage . . . No, Dwight, I'd better stick to my role as theatre reviewer for the paper. Have you cast Lady Macbeth?"

"Yes, I gave the role to Melinda. She has a certain quality for Lady Macbeth. She brought a script with her on the trip, and she's been working on her lines."

Members of the party were emerging from the castle and sauntering across the drawbridge.

"Melinda's an interesting woman," Dwight went on. He paused, waiting for an affirmative comment. When none was forthcoming, he said, "We both have apartments at Indian Village, and I've been seeing her quite often but not getting very far." There was another pause. "I'm getting the impression I might be trespassing on your territory."

"No problem," Qwilleran assured him.

"This is the first time I've lived in a town as small as Pickax, and I don't want to violate any codes."

"No problem," Qwilleran said.

When the group started climbing into the bus, everyone expressed concern about his condition, but Melinda examined the bump on his head and announced there was no bleeding.

Their destination that night was a picturesque inn converted from a bothy, with numerous additions, confusing levels, and angled hallways. The beds were comfortable, however, and the furnishings were engagingly old, with a homey clutter of doilies, knickknacks, vases of heather, baskets of fruit, and the ubiquitous tea-maker. Coils of rope were provided under the windows for escape in case of fire.

The Bonnie Scots tourists were booked for two nights, and Irma had promised them a free day, absolutely unstructured, after several days of hurtling around in the bus. They could enjoy the luxury of unpacking their luggage, putting their belongings away in bureau drawers, and hanging clothes in the wardrobes that served as closets.

After a dinner of sheep's head broth, rabbit casserole, and clootie dumplings, Qwilleran excused himself, saying he had a headache and wished to retire early, although the chief reason was a desire to get away from his fellow travelers.

From the main hall he went up half a flight of stairs, turned left into a narrow passage, then to the right and three steps down, through a glass door and up a ramp, and finally to the left, where he bumped into a bewildered Grace Utley, clutching her necklace in panic.

"Are you lost?" he asked. "It isn't hard to do."

"I took the wrong turn somewhere, dear heart," she said. "We're in Number Eight."

"Then you should be in the other wing. Follow me."

After he had conducted her to the hallway leading to Number Eight, she seemed reluctant to let him go. "Mr. Qwilleran," she began in her grating voice, "I shouldn't mention this, but . . . do you think Ms. Hasselrich is carrying on with that bus driver?"

"What do you mean by carrying on?" he asked.

"It's the way she looks at him, and they have secret conversations in a foreign language. Last night, when I looked out my window, I could see them on the moor in the moonlight . . . yes!"

"Could have been ghosts," he said archly. "They haunt the moors all the time. Pay no attention, Mrs. Utley."

"Please call me Grace," she said. "How do you feel after your accident, dear heart?"

"Just a slight headache. I'm retiring early."

Other women in the group had raised eyebrows over Irma's secret nightlife, but Lyle had said, "The woman works sixteen hours a day! She's entitled to some R&R, and ours not to question where or with whom."

Qwilleran returned to his room and changed into the red pajamas that Polly had given him for a Valentine, hoping for a few hours of solitude. The others were sipping Drambuie in front of the fire, or playing cards, or watching TV in the keeping room.

Lounging in a passably comfortable chair, he began to dictate the day's experiences into his tape recorder: "Today we visited the island where Macbeth was buried in 1057 . . ."

He was interrupted by a knock on the door.

"Now, who the devil is that?" he muttered. He hoped it was not Grace Utley. Worse yet, it was Melinda.

Four

"How do you feel, lover?" Melinda asked as she stood in the passage outside Qwilleran's room. "You seemed rather quiet during dinner."

"After conversing with the same crowd for five days, I'm running out of things to say and also the patience to listen," he said.

"May I come in? I want to check your pulse and temperature. Sit down over there, please." She entered in a cloud of scent that had enchanted him three years ago; now it seemed too sweet, too musky. She inserted a thermometer in his mouth, counted his pulse, raised his eyelids, and looked at his eyeballs. "You're still legally alive," she said as she drew a flask from her official black bag. "Would you like a little nip for medicinal purposes?"

"You've forgotten I can't have alcohol, Melinda."

"Where's your tea-maker? We'll have a nice cup of tea, as they say over here." She filled the pot with water from the bathroom tap. "How do you like the tour so far?"

"There's too much of everything. Too much food, too much conversation, too much bus travel, too many tourists."

Melinda sauntered around the room in familiar fashion. "Your room looks comfortable. The doubles are better than the singles. I'm at the end of the hall in Number Nine—for your future reference—and the furnishings give me gastrointestinal burbulence. I have a wonderful view of the loch, though. Perhaps Arch would like to exchange with me," she said with a mischievous glance.

"Does anyone know the name of this loch? They all look alike to me," said Qwilleran, an expert at ignoring hints.

"Well, tell me about you, Qwill. What have you been doing for the last three years?"

"Sometimes I wonder. The years speed by." He was in no mood to socialize or particularize.

"Apparently you're not married yet."

"It's fairly well accepted in Moose County that I'm not suitable grist for the matrimonial mill."

Melinda poured two cups of tea and splashed something from the flask into her own cup. "I was hoping we could pick up where we left off."

"I'll say it again, what I've said before, Melinda. You belong with a man of your own age—your own generation."

"I like older men."

"And I like older women," he said with brutal candor.

"Ouch!" she said and then added impishly, "Wouldn't you like a second-string girlfriend for your youthful moments?"

"This is good tea," he said, although he disliked tea. "You must have used two teabags."

"Are you as . . . uh . . . compatible with your present inamorata as you were with me?"

"What is this? The third degree? I think you're exceeding your privilege as a medical practitioner."

She was not easily deterred. "Didn't you ever think you'd like to have sons, Qwill? Polly is a little old for that."

"Frankly, no!" he said, irritated at her intrusion into his privacy. "Nor daughters. I'm a bachelor by chance, choice, and temperament, and offspring are outside my frame of reference."

"With all your money you should have heirs."

"The Klingenschoen Foundation is my sole beneficiary, and they'll distribute my estate for the benefit of the county, the population of which is 11,279, according to Big Mac. So I have 11,279 heirs—a respectable heirship, I'd say."

"You're not drinking your tea."

"Furthermore, I resent suggestions for the disposition of my financial assets."

"Qwill, you're getting to be a grouchy old bachelor. I think marriage would be good for you. I speak as your medical adviser." She transferred to the arm of his chair. "Don't move! I want to check the bump on your head."

"Excuse me," he said and went into the bathroom, where he counted to ten . . . and then a hundred and ten before facing her again. She had kicked off her shoes and was now lounging on the bed against a bank of pillows.

"Won't you join me?" she invited playfully. "I like red pajamas."

He made a point of pacing the floor and saying nothing.

"Let me explain something, Qwill," said Melinda in a reasonable tone. "Three years ago I wanted us to marry because I thought we'd have a lot of fun together. Now I have a couple of other reasons. The Goodwinter clan is dying out, and I want sons to carry on the name. I'm very proud of the Goodwinter name. So I'll make you a proposition—since one has to be conventional in Moose County. If you will marry me, you can have your freedom at the end of three years, and our children will resume the name of Goodwinter. We might even have a go-o-od time together."

"You're out of your mind," he said, suddenly suspecting that the strange look in her eyes was insanity.

"The second reason is . . . I'm broke!" she said with the impudent frankness that he had once found attractive. "All I'm inheriting from my dad is obligations and an obsolete mansion."

"The K Foundation can help you over the rough spots. They're committed to promoting health care in the community."

"I don't want institutional support. I want you!"

"To put it bluntly, Melinda, the answer is *no!*"

"Why don't you think about it? Let the idea gel for a while?"

Qwilleran walked to the door and, with his hand on the knob, said, "Let me tell you something, and this is final. If I marry anyone, it will be Polly. Now, if you'll excuse me, I need some rest . . . Don't forget your shoes."

If Melinda felt the hellish fury of a woman scorned, the Goodwinter pride prevented her from showing it. "Take a couple of aspirin and call me in the morning, lover," she said with an insolent wink as she brushed past him, carrying her loafers.

Huffing angrily into his moustache, Qwilleran dictated a few choice words into the tape recorder before snapping it off. He was reading a booklet about the Mackintosh clan when Arch Riker walked into the room at eleven o'clock.

"You're awake, Qwill! Did you get any rest?"

"Melinda dropped in to take my pulse, and I couldn't get rid of her. The girl is getting to be a nuisance."

"I guessed that would happen. You may have to marry Polly in self-defense. If Polly doesn't want you, how about Amanda? I'll let you have the lovely Amanda."

"This is no joke, Arch."

"Well, I'm ready to hit the sack. How about you? Polly's with the Lanspeaks and the Comptons, playing Twenty Questions. Amanda's winning at cards with the Mac-Whannells and Bushy; no doubt she's cheating. Dwight is out on the terrace practicing the tin whistle; he'll be lucky if someone doesn't shoot him."

"Once a reporter, always a reporter," Qwilleran commented.

"I haven't seen Irma. Her voice was very hoarse at the dinner table. Too much chatter on that blasted microphone! And her evenings in the damp night air can't do anything for her vocal cords . . . How's the bump on your head, Qwill?"

"It's subsiding, but I'd like to know who yelled 'Look out' and why!"

That was the end of Day Five.

Day Six began at dawn when Qwilleran was awakened by screams in the hall and frantic banging on someone's door.

Riker was sitting up in the other bed, saying, "What's that? Are we on fire?"

There were sounds of running feet, and Qwilleran looked out in the hall as other heads appeared in other doorways. The innkeeper rushed past them and disappeared into Number Eleven, occupied by Polly and Irma.

"Oh, my God!" Qwilleran shouted over his shoulder. "Something's happened to the girls!" As he started down the passageway, the innkeeper's wife was ahead of him.

Her husband shouted to her, "Ring up the constable! One o' the lassies had an attack! Ring up the constable!"

Qwilleran hurried to the room at the end of the hall and breathed a sigh of relief when he saw Polly standing there in her nightgown. She was weeping in her hands. Melinda, in pajamas, was bending over the bed. He threw his arms around Polly. "What happened?"

"I think she's dead!" she sobbed. "I woke up suddenly a few minutes ago and felt that ghastly sense of death. I called Melinda." Polly burst into a fresh torrent of tears.

Still holding her, Qwilleran said to Melinda, "Is there anything I can do?" Others were crowding into the room in their nightclothes.

"Get everyone out of the room—and out of the hall— until the authorities have been here. Out! Out! I'll talk to all of you downstairs, later."

The concerned bystanders wandered back to their rooms, whispering:

"Is Irma dead?"

"What was it? Does anyone know what happened?"

"This is terrible! Who'll notify her parents?"

"It'll kill them! She's their only child, and they're getting on in years."

"She was only forty-two last birthday."

Lyle Compton nudged Qwilleran. "Do you think something happened out on the moor?"

Quickly they dressed and gathered downstairs in the small parlor, and the innkeeper's wife served hot tea, murmuring sympathetic phrases that no one understood or really heard. In everyone's mind the question was nagging: *What do we do now?*

They were aware of vehicles arriving in the courtyard and then departing, and eventually Melinda walked into the parlor in robe and slippers, with uncombed hair and no makeup. She looked wan and troubled. The group fell silent as she faced them and said in a hollow voice, "Irma was the first patient to walk into my clinic—and the real reason for my coming on this trip. And I've lost her!"

When someone asked the cause of death, Qwilleran turned on his tape recorder. At this moment he could feel only compassion for this young doctor; she was so distraught.

"Cardiac arrest," Melinda said wearily. "With her heart condition she should never have undertaken this project. She had this driving ambition, you know, and she was such a perfectionist."

Polly said, "I didn't know she had a bad heart. She never mentioned her symptoms, and we were the best of friends."

"She was too proud to admit to any frailty—and too independent to take my advice or even medication. It could have saved her."

Carol said, "But, Irma, of all people! Who would think—? She was always so cool and collected. She never hurried or panicked like the rest of us."

Melinda explained, "She internalized her emotions—not a healthy thing to do."

"What was the time of death?" Qwilleran asked.

"About three A.M., I would say. Does anyone know what time she came in?"

Polly said, "I don't know. I never waited up for her. She told me not to."

"What happens now?" Larry asked.

"I'm not allowed to sign the death certificate over here," Melinda said. "A local doctor will have to do that. I'll notify Irma's parents and make whatever arrangements are necessary."

Qwilleran offered to call the Hasselriches, since he knew the father well.

"Thanks, but I feel I should do it. I can explain exactly what happened."

"We're certainly grateful that you're here, Melinda. Is there anything we can do for you—anything at all?"

"You might talk it over among yourselves and decide how to handle the rest of the tour. I'll fly back with the body. There'll be some red tape before they release it, the constable said, but they don't anticipate any problem . . . So, if you'll excuse me, I'll go up and get dressed. You can stay here and talk."

When Amanda arrived from the other bedroom wing and heard the news, she said, "I move to cancel the tour and fly home. Anybody second it? Let's cut our losses."

Polly spoke up with conviction. "Irma would want us to continue, I'm sure."

"But do we know what to do and where to go?" Lisa asked.

"Everything is in her briefcase—itinerary, confirmations, maps, and so forth. I'm sure we can follow her plan to the letter. Since we have an extra day here, we'll have time to work it out."

Riker said, "What time is it in Pickax? I want to call Junior and get him started on the obituary. It'll take some digging, because she was a very private person—would never let us do a feature on her volunteer work."

Guests from the other wing straggled into the parlor, and Bushy said, "Why so glum, kids? Did somebody die around here?"

At the breakfast table the members of the Bonnie Scots Tour halfheartedly discussed their options for the day: Go shopping in the village . . . Watch the fishing boats come in . . . Take the ferry to one of the islands . . . Loll around the inn. Larry said he would wander in the hills and study his lines for the play. Amanda thought she would go back to bed. The MacWhannells announced they were leaving the tour and would hire a car to drive to Edinburgh. They gave no reasons for cutting out, and no one bothered to ask why.

After breakfast, Qwilleran and the school superintendent strolled down the winding road to the village below. "Don't forget, Lyle. What goes down must come up," Qwilleran warned. "We have to climb this hill again."

Compton said, "I hope I didn't contribute to Irma's stress by blowing off steam about Scottish history and challenging her statements. Lisa said I should have kept my big mouth shut, but—dammit—Irma drove me up the wall with her sentimental claptrap about the romantic Jacobite Rebellion and her beloved Prince Charlie."

"Don't worry. She was a tough one. She didn't earn the name of Sergeant for nothing. They say she ran the volunteer crew at the Senior Facility like an army battalion."

They stopped awhile to admire the view: the patchwork of rooftops down below, the curve of the harbor crowded with boats, the islands beyond, floating placidly in a silver sea. Behind them the hills rose like Alpine meadows, dotted with sheep and the ruins of stone buildings.

"Lyle, you promised to tell me how the sheep took over the Highlands," Qwilleran said.

"Don't blame the sheep. Have you heard about the Highland Clearances?"

"Only superficially. Okay if I tape this?"

"Go ahead . . . Well, you know," he began, "when the Rebellion failed, the clan system was deliberately destroyed, and Highlanders were forbidden by law to wear kilts or play bagpipes. Instead of clan chieftains they now had rich landlords renting small bits of land to crofters, who shared their one-room huts with the livestock. Then, with the growing demand for meat, the big landowners found it easier and more profitable to raise sheep than to collect rents from poor crofters. Also, sheep could make money for investors in Edinburgh and London."

"Agribusiness, eighteenth-century style," Qwilleran remarked.

"Exactly! To be fair, though, I should say that not all the landlords were villains; some of the old families tried their best to help their people, but overpopulation and old-fashioned farming methods combined to keep the crofters in a state of near-starvation."

"What happened to them when the sheep took over?"

"They were driven off the land and forbidden to hunt, fish, or graze livestock. Their pitiful crofts were burned before their eyes."

"Where did they go?"

"They were sent to live in destitution in big-city slums or in poor coastal villages. Many were transported to North America, and that's another story! They were exploited by ship owners and sent to sea in leaky tubs overcrowded and without sufficient food and water . . . I shouldn't be telling you this; it shoots up my blood pressure."

The two men wandered around the waterfront and watched the fishing boats coming in, surrounded by screaming seagulls. Crewmen in yellow slickers were slinging prawn traps onto the wharf, laughing and joking. Facing the docks were freshly painted, steep-roofed cottages huddled in a row, with flowers around the doorsteps and seagulls on the chimney pots. Some of the cottage windows had cut-off curtains that allowed cats to sit on the window-sills.

Lyle said, "The Scots today are nice people—sociable, hospitable, and slyly witty—but they have a bloody history of cutting throats and pouring molten lead on their enemies."

They lunched at a pub before returning to the inn. There

they learned that Melinda had checked out and was on her way to Glasgow in a hired car, leaving a message: "Don't feel bad about my giving up the rest of the tour. This is my responsibility as Irma's friend and physician."

Lisa reported to Qwilleran, "Polly and I packed Irma's belongings to ship home. Polly's all broken up. She's in her room, saying she doesn't want to be disturbed by anyone."

"I guess that means me," he said.

For him the death of their leader was an excuse to phone Mildred Hanstable and inquire about the Siamese. They were often on his mind, although he refrained from talking about them to anyone except Polly. Grace Utley showed pictures of her teddy bears to anyone who sat next to her on the bus. Nevertheless, Qwilleran often looked at his watch, deducted five hours, and visualized the cats having their breakfast or taking an afternoon nap in a certain patch of sun on the rug. He wondered how they were hitting it off with Mildred. He wondered if they were getting fat on her cooking. He wondered if they missed him.

When he telephoned Pickax, it was eight o'clock in the morning, their time, and Mildred had heard the news of Irma's death on the radio. "They didn't give any details on the air," she said. "There'll be more in the paper when it comes out, I hope."

"It was a heart attack. She'd been under a lot of stress. Conducting a tour is a big job for an amateur guide—with a bunch of Moose County individualists in tow. The obituary will probably be in today's paper. Please save it for me . . . How are the cats behaving?"

"We get along just fine! Yum Yum is adorable. When I'm quilting she sits on the frame and watches the needle go in and out. Koko helps me read the tarot cards."

"If the Siamese were humans," Qwilleran explained, "Yum Yum would win prizes at the county fair, and Koko would discover a cure for the common cold . . . Is he there? Put him on."

Mildred could be heard talking to the cats. There was a faint yowl, then some coaxing, and then a louder response.

"Hello, Koko!" Qwilleran shouted. "How's everything? Are you taking care of Yum Yum?"

It took the cat a while to understand that the voice he knew so well was coming out of the instrument held to his ear, but then he wanted to do all the talking, delivering a series of ear-splitting yowls and even biting the receiver.

Wincing, Qwilleran shouted, "That's enough! Take him away!"

There were sounds of scuffling and arguing, and then Mildred returned to the line. "There's one unusual thing I'd like to report," she said. "Last night while I was quilting, I heard an unearthly howl coming from one of the balconies. Koko was in my bathroom, howling in the shower. It made my blood run cold. I went up and talked to him, and finally he stopped, but it really gave me a scare."

"What time did it happen?"

"Between nine-thirty and ten, when that crazy DJ was on WPKX. I turned off the radio, thinking Koko objected to the program."

"I don't blame him," Qwilleran said. "That guy makes me howl with pain, too."

After hanging up the phone, he realized that Koko had howled between two-thirty and three, Scottish time. That cat knew the moment that Irma died! . . . He had a sense of death that spanned the ocean!

Only eleven of the original sixteen travelers reported for dinner that evening, and they were quieter than usual. The meal started with cock-a-leekie soup served with small meat-filled pastries called bridies, followed by lamb stew with barley and neeps, as well as a dish of tatties and onions called stovies.

Lyle Compton asked, "Has anyone seen Bruce today?"

No one had seen the bus driver. They all agreed he deserved a day off, and they wondered if he even knew about Irma's death.

Lisa said, "According to the Bonnie Scots game plan in Irma's briefcase, Bruce is not to smoke on the job or mix with the passengers, and he must be clean and presentable at all times. For this he's getting $1,000, plus meals and lodging and whatever tips we give him. He was paid $100 up front."

"We should tip him generously when the tour ends," Larry said. "He's an excellent driver. He picks up the luggage unobtrusively while we're at breakfast and has the bus packed for departure on time. He's not friendly, but he's courteous in a businesslike way." Everyone agreed.

After dinner, Lisa said to Qwilleran, "Polly and I decided that Larry should manage the tour."

"Why? You two are completely capable, and you've studied the contents of the briefcase."

"That's the problem," she said. "If a man is in charge, he'll be considered well informed, well organized, and a good leader. Because Irma was a woman, she was called fussy, bossy and a know-it-all."

"That's preposterous, Lisa!"

"Of course it's preposterous, but that's the way it is in Moose County, and it'll take a couple of generations to change the attitude. I just wanted you to know why Larry will be calling the plays."

The next morning, Amanda was absent from the breakfast table, and Riker explained to Qwilleran, "She has a dental problem. She broke her upper denture, and she's too embarrassed to open her mouth. Until we reach Edinburgh and get it repaired, she'll have to live on a soft diet, like porridge and Scotch."

Arch Riker was wrong. At that moment, Amanda was arranging for transportation to Glasgow; she was canceling the rest of her tour.

Carol said, "We're like the Ten Little Indians. Who's next?"

After breakfasting on a compote of dried apple slices, prunes, and figs, followed by creamed finnan haddie and oatcakes, the group shook hands with the innkeeper and his wife and prepared to board the bus in the courtyard of the inn. The baggage was loaded in the bin, but Bruce was not there to help the women aboard. Neither could he be found smoking a cigarette on the grounds, nor passing the time with a cup of coffee in the kitchen. At nine o'clock there was still no driver. In fact, they never saw Bruce again.

Five

The events of the last twenty-four hours bewildered the members of the Bonnie Scots Tour as they switched from sadness at the loss of their leader to indignation at the loss of their driver. Obviously Bruce had been there earlier, picking up the luggage in the hall and loading it properly in the waiting bus. The assistant cook said she had given him his breakfast in the kitchen at six o'clock.

Some of the passengers sat in the bus waiting hopefully for his return, while others trooped back into the inn for another cup of coffee. Mrs. Utley, who had been late in rising as usual, reported that she looked out her bedroom window while everyone was at breakfast and saw a car pull into the courtyard. It left again immediately and went downhill in a cloud of dust. No one paid any attention to her.

Eventually the innkeeper called the constable, and Larry gave the constable a rough description of the missing driver. No one knew his last name, and a quick check of Irma's briefcase failed to fill in the blank. The nearest hospital also was called, but no red-haired forty-year-old male had been admitted.

Larry addressed the group seriously. "How long do we sit here, wondering if he'll show? We have a reservation at another inn tonight and a lot of traveling to do in the meantime."

"Let's not hang around any longer," Riker advised. "It's our bus, not his. Let's hit the trail."

"That is," said Larry, "if anyone is comfortable with driving on the wrong side of the road."

Qwilleran volunteered to drive, if someone else would navigate, and Dwight was elected. Larry offered to read Irma's travel notes en route, and Lyle said he would fill in the historical facts. With this arrangement in effect, the bus pulled away from the inn for Day Seven: another castle, another loch, another stately garden, another pub lunch, another four o'clock tea with shortbread.

Qwilleran was a good driver. Everyone said he was better than Bruce. "Cheaper, too," he boasted.

At lunchtime, Carol said to him privately, "I feel terribly sorry for Melinda. My father was a surgeon, and even after thirty years in the operating room he was absolutely crushed if he lost a patient. So Irma's death was a terrible blow for Melinda, coming right on top of her father's suicide and the rumors about her mother's death. She has no immediate family now. She lost her only brother while she was in med school. She and Emory were only a year apart and grew up like twins. His birth was a difficult one, and that's what started Mrs. Goodwinter's decline into complete helplessness."

Why is she telling me this family history? Qwilleran wondered.

"You know, Qwill, it's none of my business, but I wish you and Melinda had gotten together. You always say you're not good husband material, but the right woman makes a difference, and you don't know what you're missing by not having children. Forgive me for saying so."

"No offense," he said, but he suspected that Melinda had coached her.

"All aboard!" came the commanding voice of their leader. The mild-mannered Larry Lanspeak could project like King Lear on the stormy moor.

During the afternoon drive through Glencoe, with its

wild and rugged mountain scenery, Lyle entertained the passengers with the story of the Glencoe Massacre in the late 1600s.

"King James had fled," he began, "and the Scottish chieftains were forced to pledge allegiance to William of Orange—by a certain date. There was one chief who missed the deadline: Macdonald of Glencoe. When his oath finally arrived at government headquarters—late—a high official suppressed it and gave orders to exterminate the clan. A Captain Campbell was dispatched to the glen with 128 soldiers, and they lived there for a while on friendly terms with the Macdonalds, presumably accepting the chief's hospitality. Suddenly, one day at dawn, the treacherous attack took place. Campbell's men put more than forty members of the clan to the sword, including women, children, and servants . . . I never trust a Campbell," Lyle concluded.

"Don't forget, dear," said his wife, "you married one."

"That's what I mean. They make great apple pie, but I don't trust 'em." Then he went on. "The order for the attack was supposedly written on a playing card, and ever since that time, the nine of diamonds has been called the Curse of Scotland."

That night they checked into a rustic inn that had been a private hunting and fishing lodge in the days when upper-class sportsmen came up from London for grouse-shooting and fly-casting. The Bonnie Scots group entered through massive oak doors, iron-strapped and green with mold, and walked into a lobby hung with hunting trophies. An ancient leather-bound journal recorded the names of sporting notables who had bagged 86 grouse and 33 pheasant on a certain weekend in 1838.

Larry picked up the room keys and distributed them. "Hey, look! We have locks on our doors!" he announced. "We're back in the civilized world!" Then, while the other men unloaded the bus, he telephoned the previous inn to inquire about the missing driver. There was still no clue to his defection.

When the luggage was marshaled in the center of the lobby, Bushy announced, "Grab your own bags, folks, and if you can't lug 'em upstairs yourself, we'll help you."

Piece by piece the luggage was identified and removed.

"Where's mine?" Mrs. Utley demanded. "You left it on the bus!"

A quick check proved that the baggage bin was empty.

Qwilleran said, "Are you sure you placed it outside your room this morning, Mrs. Utley?"

"My sister took care of it while I was in the shower! Where is she? Somebody go and get her! Bring her down here!"

The shy Zella, acting as if under arrest and stammering in self-defense, insisted she had put the bags in the hall along with her own suitcase. Hers had arrived safely. "I always packed for Grace while she was dressing," she explained in a tremulous voice. "I brought up the jewel cases from the safe and packed them. Then I stayed in the hall with the luggage until it was picked up."

"And Bruce picked it up?" Qwilleran asked.

"I saw him."

He exchanged knowing glances with Bushy, who was now official baggage handler as well as official photographer.

"They've been stolen!" Mrs. Utley screamed. "That man! That driver! He stole them! That's why he ran off! Somebody picked him up in a car! I saw them speed away from the inn!"

Other members of the group, hearing the commotion, came down to the lobby, and the hysterical Mrs. Utley was assisted to her room.

"Does anyone have a tranquilizer for the poor woman?" Carol asked.

"At least she has her carry-on bag, so she can brush her teeth," said Lisa, "and I imagine she's well covered with insurance."

"Where did Irma hire that guy?" Compton kept saying.

Larry phoned the previous inn, describing the missing luggage, and after a search the innkeeper called back to say that no alligator bags could be found anywhere. Larry also phoned the constable in the fishing village and learned that a report of the missing articles would have to be filed in person.

Larry said, "We'll hire a car and drive tomorrow. I'll go back there with Grace."

"That's really noble of you," said Lisa.

Qwilleran asked Bushy, "Do you think you may have taken a picture of Bruce?"

"No, he'd never let me shoot him—always turned his back. I thought he was camera-shy, but now I'm beginning to wonder . . ."

The Chisholm sisters had a tray sent up to their room, while the others gathered in the dining room for a five-course dinner of smoked salmon, lentil soup, brown trout, venison, and a dessert flavored with Scotch whiskey—or whisky, as it said on the menu card. Afterward they assembled in the lounge, where hot coals were glowing in the fireplace, and the Lanspeaks organized an impromptu revue to bolster morale. Carol and Lisa harmonized "Annie Laurie" and Larry read Robert Burns's poem "To a Mouse," with a passable Scots accent. Then Dwight played "The Muckin' o' Georgie's Byre" on the tin whistle, one of the Scottish tunes in the booklet that came with his purchase.

"It didn't take you long to become a virtuoso," Polly remarked.

"I've been playing since I was a kid," Dwight explained. "I won second place in an amateur contest when I was ten."

"Amanda says a tin whistle sounds like a sick locomotive," said Riker.

"It's weird, all right. I'm thinking of using it in *Macbeth* whenever the witches are on stage."

Lisa asked, "Are any of you fellows going to buy kilts? We're scheduled to visit a woolen mill tomorrow."

"Not I," said Qwilleran promptly, although secretly he thought he would look good in one.

"I think men look sexy in kilts . . . but they've got to have sturdy, good-looking legs," she added with a telling look at her lanky husband.

Bushy said, "I heard a good story from the innkeeper this morning. There was this newspaper woman from the states, attending some Highland games over here. Men were swinging battle axes and tossing the caber, which is something like a telephone pole, and half the male spectators were wearing kilts. This was her chance, she thought, to get an honest answer to the old question: Is it true they don't wear anything underneath? So she went up to a congenial-looking Scot with red hair, who wore his kilt with a swagger. 'Excuse me, sir,' she said. 'I'm from an American newspaper. Would you mind if I asked a bold question? Is it true that—ah—*nothing is worn under your kilt?*' He answered without hesitation. 'Yes, indeed, ma'am, it's true. Everything is in perfect working order.' "

Lyle grunted, and his wife giggled. He said, "When the English Redcoats ridiculed the Scots for fighting in 'short skirts' during the Rebellion, they didn't know the reason for the national costume. It was for walking through a dense growth of heather. When the English soldiers tried it in full uniform, they bogged down."

Larry said, "Tomorrow we visit the battlefield at Culloden. Why don't you brief us, Lyle?"

"How much do you want to know? It was one of the bloodiest military mistakes ever made!"

"Go ahead," everyone insisted.

"Well . . . Prince Charlie wanted to put his father back on the throne, and the English marched north to put down the uprising. They had 9,000 well-equipped, well-trained professional soldiers in scarlet coats. They had competent officers in powdered wigs, as well as a full complement of cannon, muskets, horses, and supply wagons. The Rebels were 5,000 hastily assembled, poorly commanded Scots with broadswords, daggers, and axes."

Qwilleran had turned on his recorder.

"It wasn't just Scots against the English. There were Highlanders against Lowlanders, Rebels against Loyalists, clans against clans, brothers against brothers.

"When the Rebels fought at Culloden, several mistakes had already been made by their commanders. They chose a battlefield that gave the advantage to the enemy; their food had run out; they had marched their troops all night in a maneuver that didn't work; the men were exhausted from hunger and lack of sleep; even their horses had died of starvation.

"Then the battle started, and they received no order to advance but stood in ranks while the enemy cannon mowed them down. Desperate at the delay, some of the clans broke through in rage, blinded by smoke, screaming and leaping over the rows of their dead. Then the cannon changed to grapeshot, and there was more slaughter. Still they attacked like hungry wolves. The muskets fired at them point blank, and they rushed in and hacked at the bayonets with swords. Some discarded their weapons and threw stones like savages. When the battle was lost, the survivors fled in panic, only to be chased down by the dragoons and butchered."

Lyle stopped, and no one spoke. "Well, you asked for it," he said.

Dwight put another shovelful of coal in the grate. Then members of the group started drifting away, saying they'd step outside for a breath of air, or they'd go up to bed, or they needed a drink.

It rained on Day Eight when they visited the battlefield at Culloden, and they found it depressing. It still rained when they visited a distillery, and even the wee dram served at the conclusion of the guided tour failed to cheer them. The Bonnie Scots Tour was winding down fast. Polly blamed it on the loss of their leader. Qwilleran thought it was a let-down after the enchantment of the Western Isles and Highlands.

On the bus, Bushy grabbed the microphone and tried to elevate the general mood with stories that fell flat. "Did you hear about the Scotsman who went to visit a sick friend with a bottle of Scotch in his pocket? It was a dark night, and on the way he tripped and fell on a sharp rock, but he picked himself up and went on his way. Soon he felt a trickle of something running down the outside of his leg. It was too dark to see, but he dabbled his fingers in it and tasted it. 'Thank God! It's only blood!' he said."

Later that evening, when Larry and the Chisholm sisters returned from the scene of the crime, he said to Qwilleran, "That woman is impossible, but we got everything taken care of. What did I miss?"

"Not much. A historic battlefield is all in your head. There's not much to see."

"And the distillery?"

"Everything was spic-and-span and absolutely sterile. Too bad Amanda wasn't there for the wee dram . . . Tell me, Larry, how valuable was the stuff stolen from Grace Utley?"

"According to her, one necklace alone was worth $150,000. Some of the stone-set brooches and bracelets were estate stuff, valued up to $50,000 apiece. It was a nice haul for someone. Do you suppose the theft was impromptu on Bruce's part . . . or what?"

Day Nine was devoted to museums and shopping. Mrs. Utley bought clothing and luggage enough to see her back to Pickax. The other women shopped for sweaters and kilts. Even Arch Riker found a cashmere cardigan that he considered a bargain. And then they checked into their last inn before Edinburgh, a stately, ivy-covered mansion on extensive landscaped grounds, furnished with antiques and chintz. The bedrooms were large, with ornate plaster ceilings, lace curtains, and telephones!

"I'm expecting Junior to phone," Riker said. He was trying on his new sweater when there was a knock at the door.

Qwilleran opened it to find a young man with a tea tray. "You've got the wrong room. We didn't order tea," he said.

"Compliments of the house, sir." The waiter marched into the room and set the tray on a lace-covered tea table in front of a stiff little settee. The tray was laden with porcelain cups and saucers, a rosebud-patterned china teapot, a silver milk and sugar service, a plate of shortbread, and dainty embroidered napkins in silver rings.

"Just what I wanted. More shortbread," Riker remarked as he sat on the settee and awkwardly poured tea into the eggshell-thin cups. Qwilleran pulled up a small chair opposite.

At that moment the telephone rang. "That's Junior!" said the editor, jumping to his feet. "He's really on the ball!"

As he started toward the phone, a button of his sweater caught on the lace cloth and dragged it off the table along with the tea, milk, sugar, shortbread, and china. With the tablecover trailing from his sweater button, he answered the phone with the composure of a veteran news editor. Then he turned to Qwilleran. "It's the desk clerk downstairs. Wants to know if everything's all right."

"Tell him to send up a mop and a shovel," Qwilleran said.

It was the final calamity of the Bonnie Scots Tour, but there was one more surprise in store for Qwilleran. The telephone rang in the middle of the night, and he jumped to a sitting position before his eyes were open. He turned on the bedside lamp. It was three o'clock.

"Something's happened to the cats—or the barn!" he said to Riker, who showed signs of stirring.

As he expected, it was an overseas call, and Mildred Hanstable was on the line. "Hope I didn't take you away from your dinner, Qwill."

"Dinner! It's three o'clock in the morning!"

"Oh, forgive me!" she cried in chagrin. "I deducted five
hours instead of adding. I'm so sorry!"

"Is anything wrong? Are the cats all right?"

"They're fine. We've just had a little snack."

"When is Irma's funeral? How are the Hasselriches taking it? Have you heard?"

"That's why I'm calling, Qwill. The funeral's been post-
poned—for family reasons, it said in the paper. Actually,
the body hasn't arrived yet."

"Hasn't arrived! It left here with Melinda four days ago!"

"Yes, Melinda is home. She said the body was flown
cargo . . . but it's lost."

"How do you know?"

"Roger was at the funeral home, asking why there were
so many flowers and no body, and the Dingleberry brothers
told him it had gone astray."

"Is there any trace of it?"

"Oh, yes. It arrived from Scotland and went to Chicago
all right, but then it was shipped to Moose Jaw in Canada,
instead of the Moose County Airport."

"Is that where it is now?"

"No, it's been traced to Denver, and they think it's on
the way back to Chicago, by way of Atlanta."

Qwilleran groaned. "This is absurd, Mildred. Does Junior know what's happened?"

"Roger told him, but it's being suppressed to keep from
upsetting Irma's parents."

"Hold the line," Qwilleran told her. Turning to Riker,
he said, "Irma's body hasn't arrived. It's being shipped all
over North America. Junior is withholding the news."

The two men stared at each other, both thinking what a
headline it would make. All their training and experience
and instincts as newsmen told them to go for the headline,
but Pickax was a small town, and the *Moose County
Something* was a small-town newspaper, and attitudes were
different.

Riker nodded assent.

"Well, thank you, Mildred," said Qwilleran. "Is everything else okay? How about the cats?"

"One of them has been chewing holes in your old sweaters and throwing up."

"That's probably Koko. He hasn't done that for years! He's lonely."

"I'm terribly sorry I disturbed you, Qwill."

"That's all right. I'm glad you called. I'll be home soon—perhaps sooner than I planned."

Six

On the morning of Day Ten the members of the Bonnie
Scots Tour placed their luggage in the corridor at seven-
thirty instead of six-thirty, having voted unanimously to
amend Irma's orders and start sleeping an extra hour.
Qwilleran walked down the hall to Polly's room and
knocked on the door. "May I come in?" he asked.

"Good morning, dear. I was about to plug in the tea-
maker. Would you like a cup?"

"No, thanks. I simply want you to know I'm leaving the
tour as soon as we reach Edinburgh."

"Has something happened at home?" she asked anxiously.

"No. I simply have a strong desire to get back to Pickax,
that's all." He fingered his moustache significantly. "I'm
changing my flight."

"Would you like company, Qwill?"

"Don't you want to see Edinburgh? It's a magnificent
city. I've had many newspaper assignments there."

"Frankly, my heart isn't in this tour since Irma died, and
it may seem foolish, but . . . I'm lonesome for Bootsie."

"Give me your ticket and I'll phone the airline," he said.

In changing their flights, he also upgraded their reservations to first class. Even though he was reluctant to spend
money on transportation, he needed the extra space for his
long legs and wide shoulders, and—after ten days of small

talk with the heterogeneous Bonnie Scots family—he wanted privacy for a sustained conversation with Polly.

Twenty-four hours later they had said goodbye to their traveling companions and were airborne—Qwilleran stretching his legs luxuriously, Polly sipping champagne, and both of them enjoying the pampering of VIPs.

"I wonder if Bootsie has missed me," Polly said. "I've never left him for more than a weekend. My sister-in-law takes good care of him, but there isn't the rapport that he has with me."

"Mildred says Koko's been chewing my sweaters. That means he's lonely, even though she's feeding him haute cuisine and perverting him with dubious diversions, like tarot cards."

The champagne bottle made the rounds again, and delectable hors d'oeuvres were served, prompting Polly to say, "Do you realize we were never offered any haggis in Scotland?"

"We never heard any bagpipes, either," he added.

"Or saw anyone dancing the hornpipe."

"In fact, we never really met any Scots. We were always with our own group, a little bit of Moose County on foreign soil."

This was followed by a regretful silence until Polly said, "On the credit side, I survived the trip without bronchitis, although I decided not to take my vitamin C. The capsules were too large and hard to swallow."

"Your bronchitis in England last year was all psychological, because I wasn't with you."

"*What a sweep of vanity comes this way!*" she said, quoting Shakespeare with glee.

"A little vanity is a good thing," he retorted.

"That's a questionable aphorism, if I ever heard one! Who said that?" she demanded.

"I did."

Polly lapsed into a sentimental reverie induced by the champagne. At length she said, "I've missed you, darling. We haven't had any time to ourselves on this trip."

"I've missed you, too, Polly."

"I feel so sad about Irma, and I couldn't even attend her funeral. She was probably buried two days ago."

"I don't think so," Qwilleran said slowly and soberly. "There's been a complication."

"What do you mean?" Polly snapped out of her brooding mood, then gasped as he reported the bizarre odyssey of Irma's casket. "Well," she said after a while, "I have something surprising to report, too."

"Let's hear it."

Polly hesitated, as if pondering where to begin. "Well . . . when I turned over Irma's briefcase to Larry, I withheld one small personal file and put it in my luggage, thinking to give it to her parents. Then Bruce disappeared, and no one knew his last name, so I searched this file without finding a clue. But there was one letter that I think you should see." She rummaged in her carry-on bag and extracted a document envelope tied with tape. In it was a folded sheet of notepaper that she handed to Qwilleran. "Read this."

Dear Irma,

Thank you from the bottom of my heart! Bruce will do a good job for you. He's an excellent driver, no mistake. He's had an awful time finding work since he got out, but he's promised to stay clean now. Do give him a proper talking to. He'll listen to you. I know you two meant a lot to each other when we were young. My brother is a good sort really, and I expect he's quite learned his lesson. Bless you! Don't forget to ring me when you reach Edinburgh.

For auld lang syne,
Katie

Qwilleran read the note twice. So that was the way it was! he thought. Irma and Bruce were—what? Youthful sweethearts? Former lovers? And Bruce had been in prison—for what? Larceny? A narcotics violation? Irma apparently knew about his record. Did she hire him in spite of it? Or because of it? Qwilleran's cynicism was close to the surface where Irma was concerned. There was more to this story, he suspected.

Polly was waiting to hear his reaction to the letter. "What do you think, Qwill?"

"Did the envelope have her full name and return address?" he asked.

"There was no envelope."

"There was gossip throughout the tour about Irma's nightly excursions with Bruce. Did she ever explain to you?"

"Not a word, and I was determined not to mention it. She was a responsible adult, and it was none of my business. She always came in after I was asleep, apparently creeping around in the dark without turning on the lights or making a sound. It was considerate of her, I thought."

"If Bruce stole Mrs. Utley's luggage, he wasn't as 'clean' as Irma was led to believe."

"It would seem so," Polly agreed.

"Did she ever mention this Katie person to you?"

"No, she was secretive about her Scottish connections, but that was characteristic of her. We never knew how much was bottled up in that cool exterior."

Qwilleran said, "If we could identify Katie, the police would have something to work with, at least. One would expect Irma to carry an address book in her briefcase—or a list of phone numbers if she planned to call friends in Scotland."

"Perhaps it was in her handbag," Polly suggested. "I packed it without examining the contents and sent it home in her luggage. Melinda was to turn everything over to the Hasselriches."

"Her parents might know Katie's name and whereabouts. If not, you could ask them for the address book on the pretext of notifying Irma's Scottish friends about her death . . . In fact," he added, "Bruce might be listed."

There were signs that dinner was about to be served.

Individual tables were unfolded from the chair arms, and white tablecloths were whisked across them, followed by linen napkins, wineglasses, tiny vases of fresh flowers, and four-page menu presentations.

Qwilleran said, "We can assume that turbulence is not in their flight plan."

They ordered vichyssoise, tournedos of beef, and Caesar salad.

After a while he asked, "What will happen at the Senior Care Facility? Will they be able to replace Irma?"

"The administrators always said they'd have to hire a professional if Irma retired. Lisa wants to apply for the job."

"She'd be pretty good, I think."

"Before we left for Scotland," Polly said, "Irma was working on a project called Pets for Patients, with volunteers bringing their cats and dogs to the facility on certain days to boost morale. If it goes through, I'd be willing to take Bootsie. How about you, Qwill?"

"I'd take Yum Yum, but I doubt whether Koko would cooperate. He has his own ideas and doesn't always do what cats are supposed to do."

They ordered crème caramel for dessert, and after coffee Qwilleran presented Polly with a small white box bearing a monogram: CRM. It was a handmade silver brooch in the form of a peacock feather, combined with blue-green enamel and a smoky quartz crystal mounted in the eye of the feather.

"It's beautiful!" she cried. "I love peacock feathers! What is the stone?"

"A cairngorm from the Cairngorm mountains in Scotland. This is one of the designs being made in the Charles Rennie Mackintosh style."

"It will be perfect on my batwing cape. Thank you so much, dear."

"Are you going to watch the movie?" he asked. The screen was being lowered at the front of the cabin.

"I'd rather take a nap," she said.

"I'm going to look at this magazine, if my reading light won't disturb you."

Window shades were drawn to shut out the brilliant sunlight, while passengers either put on their earphones to watch the film, or went to sleep, or both. He held the magazine open to a feature on Tlingit art, but he was thinking rather than reading. If he could discover the bus driver's identity, he would turn the information over to the Pickax police chief and let him follow through. Reviewing the Scottish tour in his mind, Qwilleran searched for clues in the behavior of Irma as well as Bruce. The tapes he had recorded might reveal forgotten details. Their content was intended as material for "Straight from the Qwill Pen," but it could serve another purpose now . . . His magazine dropped to his lap, and he fell asleep until the cabin was again flooded with light and another meal was served.

By the time the plane landed in Chicago, and by the time they claimed their baggage and went through Customs and Immigration, it was too late to continue to Moose County. They stayed overnight at an airport inn and caught the shuttle flight in the morning. At the Moose County Airport Qwilleran's white four-door was waiting in the long-term parking structure, a new building made possible by a grant from the K Foundation.

Polly said, "I remember when the terminal was a shack without chairs or indoor plumbing."

"I remember when we had to park our cars in a cow pasture and be *very careful*," Qwilleran said, "and that was only five years ago."

"I can hardly wait to see Bootsie," she said on the way to Pickax.

"I'm looking forward to seeing my two rascals also."

When they arrived at Polly's carriage-house apartment, she ran up the stairs while Qwilleran followed with her luggage. "Bootsie!" she cried. "How's my little boy? Did you miss me?"

The husky Siamese approached with curiosity, appraised

her coolly, then turned abruptly and walked away, leaving his adoring human crushed.

Qwilleran said, "That's your punishment for abandoning him. After he thinks you've suffered enough, he'll smother you with affection. I expect the same treatment when I get home."

After two weeks of picturesque inns and impressive castles, he had forgotten that the converted apple barn was such a wondrous bit of architecture. The octagonal structure had a rough stone foundation that looked like thirteenth-century Scotland, and the weathered shingle siding was crowned by a slate roof. There were no furry creatures spying on him from the windows, however. They were in the kitchen, sitting contentedly on top of the refrigerator, watching Mildred Hanstable as she slid a casserole into the oven. They looked down on Qwilleran with condescension.

"Welcome home!" she greeted him. "How was the trip?"

"No one ever said traveling is easy."

"How about a cup of coffee?"

"As soon as I dump this luggage. I've been living out of it for two weeks." He carried his bags up the ramp to the balcony, and when he returned he had a small white box in his pocket, with CRM on the cover. The Siamese were still sitting sphinxlike on the refrigerator. "Did they ever find Irma?" he asked as he slid onto a seat at the snack bar.

Mildred poured two mugs of coffee. "Yes, she finally arrived, and they buried her yesterday, although there was some further unpleasantness. The Dingleberry brothers told Roger—off the record, of course—that the Hasselriches disagreed violently about burial versus cremation."

"Did the obit run?"

"Yes. On the front page. I left it on the coffee table. It's a lovely write-up . . . Well, apart from the tragedy, Qwill, how was your adventure?"

"I'll know better after I've spent a night in my own bed and recovered from tour trauma."

"Did you buy yourself a kilt?"

"No, just a couple of ties in the Mackintosh tartan. Speaking of Mackintosh, here's a memento of Glasgow." He pushed the small white box across the bar.

"Oh, Qwill! Thank you so much!" she exclaimed when she saw the peacock feather pin in silver and enamel. "What's the name of this stone?"

"It's a cairngorm, found only in Scotland, I believe."

"It was sweet of you to think of me."

"It was generous of you to take care of the Siamese, Mildred."

"Not a bit! It was a thrill to live in this barn, and the cats were enjoyable company. I wouldn't mind having one just like Koko."

"There's no such thing as just-like-Koko," he informed her. "He's the Shakespeare of cats, the Beethoven of cats, the Leonardo of cats!"

Hearing his name mentioned favorably, Koko rose and stretched his rear chassis, then extended his forelegs with spreading toes, after which he jumped down from the refrigerator with a thump and an involuntary grunt and ambled over to Qwilleran to sniff the foreign aromas. Who could say what scents were registered by that twitching nose? Old castles? Heather? Scotch broth? Fishing villages? Sheep? A distillery? The bones of ancient kings? A battlefield soaked with blood 250 years ago?

"Did the cats misbehave in any way?" Qwilleran asked.

"Well, one of them stole my emery boards—a whole pack of them, one at a time."

"Petty larceny is Yum Yum's department. I owe you a pack. I'll take it out of her allowance. How about Koko?"

"He did one naughty thing that gave me a scare," Mildred said. "I was getting ready to take my diet pill, and he swooped in and snatched it. I was afraid he'd eat it and get sick, but he just punctured the capsule with his fangs."

"Yes, he likes to sink them in soft, gummy things, like jelly beans," Qwilleran explained. "Do I smell macaroni and cheese in the oven? All the time I was eating nettle broth, mutton pie, boiled sheep's tongue, and tripe and onions, I was dreaming about macaroni and cheese."

"That's for our lunch," she said. "I'm leaving some left-overs in the refrigerator for the cats—meatloaf, codfish cakes, terrine of turkey—and there's beef stew for you in the freezer. I've been cooking up a storm while you were away and having a wonderful time."

After lunch, Mildred packed and moved out, and Qwilleran shut himself in his balcony suite until an operatic chorus outside his door reminded him it was time for dinner. The three of them snacked informally on the leftovers, and then he sprawled listlessly in his favorite lounge chair with no desire to read the newspaper or play the stereo or write a letter or take a walk or call anyone on the telephone. It was post-vacation lethargy. When the Siamese crowded around, having forgiven him for his unexplained absence, he stroked Yum Yum halfheartedly and told Koko without much conviction that he was a handsome fellow.

Impulsively, Koko jumped from the arm of the chair and walked deliberately to the large square coffee table, where Mildred had left a copy of the *Moose County Something*. Hopping to the tabletop, he stared down at the newsprint with a nearsighted gaze. Then, arching his back and bushing his tail and sweeping his ears back, he commenced a slow prance around the lead item on the front page. He circled it again and again in a hair-raising ritual that Qwilleran had seen before. It meant that Koko's extra senses were detecting a discrepancy that escaped human perception.

Qwilleran felt the familiar crawling sensation in the roots of his moustache. There on page one was the three-column photo of Irma Hasselrich and the half-page obituary. Koko, he remembered, had howled at the exact moment of her death. Without benefit of satellite he had known what was happening in a remote Scottish hamlet. Was it possible that the cat sensed more than that? Was Koko the source of the subliminal message urging him to return home early? Polly thought she had a remarkable rapport with Bootsie, but it was nothing compared to the mutual understanding that existed between Qwilleran and Koko.

But no, he finally decided; it was all absurd imagining. "I'm punchy from jet lag," he said to the Siamese. "Let's turn out the lights and call it a day."

Seven

Back home in his own bed Qwilleran enjoyed a good night's sleep, but in the morning he was disoriented. He didn't know what day it was. He knew only that it was Day Thirteen. After living in a tour-induced limbo, where days had numbers instead of names, he had not adjusted to the standard calendar week. Consequently, the morning after Koko's macabre dance around Irma's obituary was Day Thirteen in Qwilleran's book.

The sound of church bells ringing on Park Circle suggested that Day Thirteen might be translated into Sunday. On the other hand, it might be Saturday if the bells were celebrating a wedding. He thought of phoning the city desk at the *Moose County Something* and asking, "Is this Saturday or Sunday?" He had answered stranger questions than that when he worked for metropolitan newspapers Down Below. The local radio station was of no help; the announcer gave the time, the temperature, the wind velocity, and the relative humidity, but not the day of the week. As for the WPKX brand of daily newscasting, it was a half hour of what Qwilleran called mushy news—no less mushy on Saturday than on Sunday.

If the day proved to be Saturday, that meant he had arrived home on Friday. Yet, would Mildred Hanstable have been there on a Friday morning? She taught school and would have been in the classroom unless, of course, it was a Teacher-Optional Workday, in which case she might have opted to stay home and prepare macaroni and cheese, although that was extremely unlikely for one as conscientious as Mildred. Ergo, this had to be Sunday, and the church bells were calling the faithful to worship. That was Qwilleran's cue to walk to the drug store and pick up the out-of-town Sunday papers.

The cats were relaxing in a patch of sunlight on the rug without a thought in their sleek brown heads. What matter to them that it was Sunday—or even Thursday? Every day was Today in their scheme of things, and there was no such thing as Yesterday or Tomorrow.

"I'm going downtown," he announced to them. "Is there anything you want from the drug store?"

They looked at him as if he were demented. Or *daft,* as they said in Scotland. (Qwilleran had bought a glossary of Scottish terms at the Edinburgh airport.) The Siamese knew very well when he was talking nonsense. Or *blethering,* as they said in Scotland.

A brisk walk downtown had the effect of clearing the stupefied brain he had brought home from the Bonnie Scots Tour. He did his best thinking while walking alone. Now he resumed his ruminations begun on the plane: Irma knew about Bruce's past record . . . She might have relived her youthful passion on the moor . . . She might have vented some hidden bitterness caused by her own conviction for manslaughter . . . She might have been Bruce's accomplice in the jewel theft!

This wild scenario brought forth not so much as a tickle on Qwilleran's upper lip, but when he tried another avenue of brainstorming, his moustache bristled slightly: Irma might have been Bruce's victim. If he planned to steal the jewels, wouldn't it be logical to eliminate the one person who knew his identity? Could he have slipped her some kind of drug that would stop her heart? This was a technical detail he would have to check with Dr. Melinda—an undertaking he hardly relished. To phone her on a Sunday afternoon would give rise to sociable invitations, such as, "Come over for a drink, and we'll discuss it," or "Let's have dinner." To visit her clinic on Monday would lead to other undesirable developments, such as, "Remove everything except your socks and shoes, and the doctor will be right with you." No, he decided, it would be safer to meet her "accidentally" in some crowded or busy place, where they could exchange a few words without getting involved in anything personal.

Qwilleran found himself walking with clenched teeth. It annoyed him to be in this awkward position with Melinda after three years of an easy relationship with Polly. He resented being hounded by an overzealous female. He had terminated other liaisons without embarrassment, and he had been jilted himself without creating a rumpus. Somehow he had to get rid of that woman! Koko had never liked her. Did the cat's uncanny prescience foretell this course of events? It was not beyond the realm of imagination.

At the drug store, Qwilleran picked up several out-of-town newspapers—his way of keeping in touch with the turmoil Down Below.

"How was Scotland, Mr. Q?" asked the cashier.

"Okay."

"I heard about Ms. Hasselrich."

"Yes, it was too bad."

"Did you see the Loch Ness monster?"

"No, we were there on his day off."

On the way home Qwilleran's mind turned to the subject of Irma's address book. If he could learn the whereabouts and/or phone number of the pivotal Katie, he could turn the whole matter over to Andrew Brodie and let him make a case of it, if he wished. Andy would be interested in Koko's startling reaction to the obituary, being one of the few who knew about the cat's sensitivity to the scent of crime. A detective from Down Below had told him about it in all seriousness. To the Pickax police chief, Koko was the town psychic.

Qwilleran walked home with his newspapers via the back road, hoping to avoid questions from well-meaning townsfolk. There was little traffic on Trevelyan Road, but eventually a car stopped and the driver called to him, "Want a lift, Qwill?" It was Scott Gippel, the used-car dealer.

"No, thanks. I'm walking for my health," Qwilleran said with a comradely salute.

"How was Scotland?"

"Fine."

"Sorry about Irma Hasselrich."

"Very unfortunate."

"Bring back any Scotch?"

Arriving home with several pounds of newsprint under his arm, Qwilleran all but stumbled over a moving hump in the foyer rug. It was a familiar occurrence, meaning that a cat had hidden stolen goods and was trying to retrieve the loot. He threw back a corner of the rug and exposed Yum Yum huddled over a playing card. It was face down, and when he turned it over, he recognized a card from Mildred's tarot deck. He also recognized the two perforations in the corner. Koko had been the thief; he always left his mark, like the Black Hand.

The picture on the card was a pleasant scene: a grape arbor with a woman in flowing robes, a bird perched on her wrist. They were surrounded by nine gold circles, each with a five-pointed star in the center. Qwilleran remembered the card from Mildred's reading prior to the Scottish venture. Dropping his stack of newspapers, he found his recording of the episode and slipped it into a player. The following familiar dialogue unreeled:

"Do you mind if I tape this, Mildred?"

"Not at all. I wish you would."

"What did you learn?"

"Strangely, when I asked the cards about you, the answers concerned someone else—someone in danger."

"Man or woman?"

"A mature woman. A woman with strict habits and upright values."

"What kind of danger?"

"Well, the cards were rather vague, so I brought the pack with me, and I'd like to do another reading—in your presence." (Pause.)

"Yow!"

"Want me to lock him up, Mildred?"

"No, let him watch. (Pause.) I'm using the Celtic pattern for this reading. This card is the significator. (Pause.) I see a journey . . . a journey across water . . . with stormy weather ahead."

"Glad I packed my raincoat."

"Stormy weather could stand for dissension, mistakes, accidents, or whatever."

"Too bad I didn't know before I paid my money."

"You're not taking this seriously, Qwill."

"Sorry. I didn't mean to sound flippant."

"This final card . . . is not auspicious . . . You might consider it a warning."

"Looks like a happy card to me."

"But it's reversed."

"Meaning . . ."

"Some kind of fraud . . . or treachery."

"Yow!"

"In conclusion . . . I urge you to be prepared . . . for the unexpected." (Pause.)

"Very interesting. Thank you."

Click.

As the tape slowly unreeled, the Siamese were alerted, having heard another cat inside the black box, and both of them circled the player with curiosity. Perhaps they also recognized the voices of Qwilleran and Mildred. It was significant that Koko had yowled at her mention of treachery. At the time of the reading, Qwilleran had thought the cards referred to Polly. Now it was obvious that Irma was the woman in danger; it was she who would be the victim of treachery . . . That is, Qwilleran reminded himself skeptically, if one took the cards seriously.

He looked up Mildred Hanstable's number. It was Sunday morning, and she would probably be at home, cooking or quilting. "Good morning," he said. "The meatloaf was delicious. The Siamese let me have some of it for dinner last night."

"There's beef stew in the freezer for you, don't forget," she said.

"I feel twice blessed. I'm calling, Mildred, to ask if you've lost one of your tarot cards. I'd hate to see you playing with a short deck."

"I don't know. Let me check." In a moment she returned to the phone. "You're right. There are only seventy-seven."

"I'm afraid Koko stole one. He left his fang marks in it. I hope that doesn't affect the—ah—authority of the deck."

"Where did you find it?"

"Hidden under a rug. It's a card I remember from your reading before I left for Scotland." He described the woman in the grape arbor.

"Yes, I recall. It was reversed when I read for you, and I predicted treachery."

"And you were right! Grace Utley's jewels were stolen by a trusted bus driver." He avoided mentioning his suspicions about Irma's death.

"Grace was crazy to take them on the trip," Mildred said, "but no one ever said that woman was in her right mind."

"Shall I mail the card to you?" he asked. "Or shall we have dinner some evening—soon."

"I'd love it!" Her voice rang with pleased surprise.

"We'll include Polly and Arch," he added hastily, "and the three of us will tell you all about Scotland."

"Say when. I'm always free. Just hang on to the nine of pentacles until then."

"What is the significance of pentacles?" he asked.

"They correspond to diamonds in regular playing cards."

An odd coincidence, Qwilleran thought as he hung up. The nine of diamonds! The Curse of Scotland!

Now he was impatient to talk with Polly about the address book. He waited until he thought she would be home from church, but there was no answer when he called. She might have gone to Sunday brunch with her sister-in-law, or she might be visiting the Hasselriches.

A few hours later Polly called in great excitement. "I have it! I have the address book!" she cried.

"How did the family react to your request?"

"When I phoned about it, they were most appreciative and invited me to dinner after church. It was a painful occasion, but we talked about Irma lovingly, and they said they consider me their surrogate daughter now. I was deeply touched."

"Did they know anything about Katie?"

"Only that she and Irma had been in art school at the same time. When I brought the book home, I searched it for a Katie with an Edinburgh address and discovered one Kathryn Gow MacBean. It looks as if MacBean might be her married name, in which case Bruce would be a Gow." Polly sounded excited about her first attempt at detection and deduction.

"Good work, Polly!" Qwilleran said. "Give me the Edinburgh phone number, and I'll see what I can find out." He avoided mentioning Koko's death dance around the obituary or his own murder theory.

She said, "I'd invite you over for coffee or something, but I need to do some laundry and get myself together for work tomorrow. Let me know what luck you have."

After hanging up, Qwilleran checked his watch. It was too late to call Edinburgh, but the next morning he took his first cup of coffee to the telephone desk, locked the meddlesome Koko in the loft, and placed a call to Katie. He said, "This is Jim Qwilleran, a friend of Irma Hasselrich." He used a sincere and cordial tone of voice intended to inspire confidence.

"Yes?" the woman replied warily.

"I'd like to speak to Kathryn Gow. Or is it Kathryn MacBean?"

"I'm Mrs. MacBean."

"I'm phoning from the States—from Irma's hometown of Pickax."

"Where is she?" came a sharp reply. "I mean, I expected her to ring me up."

"She never reached Edinburgh, I'm sorry to say," Qwilleran said, introducing a grieved note to prepare his listener for bad news. "I was a member of her Scots Tour, and while we were still in the Western Highlands, she suffered a heart attack and died."

"*Died!* . . . That's perfectly awful!"

"It pains me to break the news, but her family felt you'd want to know."

There was a blank silence.

"Hello? Hello?" he said.

In a softer voice Katie said, "I do declare, this is a bit of a shock! I mean, she was fairly young."

"Her body was flown back here, and she was buried two days ago. We're notifying a list of her friends."

"Was the rest of the tour canceled? My brother was the driver. Odd that he didn't notify me."

"Bruce Gow! Is he your brother?"

"Ah . . . yes."

"He's an excellent driver, and he was very courteous to a busload of crotchety American tourists."

"Yes, he's . . . very good. What is your name, did you say?"

"Jim Qwilleran. My mother was a Mackintosh. We're branches of the same clan. There was a MacBean, a giant of a man, who fought at Culloden and killed thirteen English with his broadsword, fighting with his back to a wall." This was intended to proclaim his Scottish sympathies and win her good will.

"Ah . . . yes . . . there's a fair number of Mackintoshes about." Her attention was wandering as if she were concerned about her brother. "When did it happen?"

"Almost a week ago."

"Honestly, I'm in a state! I'm not sure I know quite what to say, Mr. . . . Mr. . . ."

"Qwilleran. It would help to console Irma's parents if you would write them a note. How long had you known her?"

"More than twenty years. We met in art school. In Glasgow." She seemed to be speaking in a guarded way.

"Do you have any snapshots or other memorabilia that you could part with? I'm sure her parents would welcome any little memento."

"I expect that's the least I can do, isn't it?"

"Do you have the address?"

"Goodwinter Boulevard? Yes, of course."

"I'll send you a clip of the obituary that ran in the local newspaper. It has a very good photo of Irma."

"That would be kind of you. If you could spare two cuttings . . ."

"Glad to do it, Mrs. MacBean."

"And thank you for calling, Mr. . . ."

"Qwilleran."

He verified her address before concluding the conversation and hung up with a strong feeling of satisfaction. Now he was ready to talk with Chief Brodie.

He walked briskly downtown to the police station, and the sergeant at the desk nodded him into the inner office before a word was spoken.

Brodie looked up in surprise. "When did you get back, laddie?"

"Saturday. Did you hear the bad news?"

The chief nodded. "I played the bagpipe at her funeral."

"You probably heard that she had a fatal heart attack, but there's more to the story than that, and I'd like your advice." Qwilleran glanced toward the outer office and closed the door.

"Pour a cup of coffee and sit down. How was Scotland, apart from that?"

"Beautiful!"

"Get your fill of bagpipes?"

"Believe it or not, Andy, we didn't hear so much as a squeal, all the time we were there."

"You went to the wrong places, mon. You should come to Scottish Night at my lodge. We'll show you what piping is all about . . . So, what's buggin' you?"

Qwilleran pulled up a chair. "Well, there were sixteen of us on the bus traveling around Scotland," he began, "and our driver was a Scot named Bruce, a sullen fellow with red hair who spoke only to Irma. They conversed, I believe, in Gaelic."

"She knew Gaelic? That's a tough language."

"They seemed to communicate all right. Then one morning she was found dead in bed by her roommate, Polly Duncan. Cause of death: cardiac arrest, according to Dr. Melinda, who was traveling with us. The next day the bus driver disappeared, and so did Grace Utley's luggage, containing a small fortune in jewels. I suppose you know about her spectacular jewelry—and the way she flaunts it."

"That I do! She's a walking Christmas tree!"

"We notified the village constable and gave a description of Bruce, but no one knew the guy's last name except Irma, and she was dead!"

"And Scotland is full of redheads by the name of Bruce. So what's the advice you want?"

"I have reason to believe," and here Qwilleran smoothed his moustache proudly, "that the heart stoppage was drug-induced. We hear of young athletes dropping dead because of substance abuse. If it can happen to them, it can happen to a forty-year-old woman with an existing heart condition."

"You can't tell me that Irma was doing drugs. Not her! Not that woman!"

"Listen, Andy. Every night after dinner she went out with Bruce. There was a lot of gossip about it."

"Why would a classy dame like her hang around with a bus driver?"

"We've since found out—from correspondence in her briefcase—that he was an old flame. Also, it appears, an ex-con. If he was plotting a jewel heist, wouldn't he get rid of the one person who could identify him? I suspect he slipped her some kind of drug."

Brodie grunted. "Do the police over there know that you suspect homicide?"

"No, it's a new development. But here's the good news, Andy." Qwilleran waved a slip of paper. "We've found the name, address, and phone number of Bruce's sister in Edinburgh, and through her we learned his last name is Gow."

"Give it here," said the chief, reaching across the desk. "Also the name of the town where you reported the larceny. Do you know what we're getting into? They'll want to exhume the body!" Then he added, partly in jest and partly because he believed in Koko's extraordinary gifts, "If Scotland Yard can't find the suspect, we'll assign your smart cat to the case."

"Yes," said Qwilleran, going along with the gag. "Too bad Koko wasn't there!"

He left the police station with a light step, knowing he had contributed vital information to the investigation, and he treated himself to a good American breakfast of ham and eggs at Lois's Luncheonette, with a double order of her famous country fries.

His elation was short-lived, however. When he returned home, the barn was a scene of havoc: torn newspapers everywhere, books on the floor, the telephone knocked off its cradle, and the rest of Qwilleran's morning coffee spilled on the desk and floor, while Koko was in the throes of a catfit. He raced around and around the main floor, almost faster than the eye could see, then up the circular ramp to the catwalk under the roof, where he screamed like a banshee before pelting down the ramp again, rolling on the floor, and fighting an imaginary adversary.

Qwilleran watched in helpless astonishment until the cat, having made his point, sat down on the coffee table and licked himself all over. He had staged catfits before, and it was always a desperate attempt to communicate.

"What's it all about, Koko?" Qwilleran asked as he cleaned up the mess. "What are you trying to say?"

It was Irma's obituary that had been shredded, and he was trying to convey that she had not died of natural causes; of that Qwilleran was sure. He had learned to read Koko's body language and the nuances of his yowling. The varying inflections and degrees of intensity—like the subtleties of Oriental speech—registered affirmation or negation, approval or disapproval, excitement or indifference, imperious demand or urgent warning.

Now, as Qwilleran watched that rippling pink tongue grooming that snowy white breast, an idea flashed through his head. It was a wild shot but worth trying. He would interrogate Koko! He waited patiently until the fastidious toilette was finished, then sprawled in the roomy lounge chair where the three of them always gathered for enjoyment of quality time. Yum Yum hopped onto his lap, landing weightlessly like a squirt of whipped cream, while Koko settled on the wide arm of the upholstered chair with perfect composure.

Solemnly, Qwilleran began, "This is a serious discussion, Koko, and I want you to give it your personal best."

"Yow," the cat replied, squeezing his eyes agreeably.

The man turned on the tape recorder, which was never far from his trigger finger. "Are you aware of the death of Irma Hasselrich?"

"Yow!" came the prompt reply, an obvious affirmative.

"Was she murdered?"

Koko hesitated before saying "Yow!" in a positive way.

"Hmmm," Qwilleran said, patting his moustache. "Did the bus driver cause her to ingest a substance that stopped her heart?"

Koko gazed into space.

"I'll rephrase that. Did the bus driver slip her a drug that killed her?"

Koko was mute. He looked from side to side, and up and down, with convulsive movements of his head.

"Pay attention!" Qwilleran rebuked him, and he repeated the question. "Did the bus driver—"

"Yow," Koko interrupted but without conviction.

It was not the definitive response that Qwilleran had hoped for, and he thought it wise to ask a test question: "Koko, is my name Ronald Frobnitz?"

"Yow!" said the town psychic as he leaped to catch the fruit fly he'd been tracking.

Eight

After the unsatisfactory interrogation of the redoubtable Koko, Qwilleran decided that the cat was a charlatan. Or he was a practical joker who delighted in deluding the man who gave him food, shelter, respect, and admiration. Despite Koko's past record, there were moments when Qwilleran seriously doubted that he was anything but an ordinary animal, and his so-called insights were all a matter of coincidence.

The telephone rang, and Koko raced him to the instrument, but Qwilleran grabbed the handset first.

"Qwill! You're home!" said the pleasant voice of Lori Bamba, his part-time secretary. "How was Scotland?"

"Magnificent! How's everything in Mooseville?"

"Same as always. We're all very sorry about Irma Hasselrich. She was a wonderful woman."

"Yes, that was a sad happening . . . Did you have any problems with my correspondence?"

"Nothing that I couldn't handle. Did it rain a lot while you were there?"

"Mornings were misty. That's what keeps the Scottish complexion so fresh and the Scottish landscape so verdant—just the way it looks in the whiskey ads."

"Do you think the cats missed you while you were away?" Lori asked.

"Not much. Mildred Hanstable cat-sat, so they ate well."

"There are several letters for you to sign, Qwill, and Nick can drop them off this afternoon. Will you be home around three-thirty?"

"I'll make it a point to be here," Qwilleran said. He found the Bambas an attractive young couple—Lori with her long, golden braids, Nick with his dark, curly hair and alert, black eyes. The best of the next generation, Qwilleran called them. Lori had been Mooseville postmaster before retiring to raise a family and work out of her home. Her husband, trained as an engineer, worked for the state prison near Mooseville, and since Nick shared his interest in crime, Qwilleran looked forward to seeing him and relating the case of the missing bus driver.

Meanwhile, he had a cup of coffee and listened to one of the tapes he had recorded during the tour. The Siamese listened, too, with Koko making an occasional comment from the top of the fireplace cube.

> "Tonight we are comfortably lodged and extremely well fed in another historic inn. I suspect Bonnie Prince Charlie slept here 250 years ago. One can hardly buy anything without his picture on it. Irma likes to talk about the heroic women who aided the prince's cause. Flora Macdonald dressed him in women's clothing and passed him off as her maid as they traveled through enemy lines. And then there was Lady Ann Mackintosh, who raised regiments to fight for the prince, while her husband was off fighting for the other side."

Koko responded to the sound of a familiar voice with a happy gurgling sound, but as the tape unreeled he seemed to hear something else.

> "Bushy is taking hundreds of pictures on this trip. At first, when Irma stopped the bus for a spectacular view, we all piled out with our cameras, but now Bushy and Big Mac are the only ones who take pictures. The rest of us, jaded with spectacular views, remain in our seats.

Occasionally Bushy photographs members of our group
in different settings, especially Melinda. He seems to
think she's a good model."

Koko jumped on and off the desk when he heard this segment, and Qwilleran recalled Lori Bamba's theory—that
cats respond to the palatal *shhhh* sound. (Her own cats,
for that reason, were named Sheba, Shoo-Shoo, Natasha,
Trish, Pushkin, and Sherman.) Evidently "Bushy" was the
trigger sound here.

"Today I was talking to Lyle Compton about the famous medical school at Glasgow University, and he
mentioned that the infamous Dr. Cream was a Glaswegian. He was the nineteenth-century psychopath who
became a serial killer in England, Canada, and the
United States—not as legendary as Jack the Ripper but
noted for 'pink pills for pale prostitutes,' as his M.O.
was described."

Koko reacted excitedly to this reference, leading Qwilleran
to assume that he heard the word "serial" and confused it
with the crunchy "cereal" that was his favorite treat.

In mid-afternoon Qwilleran walked downtown to the offices of the *Moose County Something,* to pick up a few
more copies of Irma's obituary. He also left a small white
box with a CRM monogram on the desk of Hixie Rice, the
advertising manager, who had been his friend and neighbor
Down Below. Then he dropped into Junior Goodwinter's
office.

"You're back early," the managing editor said. "We don't
expect Arch till tomorrow or Wednesday. Tell me about
Scotland. What did you like best?"

"The islands," Qwilleran answered promptly. "There's
something wild and mystic and ageless about them. You
feel it in the stones under your feet—the ancient presence
of Picts, Romans, Saxons, Gaels, Angles, Vikings—all that
crowd."

"Wow! Write it up for the 'Qwill Pen' column!" Junior suggested with his boyish enthusiasm.

"That's my intention eventually, after I've had a chance to sort out my impressions. But I came in to compliment you on the obit, Junior. A beautiful piece of copy! We're sending clips to Irma's friends in Scotland . . . How about the local scene? Any momentous news in Moose County?"

"Well, we're carrying a series of ads on the liquidation of Dr. Hal's estate. Melinda's selling everything in a tag sale. I hope she rakes in some dough, because she needs it. After that, the house will go up for sale, and we'll have another empty mansion on Goodwinter Boulevard."

"Did you attend Irma's funeral?" Qwilleran asked.

"Roger covered it, but I didn't go. The cortege watchers counted forty-eight cars in the procession to the cemetery."

"I hear there was some kind of argument about the disposition of the remains."

"Oh, you heard about that? Melinda said they'd had a doctor/patient discussion about living wills. She said Irma preferred cremation and no funeral. Mrs. Hasselrich wanted to go along with her daughter's wishes, but her husband—with his legal mind-set, you know—said it wasn't in writing. So Irma was buried in the family plot with full obsequies—eulogies, bagpipe, tenor soloist, and marching band. You know how Pickax loves a big funeral production!"

Qwilleran said, "I ought to write a column on living wills."

"Can you rip off a piece on Scotland for Wednesday? Your devoted readers are waiting to hear about your trip."

"We saw a lot of castles. I'll see if I can write a thousand words on castles without having to think too much," Qwilleran promised as he started out the door.

Walking home from the newspaper office, he let his mind wander from castles to the baronial mansions on Goodwinter Boulevard. The only solution to the local problem, as he envisioned it, would be rezoning . . . or a bomb . . . or an earthquake, and the old-timers in Pickax would prefer either of the latter to rezoning. He was walking along Main Street toward Park Circle when a car in a southbound lane caught his attention. It had what he thought was a Massachusetts license plate, its light color like a white flag among the dusky, dusty local plates. But it was not the old maroon car he had seen and suspected at the time of the prowler scare. It was a tan car, and it was soon lost in traffic. He thought, It could be the same guy in a new car; it could be the same car with a new paint job.

Qwilleran felt it wise to alert Polly, if he could do so without alarming her, and when he reached the library he went in, nodded to the friendly clerks, and climbed the stairs to the mezzanines. She was sitting in her glass-enclosed office, listening sympathetically to a young clerk who was pregnant. The young woman left immediately when her boss's special friend appeared in the doorway.

"Anything new?" Polly asked eagerly.

"I had a long telephone conversation with Katie," Qwilleran said, "and it appears her brother's name is in fact Gow. She was surprised he hadn't notified her of Irma's death—or so she said . . . By the way, did you and Irma ever discuss living wills? Or last wishes? Or anything like that?"

"No. She never mentioned death or illness. Why do you ask?"

"I thought I might write a column on living wills. It's a hot topic right now. When you two got together, what did you talk about, anyway? Besides me," he added to give the discussion a light touch.

Her smile was mocking, but her reply was serious. "We talked about my problems at the library . . . and her work at the facility . . . and clothes. She had a great interest in fashion. And naturally we talked about birds. Irma's life list included the Kirtland's warbler, the red-necked grebe, and the white-winged scoter. She had traveled around the country on bird-counts."

Polly stopped and regarded him wistfully, and he squirmed in his chair, knowing she would expect him to go birding in Irma's place. Clearing his throat to signal a change of subject, he asked casually, "Have you noticed any more suspicious characters around town since we returned?"

"Well . . . no . . . I haven't really been looking."

"In times like these a woman should keep her eyes open and her wits about her, no matter where she is."

"Oh, dear! I suppose you're right, but it sounds so threatening!"

He avoided pursuing the unpleasant subject but tossed off a parting reminder to be careful, with no mention of the tan car with a Massachusetts plate. Later in the afternoon he reported it to Nick Bamba, however. Nick had an eagle eye for anything automotive: car makes and models, license plates, bumper stickers, drivers, and even the driving habits of individual motorists.

When Nick arrived to deliver his wife's typing, his first words were, "I see you've got a new car."

"Not new, just different," Qwilleran said. "My old one conked out, and I hate to let Gippel skin me on a new model. The prices are outrageous. My first car, when I was sixteen, was $150."

"How come you got a white one?"

"Does it look like a diaper service? It's all they had on Gippel's lot—that is, the only car where the floor of the backseat would accommodate the cats' commode . . . Nick, how would you like a wee dram of Scotch, hand-carried from the distillery for a moment such as this?"

"Sure would, but don't make it too wee."

They sat in the lounge area, Nick sipping Scotch on the rocks, Qwilleran sipping white grape juice, and both of them dipping into bowls of Mildred Hanstable's homemade sesame sticks. Then the Siamese started parading in front of them. Whenever the Bambas visited the barn, Koko and Yum Yum made themselves highly visible, walking back and forth languorously, pivoting and posing like models on a fashion-show runway.

"So what did you think of Scotland?" Nick asked.

"The Western Isles and Highlands are fascinating," Qwilleran told him. "The landscape is almost spooky, with a haunting melancholy in spite of all the tourists and back-packers."

"How were the country inns?"

"Pleasant, hospitable, comfortable. The food was different, but good. Have you and Lori given any more thought to opening a bed-and-breakfast?"

"We talk about it all the time. With the tourist business increasing, we think we should act now and get in on the ground floor, but it'll take a lot of nerve to quit my good job with the state."

"Is the tourist season long enough to make it worthwhile?"

"Right now there's a seven-month season for boating, camping, hunting, and fishing, and there's talk about developing a winter sports program."

"May I touch up your drink, Nick?"

"No, thanks. One's enough. It's really smooth. Did you see them making it?"

"Not exactly. This stuff has been lying around in a cask for fifteen years."

The Siamese were still making themselves conspicuous, and Yum Yum carried something in her jaws and laid it at Nick's feet.

"Hey, what's this?" he asked.

Qwilleran said, "It's an emery board. She was stealing them from our cat-sitter, and I keep finding them around the house. You should be flattered that she's parting with one of her treasures."

"Thanks, baby," Nick said, leaning over to scratch her ears. "If we open a country inn, Qwill, we're going to permit pets. I don't know how practical it'll be, but we'll work it out somehow."

"Good for you! When I drove to the mountains earlier this year, I stopped at a motel that actually provides an overnight cat for guests who don't have their own. They do a brisk business at two dollars per cat, per night."

"Lori and I never knew why you canceled that trip," Nick said.

Confidentially, Qwilleran explained the prowler episode. "I don't want this to go any further," he said, "but I had reason to believe he wanted to grab Polly and hold her for ransom."

"No! You don't mean it! Did the police do anything about it?"

"Brodie offered her protection, and I came home immediately. The prowler had a wild beard, and I saw a young man of that description at the library, acting suspiciously. He drove an old maroon car with a Massachusetts plate. Later, the state police saw him leaving the county, and there's been no further sighting—until today."

"What happened today?"

"I saw a car with a Massachusetts plate, and they're rare around here, if not virtually unknown."

"You're right about that," said Nick. "I hardly ever see a New England car. Funny, isn't it?"

"This was not the original maroon car, but it had the original bushy beard behind the wheel. I didn't catch the license number."

"I'll watch for it." Nick's eye had been sharpened by his job at the prison.

"It's a tan car. Try to get the number. Brodie ran a check on the previous vehicle. It's registered to one Charles Edward Martin."

"Will do, Qwill. Now I've got to get home to dinner. Here are your letters to sign. Anything to go?"

"Only this." Qwilleran handed him a small white box with CRM on the cover. "A souvenir of Scotland for Lori."

"Gee, thanks. She really likes that cape you brought her from the mountains." Nick had to wade through a tangle of legs, tails, and undulating bodies on his way to the door. "And thanks for the Scotch. It's good stuff!"

Qwilleran had still another gift to deliver that day, and he walked downtown for the third time. The three commercial blocks of Main Street constituted a stone canyon. In the nineteenth century, the surrounding countryside had been quarried to pave Main Street and build the stores and civic buildings. Squeezed between the imitation forts, temples, and castles was the Old English storefront housing Amanda's Studio of Interior Design. When he walked into the studio, he was greeted by Fran Brodie, who was always as chic and personable as her boss was dowdy and cranky.

"How's Amanda?" he asked. "Did she recover from the tour?"

"Oh, yes," Fran replied with an airy wave of the hand. "Dr. Zoller repaired her denture, and she's once more her old, sweet, smiling self. She left on a buying trip this morning. What did you think of Scotland?"

"Ask me what I think of tourists! We travel to a foreign country and never really leave home. We take our own egos, preferences, hobbies, dislikes, and conversation and never really appreciate what we see and experience. In Glasgow I went exploring at my own pace and enjoyed it more. You'd like the Charles Rennie Mackintosh exhibits, Fran." He handed her a small white box. "Here's what the contemporary artists are doing in the Mackintosh tradition. I thought you'd like it."

"It's lovely! It's Art Nouveau! What is this unusual stone?"

"A Scottish cairngorm."

She pinned it on the lapel of her bronze-toned suit and gave him a theatrical kiss. "You're a darling! Will you have coffee?"

"Not this time, thanks. It's late, and you're probably ready to close up. I just wanted to ask when you start rehearsals for *Macbeth*. How are you going to get the show on the boards by the last week in September?"

"We're used to chaos in community theatre, Qwill, but it always works out by opening night. Dwight did the casting and blocking before he left, and I worked with the supporting cast while you were away—the witches, the bleeding captain, the porter, and so forth. Derek Cuttlebrink is doing the porter in act two, scene three. *Knock, knock, knock! Who's there?* He'll provide our comic relief."

Before leaving, Qwilleran said, "About that fragment of the Mackintosh kilt—I'll take it. Now that I've seen the battlefield at Culloden, it has some meaning. Go ahead and have it framed . . . and I may see you at one of the rehearsals," he said as he left the studio.

On the sidewalk he stopped abruptly. Parked at the curb was a tan car that had not been in evidence when he arrived a few minutes before. He walked behind it and wrote down the license number. Then, hurrying back into the studio just as Fran was preparing to lock the door, he demanded, "What's that tan car parked out in front?"

"Is he there again?" she said indignantly. "He's supposed to park in the rear. I'm going to complain to the hotel."

"Who is he?"

"The new chef they've just hired. God knows they needed one! The menu hadn't been changed for forty years."

"Where did they get him? Where's he from?"

"Fall River."

"Fall River, Massachusetts? That's not exactly the gourmet capital of the east coast!"

"No, but he's offering things like chicken cordon bleu instead of pig hocks and sauerkraut, and that's an improvement."

"Does he have a beard?" Qwilleran asked.

"Yes, a shaggy one. He wears it in a hairnet to cook."

"What does he give as his name, do you know?"

Fran said hesitantly, "I think it's Carl. I'm not sure. You seem unusually curious about him."

"May I use your phone?"

"Sure. Go ahead. We'll put it on your bill," she said archly.

"As we say in Scotland," he admonished her, "don't be *pawky!*"

He called the police station.

Nine

The telephone at the apple barn rang constantly Tuesday morning, keeping Koko in a frenzy; he considered it his responsibility to monitor all calls. The barrage started with thank-yous from Lori Bamba and Hixie Rice, each of whom had to be told the significance of CRM, the Art Nouveau background of the peacock feather, and the name of the semiprecious stone.

Then came a report from Chief Brodie: The tan car with the Massachusetts license was registered to one Karl Oskar Klaus of Fall River. He spelled the name. Klaus was the new chef at the hotel, he said.

"Do you know anything about him?" Qwilleran's attitude was challenging.

"Only that he hasn't robbed the bank yet," Brodie quipped. "What do you have against Massachusetts?"

"Nothing. In fact, my mother was born there. I'm a second-generation codfish."

Next, a weary traveler phoned from Lockmaster.

"Welcome home, Bushy," Qwilleran said. "How was your flight?"

"Not too bad. As soon as I catch up on my sleep, I'll start developing my black-and-white film. I think I've got some good shots."

"Hear any news about the jewel theft before you left?"

"Nope. Nobody was feeling too sorry for Grace Utley.

It's hard to shed tears over lost diamonds when all you have is a $50 watch."

Qwilleran said, "I'm looking forward to seeing your pictures, Bushy. When will you have prints? Bring them up here and I'll buy lunch."

"In a couple of days, okay? And Qwill . . . I'll be wanting to talk to you about a problem."

"What kind of problem?"

"Personal." He sounded discouraged for a young man who was usually so exuberant.

The next call came from Arch Riker. "When did you get in?" Qwilleran asked him.

"Three o'clock this morning! How long have you been home? Three days? And you haven't written a line of copy!"

"Sounds as if you're at the office. Go home and go to bed, Arch. Everything's under control. Junior's saving me a hole on page two for tomorrow. Have I ever missed a deadline?"

"Another thing!" Riker shouted into the phone. "I came home on the same flight with Grace Utley—in the same row, for God's sake! And I wish you'd call her and get her off my back." For a veteran deskman, usually so placid, this was a surprising outburst.

"What does she want?"

"She wants to publish a book about her teddy bear collection, and she wants someone to do the writing and editing. You could do it. You don't have anything else to do."

"You must be kidding, Arch."

"She'll pay. You could pick up a few bucks."

"Sure. Just what I need," Qwilleran said. "Go home and sleep it off, chum. You're pooped after that long flight, or *ramfeezled,* as the Scots say."

"At least talk to her and get me off the hook. I've got a paper to publish."

Qwilleran muttered a protest but agreed to follow through, after giving her a day to recover from jet lag. He promised to get rid of her in one way or another.

"Try murder!" Riker said and slammed down the receiver.

Before writing his column on castles, Qwilleran refreshed his memory by listening to a tape that he recorded after bumping his head on a stone lintel.

"There are said to be more than a thousand castles in Scotland, some with very low doorways. They were first built in medieval times by conquerors of Scotland, as fortresses from which to rule the rebellious natives. A livable castle consisted of an impregnable wall as much as fourteen feet thick, a ditch or moat, a tower called a keep, an iron gate called a yett, an inner courtyard, and housing for the conqueror's family, retainers, and soldiery. This stronghold also had a pit for prisoners, and gun-loops and battlements from which defenders could hold the fort, as the saying goes, and pour boiling oil on attackers.

"Many of these historic castles now lie in ruins. What is more stirring to the imagination than a noble ruin on a mountaintop, silhouetted against the sky . . . or on a cliff overlooking the sea . . . or on a lonely island, reflected in the silvery water of a loch? Other castles have been restored as museums or palatial residences whose owners admit the public for a fee.

"Today we visited the island where Macbeth was buried in 1057" . . . (Sound of knocking.) "Now who the devil is that?"

(Pause.)

"How do you feel, lover? You seemed rather quiet during dinner."

"After conversing with the same crowd for five days, I'm running out of things to say and also the patience to listen."

"May I come in? I want to check your pulse and temperature. Sit down over there, please."

As soon as Melinda's voice issued from the player, Koko began protesting in a piercing monotone. After three years' absence, she still aroused his antagonism, the cause of which had never been clear. Had he objected to her perfume? Did he detect her hospital connection? Anything associated with a hospital was on Koko's hate list. No, more likely he had sensed her motives; Koko was dedicated to keeping Qwilleran single.

Qwilleran retired to his studio to write a thousand words on castles, and the Siamese retired to some secret hideaway. Before he left the barn to deliver his copy, however, he made a routine check. He never left home without knowing their whereabouts. This time they were not sleeping on the chairs in the lounge area, not huddled on the fireplace cube or the refrigerator, not hiding under a rug or behind the books on the shelves. They were in one of those voids in another time warp into which cats are able to vanish at will. It happened frequently, and the only way to rout them out was to shout the secret password: *Treat!* Then they would materialize from nowhere to claim their handful of crunchy cereal or morsel of cheese. It was the only guaranteed method, and to ensure its efficacy he never used the T word unless he meant to deliver.

So Qwilleran yelled "Treat!" and they suddenly appeared in the kitchen. "I'm going out," he told them as he dispensed their snack. "Don't answer the phone if it rings."

Being on a short deadline, he used the quick route downtown, through the woods that gave the apple barn its countrified seclusion, and he was able to deliver his copy to Junior Goodwinter in time for Wednesday's edition.

"Is this your piece on castles?" the editor asked. "I've been waiting to read it. Everyone likes castles."

"While churning it out," Qwilleran said, "I figured out how to solve the Goodwinter Boulevard problem. Turn it into an avenue of castles and sell tickets to tourists. The owners can reserve seven or eight rooms for their families, while the public tramps through the other ten or fifteen at $5 a head. The revenue from admissions will take care of taxes and maintenance."

"I wish you weren't only kidding," Junior said.

"Do you know anything about the new chef at the hotel? Have you eaten there since they hired him?"

"No, but I hear he's pretty good, although *anyone* would be an improvement."

Using Junior's phone, Qwilleran called Polly at the library. "Are you feeling adventurous? Would you like to have dinner at the hotel? They have a new chef."

"That's what I heard. Is he good? What is his background?"

"He's from Fall River, Massachusetts." Facetiously he added, "They say he's a legend in Fall River."

It had to be an early dinner, because Polly had scheduled one of her frequent committee meetings at the library, and the members were gathering at seven-thirty. He often wondered how a small library in a small town could keep so many committees busy with whatever it was they did. Meanwhile he killed time by listening to a few more of his Scottish tapes. The Siamese listened, too. When their dinner hour was approaching, their empty stomachs stimulated their interest in everything that Qwilleran did.

One tape launched him on a new train of thought and aroused certain suspicions. It was a conversation with Lyle Compton toward the end of the tour. Lyle was saying:

"Too bad we didn't see any smugglers' caves. I used to read about Dick Turpin, the notorious smuggler and highwayman, but Irma never mentioned smuggling at all. I wonder why. At one time in history it was a national industry. The ragged coastline, you know, with all those hidden coves and sheltering islands, was ideal for bringing in contraband by ship."

"What did they smuggle, Lyle?"

"Luxury items like rum, wine, tea, tobacco, lace, diamonds, and so on. From Scottish coastal villages they were transported to major cities in Britain by wagon and stagecoach—disguised as something else, of course. It drove the government crazy, but it must have been an exciting operation. They had a network of tunnels and hiding places, including caves along the shore. A whole string of inns was involved."

"With a great natural resource like the coast of Scotland, you can't tell me that they're not exploiting it today."

"You're right, Qwill! Probably for drug smuggling." Click.

There was no vocal response from Koko during this tape, although his ears twitched whenever he heard Qwilleran's voice. Then it was five-thirty and time to pick up Polly at the library.

Qwilleran was wearing his new suede sports coat ordered from Scottie's Men's Store before the tour. He had never spent that much money on any item of clothing, but Scottie had assumed his Scots brogue and talked him into it. It was camel beige, and he wore it with brown trousers. Polly said he looked wonderful. She was wearing a black and yellow kilt purchased in Inverness.

"It's a MacLeod tartan, but it goes with my black blazer," she explained.

"So much for clan loyalty," he said.

The "New" Pickax Hotel had been built in 1935 after the Old Pickax Hotel burned down, and now the locals were saying that it was time for another fire. In 1935 the public rooms had been furnished in Early Modern—not comfortable, not attractive, but sturdy. Recently a runaway snowplow had barged into the front of the building, demolishing the lobby but not the sturdy oak furniture.

Qwilleran and his guest were the first to arrive in the dining room, and the hostess seated them at a window table overlooking Main Street. He remarked, "I hear you have a new chef."

"He's completely redone the menu," she said. "It's very exciting! Would you like something from the bar?"

After ordering dry sherry for Polly and Squunk water with a twist for himself, Qwilleran scanned the menu card. Only a diner familiar with the hotel for the last forty years would consider the selection exciting: French onion soup instead of bean, grilled salmon steak instead of fish and chips, chicken cordon bleu instead of chicken and dumplings, and roast prime rib instead of swiss steak.

When the waiter brought the drinks, Qwilleran asked, "Is the chicken cordon bleu prepared in the kitchen, or is it one of those frozen, prefabricated artifacts shipped in from Ontario?"

"No, sir. The chef makes it himself," the waiter assured him.

Qwilleran decided to try it, but Polly thought the ham and cheese stuffing would violate her diet; she ordered the salmon.

The previous cooks had merely dished up the food; the new chef arranged the plates: parsley, boiled potatoes, broccoli, and a cherry tomato with the salmon; broccoli, a cherry tomato, and steamed zucchini straws with the chicken cordon bleu.

"I see they've gone all-out," Qwilleran commented.

Surveying the neat bundle on his plate, he plunged his knife and fork into the chicken, and a geyser of melted butter squirted fifteen inches into the air, landing on his lapel and narrowly missing his left eye.

"This isn't what I ordered!" he said indignantly as he brushed the greasy streak with his napkin. "Waiter! Waiter!"

"It's chicken Kiev!" Polly cried.

Qwilleran said to the young man, "Is this supposed to be chicken cordon bleu?"

"Yes, sir."

"Well, it's not! It's something else. Take it back to the kitchen and tell Karl Oskar I want chicken cordon bleu."

"Your coat is ruined!" Polly said in dismay. "Do you think the cleaner can get it out?"

The waiter soon returned with the plate. "The chef says this *is* chicken cordon bleu, like it says on the menu."

Blowing furiously into his moustache, Qwilleran said, "It may be so described in Fall River, but it's chicken Kiev in the rest of the civilized world! . . . Come on, Polly. We're going to the Old Stone Mill." To the bewildered hostess he said, "I'm sending you the bill for a new suede coat, and if I hadn't ducked, you'd be paying for an eye, too."

Over dry sherry and Squunk water at their favorite restaurant, the pair tried to relax, but Qwilleran was in a bad humor, and he plunged recklessly into a subject that had been on his mind for a couple of days, his suspicions augmented by the tape he had heard before coming to dinner. "You know, Polly," he blurted out, "I'm beginning to wonder if Irma's death could have been murder."

Polly recoiled in horror. "Qwill! What makes you say that? Who would do such a thing? And why?"

"How well did you really know Irma?"

She hesitated. "She was just a casual acquaintance until recently, when we started to go birding together. Out there on the riverbank or in the wetlands, where it was quiet and peaceful, it was easy to exchange confidences—"

"Did she ever tell you what she did on her frequent trips to Scotland?"

"Not in detail. I know she went birding in the islands. She always mentioned puffin birds and the red-necked phalarope—"

"Hmmm," he murmured cynically, thinking that bird-watchers on the islands would make good lookouts, especially if equipped with radios. "I hate to say this, Polly, but I always received the impression that Irma was hiding something behind a somewhat artificial facade, and now it occurs to me that the Bonnie Scots Tour may have been a cover for something else—a scam that backfired."

"*What!*" Polly's throat flushed. "What in God's name are you talking about?" She pushed her sherry away in an angry gesture.

"For centuries the Scottish coastline has lent itself to smuggling. Today the contraband is probably drugs."

Shocked, Polly demanded, "Are you suggesting that Irma was involved in *smuggling drugs?* Why, that's unthinkable!"

Qwilleran thought, Irma was fanatically devoted to raising money for charity, and fanaticism makes strange bedfellows. He said, "She never told you anything about her friends in Scotland. What about this man she sneaked away with every night—always in wild, secluded country where the inns had no names? What were they doing? And did something go wrong? He could have slipped her a drug because she became a threat. He had a police record. Obviously he was planning to steal the jewels. Did Irma know about that?"

Polly snatched the napkin from her lap and threw it on the table. "How can you make such malicious assumptions when she's not here to defend herself? It was a heart attack! Melinda said so!"

"Melinda could be wrong."

"I refuse to listen to this assault on Irma's integrity!"

"I'm sorry, Polly. Perhaps Irma was an innocent victim, murdered because she could identify Bruce after he committed his crime . . . Finish your drink, and we'll ask for the soup course."

"No!" she said bitterly. "You have your dinner. I'll wait in the lobby."

He signaled the waitress. "Check, please, and cancel our order."

They drove back to town in silence, but he could feel the waves of anger emanating from the passenger seat. When they reached the library, Polly stepped out of the car and said a curt thank you.

At the barn, he was met by two alert Siamese with questioning tails, as if they felt the tension in the air. Now Qwilleran felt hungry, as well as uneasy about the scene with Polly and indignant about his suede coat. He threw it on a kitchen chair and searched the refrigerator for the makings of a sandwich. Yum Yum, as if she wanted to comfort him, presented him with an emery board.

"Thank you, sweetheart," he said.

As he swallowed his sandwich and gulped his coffee, he admitted to himself that he had been tactless in linking Polly's friend with illegal activity. Yet, there was something about the events in the Highlands that made his moustache bristle, and he was floundering in his search for a clue.

He played some more tapes, hoping for enlightenment:

> "At the inn where we're lodged tonight, the fireplace mantel is draped with a fringed scarf; the lamp shades are fringed; and there are rugs thrown over the sofas—all very cozy. Blankets are used for draw draperies over the windows, which should say something about winters in the Highlands. The mantel shelf is adorned with the usual clock, some pieces of china, and a live but apathetic cat. The cats in the Scottish Highlands are not as nervous as American cats. They walk in slow motion, stretch lazily instead of purposefully, and spend their time resting on wharf pilings, fences, doorsteps, windowsills, rooftops, or fireplace mantels."

It surprised Qwilleran that the Siamese failed to respond to this segment of the tape. There was something about the sound of the word "cat" that usually commanded their immediate attention. When they were sleeping, he had only to whisper "cat" and their ears would twitch. The tapes rolled on:

> "Today I did my neighborly duty on the bus, sitting with Zella in the morning and Grace in the afternoon. When we're on the road, Zella looks out the window and enjoys the scenery. Grace never stops talking about life back home. She's an encyclopedia of Pickax scandal, and what she doesn't know, she invents. That, at least, is her reputation. It appears that the only Moose

County families without skeletons in the closet are the Chisholms and the Utleys, and even the Utleys have a few bones rattling under the stairs."

Qwilleran kept glancing at his watch. He half expected Polly to phone and say, "Qwill, I'm afraid I overreacted." He thought she would call about nine o'clock, after the committee meeting, but the telephone was exasperatingly silent.

"After dinner tonight Irma did her usual vanishing act, and Larry, Melinda, and Dwight went into the garden to work on *Macbeth*. I'd hear Larry's magnificent voice: *'Is this a dagger which I see before me?'* He'd repeat it several times with different emphasis. Or I'd hear Melinda screaming, *'Out, damned spot! Out, I say!'* How do these intrepid actors endure the midges that swarm up out of the bushes in millions?"

It was a disappointing session for Qwilleran, with no clues on the tapes and no pertinent comments from Koko. Neither cat, he now realized, had been in evidence for some time—not, in fact, since he had returned home. Where were they? Reluctant to overdo the T word, he wandered about the barn, searching all levels, calling their names, hoping to find one or the other. No luck! And where, he asked himself, was his suede coat?

Ten

When Qwilleran found his suede sports coat, he had a wild impulse to phone Polly and relate the incredible circumstances: how he had found it under a kitchen chair . . . how the suede surface was furred with cat hair . . . and how the streak of melted butter had completely disappeared. There was not even a trace of it! The left-hand lapel was now more roughly sueded than the right, but the grease spot was gone.

Before he could pick up the phone, however, he thought about their disagreement at the restaurant. They'd had spats in the past, which were always resolved when one or the other decided the triumph was not worth the battle. This time he was in no mood to wave the white flag. She should have been more understanding, he thought. She should have known he was blowing off steam after the infuriating chicken episode. She was well acquainted with his reckless surmises when faced with unanswered questions. Furthermore, he had apologized—somewhat—in the restaurant, and he was in no hurry to make further amends.

Perhaps there was an element of suppressed guilt lurking under his rationalizations, calling for atonement, and that was why he telephoned the Chisholm sisters the next morning with such a pretense of bonhomie. Grace Utley answered.

"Good morning," he said in his most ingratiating tone.

"This is your erstwhile traveling companion, Jim Qwilleran. I trust you two lovely ladies had a pleasant journey home."

"Oh, Mr. Qwilleran! It's so nice of you to call!" she said, with excitement heightening the rasp in her voice. "We had an enjoyable flight. Mr. Riker was our seatmate, and he's a most interesting man."

"He enjoyed your company, too. That's why he asked me to call. He says you have an idea for a book that you want to discuss."

"About our teddy bear collection . . . yes! He was quite excited about the idea. Would you be willing to help us? I know you're a very busy man . . ."

"Not so busy that I'd turn down a stimulating challenge! I'd like to explore the possibilities—perhaps this afternoon."

"So soon?" she crowed with delight. "Then you must come for lunch, dear heart. Zella is a wonderful cook."

"I'm sure she is," he replied, "but I have a previous engagement. How about two o'clock?"

"Then we'll have tea," she said with finality. "We brought some shortbread from Edinburgh. Do you like Scotch shortbread?"

"My favorite treat!" If Qwilleran was atoning, he was doing it with panache.

To fortify himself for the appointment he had a good lunch at the Old Stone Mill—crab bisque, a Reuben sandwich, pumpkin pie—and before driving to Goodwinter Boulevard he picked up a bunch of mums at the florist shop. Mums were Moose County's all-purpose flower for weddings, funerals, and table centerpieces. On second thought, he bought two bunches, one rust and one yellow.

The sisters lived in one of the larger stone mansions on the boulevard, next door to the residence of the late Dr. Halifax Goodwinter. The Chisholms and the Utleys had been among the founders of Moose County. Yet, like many of the old families, they were disappearing as the later generations stayed single or remained childless or moved away after marrying outsiders from such remote areas as Texas and the District of Columbia. It was said that Grace Utley had two daughters Down Below, who would have nothing to do with her. So the widow and her unmarried sister lived by themselves in the big house. According to Junior Good-winter, they were among the old-timers who would fight rezoning to their last breath.

Upon arriving, Qwilleran had hardly touched finger to doorbell before the door was flung open.

"Welcome to Teddy Bear Castle!" cried Grace in her abrasive voice, while Zella hovered in the background, wringing her hands with excitement. She was wearing her gold teddy bear with ruby eyes. Grace, bereft of everything but what she had on her person at the time of the theft, was reduced to a few gold chains and a frog brooch paved with emeralds.

With a courteous bow Qwilleran presented his flowers, rust for Grace and yellow for Zella, who squealed as if she had never before received a floral token.

"So good of you to come!" said Grace. "Zella, dear, put these in water." Then grandly she waved an arm about the foyer. "How do you like our little friends, Mr. Qwilleran?"

Being familiar with boulevard architecture, he knew what to expect: grand staircase, massive chandelier, carved woodwork, stained glass, oversize furniture. But he was unprepared for the hundreds of shoe-button eyes that stared at him—charmingly, impishly, crazily—from tabletops, cabinets, chairseats, and even the treads of the wide stair-case.

"We're collectors," Grace explained with pride.

"So I see." Feeling a presence behind him, he turned to find a plush animal somewhat larger than himself.

"That's Woodrow, our watch bear," said Grace.

"How many do you own?"

"Zella, dear, how many do we have now?" she shouted toward the kitchen.

"One thousand, eight hundred, and sixty-two," came the small voice.

"One thousand, eight hundred, and sixty-two . . . yes. Zella has them catalogued for insurance purposes." She led Qwilleran to a locked vitrine in the drawing room. "This is Theodore, our button-in-ear Steiff. One just like him sold for $80,000."

Other bears sat on chairs, windowsills, the fireplace mantel, and the grand piano.

"That's Ignace on the piano bench—Zella's special friend. She took him to Scotland. I took Ulysses, the one on the rocking horse," Grace said. "Fortunately Ulysses was traveling in Zella's luggage."

Other bears sat at the dining room table with a full setting of china, crystal, and silver at each place and a napkin on each lap. Several, wearing eyeglasses, were reading books in the library or working at the desk. Throughout the house they were arranged in tableaux: playing croquet, trimming a Christmas tree, sailing toy boats in a tub of water, wheeling a baby bear in a stroller, gardening with a toy wheelbarrow. Although they all seemed to have the same perky ears, felt snout, stitched mouth, and shoe-button eyes, they had individual facial expressions and personalities. Many were in costume. Some squeaked, or laughed, or blinked battery-operated eyes.

Qwilleran, who had seen everything as a newsman Down Below, had never seen anything like this.

"Zella, dear, you may serve the tea now," Grace said as the tour ended.

A few distinguished bears were invited to join the party. They had their own tiny cups and saucers, and Zella poured tea for them.

Grace said to Qwilleran, as sweetly as she could with her rasping voice, "We're going to name our next little friend after you, and you must attend the christening party."

Asking permission to use a tape recorder, he asked the routine questions: Why do you collect bears? When did you start? Which have you had the longest? Where do you find them? Who makes the costumes? How do you keep them from catching dust? Do you have a good security system?

"The best!" said Grace. "We also have a watchman living in the caretaker's apartment over the garage, and his wife vacuums the bears in rotation."

Meanwhile, Qwilleran drank tea without pleasure and ate shortbread dutifully, asking himself, What am I doing here? . . . Are the women crazy? . . . Are they pulling my leg?

With his third cup of tea he made a desperate effort to change the subject. "Well, it looks as if you're going to have some excitement next door—the liquidation sale."

Grace erupted in indignation. "It's absolutely dreadful! Zella and I are leaving town until it's over. No one should be allowed to have a tag sale in a neighborhood like this! How will they handle the crowds? Where will they park? Everyone in Moose County adored Dr. Hal and will want to buy something as a memento. I'll tell you one thing: Dr. Hal would never have permitted such a sale! But his daughter is another breed. She does as she pleases without regard for anyone else. The entire contents of the house should have been moved to the Bid-a-Bit auction barn."

"Why didn't Dr. Melinda do that?" he inquired.

"Why? Because she can make more money with a tag sale on the premises!"

"Did you know the Goodwinter family well?"

"All my life! . . . Zella, dear, this tea is cold. Would you bring a fresh pot?" When her sister had left the room, she said in a hushed voice, "Zella could have married Dr. Hal, but she missed her chance by being too meek, and he had the misfortune to marry a woman with bad blood. Mrs. Goodwinter's father died of a disease that the family never mentions, and her brother embezzled money in Illinois and went to prison. Melinda was their firstborn, spoiled from the cradle. Their son—we always knew he'd be the black sheep of the family. He finally left town and was later killed in a car accident. Everyone said it was a blessing in disguise because he was an embarrassment to his father and a worry to his mother, who was a chronic invalid."

Before making his escape, Qwilleran asked, "Would you ladies allow the *Moose County Something* to photograph your collection for a feature story?"

"We'd be flattered, wouldn't we, Zella? That is, Mr. Qwilleran, if you'll promise to write the article yourself. You write so well!"

"I think that could be arranged. And now, thank you for a memorable adventure and delicious tea."

Blushing furiously, the shy sister stepped forward, saying, "This is for you!" She handed him a brown velvet teddy bear, hardly three inches high.

"Oh, no! I wouldn't think of robbing your collection," he said.

"But we want you to have it,' Grace insisted. "Please accept it."

"His name is Tiny Tim," Zella said.

With Tiny Tim in his pocket, Qwilleran left the house, saying to himself, *Whew!*

Back home at the barn, his first move was to phone Riker at the office. He said, "Arch, you owe me one! I've just spent a tedious afternoon with the Chisholm sisters, drinking tea and eating shortbread, and they want me to be godfather to their next teddy bear."

"What about their idea for a book?"

"They never mentioned a book. They just wanted someone to visit and be impressed by their collection, but I think we should do a story. Send a good photographer over there, like John Bushland, and I'll bet the wire services will pick it up!"

While he was on the phone, the Siamese were rifling his jacket pocket. They knew instinctively that something new had arrived.

"Oh, no, you don't!" he scolded when he finished the phone call. They were sinking their fangs into the spongy body. He hid Tiny Tim in the kitchen drawer where he always tossed his car keys.

Then he checked the answering machine; there was still no call from Polly, all the more reason why he wanted to consult Melinda. If she agreed that Irma's attack could have been drug-induced, he would be in the clear. The entire cast was scheduled to rehearse that night; he could get an answer from her during a break, without personal complications.

The K Theatre, built within the fieldstone shell of the former Klingenschoen mansion, was small—only 300 seats—but it was large enough for the Pickax Theatre Club. The auditorium was a steeply raked amphitheatre with a thrust stage, and there was a gracious lobby. When Qwilleran arrived there Wednesday night, he found Larry Lanspeak in the lobby, bent over the drinking fountain.

"Your beard looks promising," he told the actor.

Larry rubbed his chin. "In two more weeks it should be good enough for an eleventh-century Scottish king."

"How's the play shaping up?"

"Not bad. Not bad at all! When we were away, Fran worked with the supporting cast in the eleven scenes where Melinda and I don't appear, and she did a good job. This is our first full-cast rehearsal."

Larry returned to the stage, and Qwilleran slipped into the back row. Some of the actors were draped over the front seats, awaiting their scenes. Dwight was in front of the stage directing performers who were running lines without the book. One of them, playing a messenger, was making his exit, and Lady Macbeth was saying, *"Unsex me here, and fill me from the crown to the toe top full of direst cruelty!"*

"Hold it!" the director said. "Bring the messenger back, and take it again, Melinda, from *Thou'rt mad to say it!* Give it some *fire!*"

They repeated the scene. Then Larry made his entrance. *"My dearest love, Duncan comes here tonight!"*

Melinda replied, *"And when goes hence?"*

"Tomorrow—" Larry interrupted his own line, saying, "Dwight, how do I play this? Is Macbeth honored that the king is going to stay under his roof? Or is he already planning to kill him? What is he thinking at this moment?"

The director said, "Lady Macbeth plants the idea of murder in his head with her line, *And when goes hence?* That means, Melinda, that you've got to give her question some powerful innuendo. *And—when—goes—hence?* The audience should feel a chill up the spine . . . Got it, everybody?"

"Got it," said Larry. "She plants the idea, and I pause before *Tomorrow*. In that split second the audience realizes the king will never leave the castle alive."

Qwilleran was impressed with Dwight's direction and told him so during the break, intercepting him on the way to the drinking fountain.

"Thanks," he said. "Larry's a joy to direct, let me say that. Now I know why he has such a great reputation in community theatre. I'd heard about him in Iowa before I knew there was any such place as Pickax."

"Will the show be ready by the last Thursday in the month?"

"It's got to be! The tickets are printed."

Carol walked up the aisle to get a drink of water, and Qwilleran said to her, "Why don't you ask the K Foundation to give you a drinking fountain backstage?"

"Not a bad idea. It would save wear and tear on the aisle carpet . . . Did I hear someone mention tickets?" she asked. "We could use some help in the box office, Qwill. Are you available?"

"If it doesn't require any rare skills or mental acuity."

To Dwight she said, "Qwill lives right behind the theatre—in an apple barn!" Then she went on her way to the lobby.

"I've heard about your barn," the director said. "I'm partial to barns."

"Stop in for a drink some night after rehearsal."

"I'll do that. I'll bring my tin whistle, and you can tell me how you react to my witch music."

There was a whiff of perfume, and Melinda sauntered up the aisle en route to the drinking fountain. "Hi, lover," she said with surprise and pleasure. "What are you doing here?"

Dwight gave a quick look at both of them and drifted away to the lobby.

"Just snooping," Qwilleran said, "but since you're here, I'll ask you a couple of questions. If I write about the liquidation of your father's estate in the 'Qwill Pen' column, will that be okay with you?" He knew it would be, but it was an opener.

"God, yes! Every little bit helps," she said. "I need to sell everything. The preview will be a week from Friday. Would you like a preview of the preview?" she asked teasingly. "Hang around, and I'll take you over to the house when we finish here."

"Thanks, but not tonight," he said.

"Wouldn't you like to see *everything*—without people around?"

He employed the journalist's standard white lie. "Sorry, I have to do some writing on deadline. But before I go, here's one more question. It's about Irma's death. As you probably know by now, the bus driver disappeared after you left, along with Grace Utley's jewels, and Irma was the only one who knew his name or anything about him. It occurred to me that Bruce could have given her some kind of fatal drug to conceal his identity."

"No, lover, it was cardiac arrest, pure and simple," she said with a patronizing smile, "and considering her medical history and the pace of her life, I'm surprised it didn't happen sooner."

Qwilleran persisted. "The police now know the driver has a criminal record, so murder is not beyond the realm of possibility, considering the size of the haul."

Melinda shook her head slowly and wisely. "Sorry to disappoint you, Qwill," she said with a tired, pitying look. "It would have made a good story, and I know you like to uncover foul play, but this was no crime. Trust me." She brightened. "If you would like to go somewhere afterward and talk about it, I could explain. We could have a drink at my apartment—or your barn."

"Another time, when I'm not on deadline," he said. "By the way, your Lady Macbeth is looking good." He turned and was halfway across the lobby before she could react to the weak compliment.

He walked home through the woods, swinging a flashlight and thinking ruefully, So it wasn't murder! Now I suppose I should square things with Polly.

The telephone was ringing when he unlocked the door, and Koko was racing around to inform him of the fact.

"Okay, okay! I'm not deaf!" he yelled at the cat as he snatched the receiver. "Hello? . . . Hi, Nick. I just got in the house. What's up?"

"You know the Massachusetts car you told me about? I saw it!" said Nick triumphantly.

"The tan car? Forget it! It belongs to the new chef at the hotel. He's from Fall River."

"No, not the tan job, Qwill. The original maroon car! It's back in town."

"Where did you see it?"

"I was driving north on the highway to Mooseville, and I saw this car turn west on the unpaved stretch of Ittibittiwassee Road. You know where I mean? The Dimsdale Diner is on the corner."

"I know the road," Qwilleran said. "It leads to Shantytown."

"Yeah, and the car was beat-up like the kind you always see turning into that hell hole."

"Did you follow it?"

"I wanted to, but I was driving a state vehicle and didn't think I should. He'd get the idea he was under surveillance.

But I thought you should know, Qwill. Tell Polly to be careful."

"Yes, I will. Thanks, Nick." Qwilleran hung up slowly, his hand lingering on the receiver. So the Boulevard Prowler was back in town! He punched a familiar number on the phone.

It was ten-thirty P.M., and Polly would be winding down, padding around in her blue robe, washing her nylons, doing something with her face and hair. He had been a husband long enough to know all about that routine.

She answered with a businesslike "Yes?"

"Good evening, Polly," he said in his most seductive voice. "How are you this evening?"

"All right," she said stiffly without returning the polite question.

"Was I an unforgivable bore last night?"

After a moment's hesitation, she replied, "You're never a bore, Qwill."

"I'm grateful for small compliments, and I admit it was bad form to bring up a painful subject at the dinner table."

"After what happened to your new coat, I believe you could be excused." She was softening up. "Did you take it to the cleaner?"

"That wasn't necessary. It was chicken-flavored butter, and the cats took care of it. You'd never know anything happened!"

"I don't believe it!"

"It's true."

There was a pause. It was Polly's turn to say something conciliatory. Qwilleran thought he was handling it rather well. Finally she said, "Perhaps I overreacted last night."

"I can't say you weren't justified. It was my fault for pursuing the subject so stubbornly. Blame it on my Scots heritage."

"I know. Your mother was a Mackintosh," she said, adding a light touch to the sober conversation. The Mackintosh connection was a running joke between them.

"Did you have a good day?" he asked.

"Interesting, at best. One of my clerks was rushed to the hospital in labor, and Mr. Tibbitt pressed the wrong button and was trapped in the elevator. We checked out 229 books and 54 cassettes, collected $3.75 in overdue fines, and issued 7 new-reader cards . . . Did you have a good day?"

"I did an assignment for Arch, and earlier this evening I audited a rehearsal at the theatre. Were you out at all tonight?"

"No, I had dinner at home and spent the evening reading and putting my wardrobe in order."

"If you have occasion to leave your apartment after dark, Polly, I'd rather you didn't drive alone. These are changing times. We have to face the fact that strangers are coming into Pickax. If you have an evening engagement, call me and I'll provide chauffeur service."

"Why this sudden concern, Qwill? Has anything happened? If it's because of that prowler last June . . . that was three months ago!"

"It's your neighborhood I worry about," Qwilleran said. "There are so many vacant houses. It behooves you to be careful. Meanwhile, would you like dinner tomorrow night? I'll be on my best behavior."

"The library will be open, and it's my turn to work."

"How about Friday?"

"The Hasselriches invited me to dinner. They're having Irma's favorite rolladen cooked in red wine."

Qwilleran huffed into his moustache. That was twice in one week! Now that she was their "surrogate daughter," they would be monopolizing her time. "Then how about Saturday? We could drive to Lockmaster and have dinner at the Palomino Paddock," he said, one-upping the Hasselriches' rolladen. In a state-wide dining guide the Paddock was rated ✳✳✳✳ for food and $$$$ for price.

Polly gasped as he hoped she would. "Oh, that would be delightful!"

"Then it's a date."

There was a pause.

"All's well, then?" he asked gently.

"All's well," she said with feeling.

"À bientôt, Polly."

"À bientôt, dear."

He immediately phoned the Paddock to reserve a good table. It was short notice for the celebrated restaurant, but the mention of his name commanded special consideration even in the next county, the K Foundation having recently funded a swimming pool for the youth center in Lockmaster.

Then he started up the ramp to change into pajamas and slippers. He was halfway to the first balcony when Koko rushed up behind him at a frantic speed and lunged at his legs, throwing him off balance and nearly knocking him to the floor.

"Say! Who do you think you are?" Qwilleran yelled. "A Green Bay linebacker? You could break my neck, you crazy cat!"

Koko, who had bounced off his target, picked himself up and sat on his haunches with head lowered as he licked his paw and passed it over his mask, stopping between licks to stare at the forehead of the man who was scolding him.

Qwilleran passed his own hand over his moustache as he thought, Can he smell Melinda's perfume? I spent two minutes with her, and he knows it! . . . And then he thought, Or is he trying to tell me something? I'm following the wrong scent; he's trying to push me back on track. *What does he want me to do?*

Eleven

The morning after Koko's flying tackle, there was no more domestic violence in the apple barn, but Koko stared at Qwilleran pointedly, as if trying to communicate. Over coffee and a thawed breakfast roll, the man tried to read the cat's message, thoughtfully combing his moustache with his fingertips. Could it be, he wondered, a warning about the Boulevard Prowler? Precognition was one of Koko's rare senses.

In sheer uncertainty mixed with curiosity, Qwilleran drove his car north that morning, turning left at the Dimsdale Diner onto the unpaved extension of Ittibittiwassee Road. This neglected stretch of gravel dead-ended at the abandoned Dimsdale Mine, with its rotting shafthouse and red signs warning of cave-ins. Nearby, where the thriving town of Dimsdale used to stand, there was only an eyesore called Shantytown.

It was a slum of shacks and decrepit travel trailers, rusty vehicles, and ramshackle chicken coops. They were scattered in a patch of woods, and the transients who lived there were actually squatters on Klingenschoen property. Shantytown was known as a hangout for derelicts, but poor families also lived there, and children played in the dust that surrounded the substandard housing. Efforts by the county and the K Foundation to "do something about Dimsdale" never achieved much. As soon as families were helped to move on to a better life through skill-training, employment, and a healthy environment, more families moved in to take their dreary place.

On this occasion, Qwilleran chose not to drive into the Shantytown jungle, thinking that his white car would be too conspicuous, but he peered through the woods with binoculars for a glimpse of a maroon vehicle and saw nothing that fitted that description. Leaving the area, he stopped for lunch at the diner, chiefly to confirm that it was as dismal as he remembered. The windows were still opaque with grime; two more seats had fallen off the stools at the counter; and the coffee lived up to its reputation as the worst in the county. Nevertheless, he recalled one dark and anxious night when he was stranded on the way home from North Middle Hummock with his car upside down in the ditch; the cook at the diner had sent him hot coffee and stale doughnuts on-the-house, a gesture that was much appreciated at the time.

A chalkboard announced the diner's Thursday specials: TOM SOUP, TUNA SAMICH, AND MAC/CHEEZ. Qwilleran, who had never encountered a plate of macaroni and cheese he didn't like, ordered the special with sanguine expectation but found the pasta cooked to the consistency of tapioca pudding. As for the sauce, library paste could have tasted no worse.

When he returned to the barn, ill-fed and somewhat ill-tempered, Koko was hopping up and down like a puppet on strings, a performance that signified a message on the answering machine. The call was from John Bushland in Lockmaster: "Qwill, it's Bushy. Making a delivery in Pickax this afternoon. Will drop by. Hope you're there. Got some good pix."

The photographer's van pulled into the barnyard about two o'clock.

"How come you're making a delivery in the backwoods?" Qwilleran asked. Lockmaster, with its horse breeders and golf courses, considered itself more civilized than its rural neighbor to the north, where potato farms and sheep ranches were the norm, and feed caps and pickup trucks were high fashion.

Bushy said, "Arch wanted to know if I had any shots of the Bonnie Scots gang with Scottish landmarks or local color. He said he'd run a spread, maybe a double-truck."

"Could you help him?"

"Oh, sure. I delivered more than a dozen prints, and I brought a set to show you, plus some scenics that are kind of different. Where can we spread them out?" There were three yellow boxes filled with 8x10 black-and-white glossies. "I'll have the color later," he said. "Here we are when we had lunch at Loch Lomond . . . and in this one we're waiting for the ferry at Mull. Here are some of the gals on the bridge at Eilean Donan Castle. The only complete group is around the bus at Oban; I even jumped into the picture myself."

"Wait a minute," Qwilleran said as he went to the desk for a magnifying glass. "Isn't that the bus driver in the background?"

Bushy studied the print with the glass. "You're right! He didn't duck his head for this one! I can blow it up and make a mug shot for the police."

"This calls for a celebration! How about Scotch with a splash of Squunk water?"

The photographer followed Qwilleran to the serving bar. "I know how it happened, Qwill. I was using the tripod, and I set the timer so I could run and get in the picture, and because I wasn't behind the camera, Bruce didn't realize he was being photographed . . . Hey! The cat's licking the prints!"

"Koko! Get away!" Qwilleran clapped his hands threateningly, and Koko darted guiltily from the vicinity.

"It must be the emulsion he likes," Bushy said. "Maybe I should put them back in the boxes . . . Guess what!" he said with more incredulity than enthusiasm. "Arch wants me to photograph the teddy bears for a story you're writing!"

"Be prepared for a wacky experience!"

"I know. Grace hired me to shoot her jewelry for insurance purposes before we left on the trip, and she hasn't paid me yet!"

Qwilleran huffed into his moustache. "What do you bet she's giving us the teddy bear story so she'll get free photos for the same purpose?"

The photographer sipped his drink moodily for a while and then said, "Do you think Pickax could support a photo studio, Qwill?"

"Why? Do you want to open a branch?"

"I'm thinking of moving my whole operation up here," Bushy said morosely. "That's the problem I told you about. Vicki and I are breaking up. My studio and darkroom are in the house, and I've got to get out. She's turning it into a restaurant."

"Sorry to hear about that, Bushy. I thought everything was going great with you two."

"Yeah . . . well . . . it looks like we won't have a family, so she's been hot for a career, which is okay with me, but she's gone crazy over her damned catering business! And now some guy at the riding club wants to back her financially if she'll open a restaurant. He comes on pretty strong, if you know what I mean. He's not just interested in food."

Qwilleran shook his head sympathetically. "I've been through that kind of mess myself, and let me offer some advice: Whatever you do, don't let them grind you down. *Illegitimi non carborundum,* as they say in fractured Latin."

"Yeah, but not so easy to do," Bushy said grimly. "Anyway, do you think a photo studio would go up here?"

"With the right kind of promotion . . . definitely! Pickax could use your talent and energy. If you don't mind working for a paper, the *Something* could give you plenty of assignments. And with your kind of enthusiasm, I predict you'll be president of the Boosters Club within a year!"

"Thanks, Qwill, I needed that! Those are the first upbeat words I've heard since I got back from Scotland . . . And now I've got work to do. I'll bring the mug shot of the bus driver tomorrow when I come up to shoot the bears."

"Deliver it to Andy Brodie," Qwilleran advised. "Start making points with the police chief."

When the photographer had left, he opened the yellow boxes on the dining table, where he could spread the prints out, and he was astounded at what he saw. Bushy had used unorthodox camera angles and different lenses and exposures to produce a startling kind of travel photography: impressionist, partially abstract in some shots, surreal in others. He went to the phone to call Arch Riker.

"Got an idea for you," he told the publisher. "I've just been talking to Bushy."

"Yes, we're running his Bonnie Scots pix Monday. How about writing some cutlines? We'll need them by noon tomorrow."

"Do I get a by-line?"

"Depends on how good they are. We'll go with the teddy bears Tuesday. That means copy's due Monday morning . . . Now what's your idea?"

"I've been looking at Bushy's scenic photos, and that guy definitely has a different way of looking at castles, mountains, sheep, fishermen, and all the other stuff. They're exhibition quality, Arch! Why couldn't the *Something* sponsor an exhibition of his travel photos?"

"Where?"

"In the lobby of the K Theatre, to tie in with the opening of *Macbeth*. He also has interesting shots of Larry and Melinda rehearsing in the courtyards of old inns."

There was a pensive pause before Riker said, "Once in a while you come up with a good one, Qwill."

As Qwilleran returned to the dining area, feeling pleased with himself, he was abashed to hear a telltale sound that was not good; Koko was slurping photos.

"NO!" he yelled. "Bad cat!"

Koko leaped from the table with a backward kick, scattering prints in all directions.

"Cats!" Qwilleran grumbled as he segregated the damaged glossies. Several had been deglossed in spots by the cat's sandpaper tongue and potent saliva.

* * *

He mentioned Koko's aberrant behavior to Polly as they drove to Lockmaster Saturday evening. "It's not the first time he's done this."

"Bootsie never does anything like that," she said.

Sure, Qwilleran thought. Bootsie never does anything— but eat.

The exclusive Palomino Paddock was located in lush horse country, and they found a parking place between an Italian sports car and a British luxury van. Eight o'clock guests in dinner jackets and long dresses were beginning to arrive—one pair in a horse-drawn surrey. The building itself, in purposeful contrast to the exquisite food and elegant customers, resembled an old horse stable—which it may well have been—and the interior was artfully cluttered with saddles, bales of hay, and portraits of thoroughbreds. Informality was the keynote, and the waitstaff—all young equestrians—were dressed like grooms. Early diners in hunting pinks, sipping their exotic demitasses, sprawled in their chairs with breeched and booted legs extended stiffly in the aisles.

Qwilleran and his guest were conducted to a cozily private table in a horse stall, where a framed portrait of a legendary horse named Cardinal was enshrined, with credit given to the Bushland Studio.

When a young wine steward wearing the keys to the cellar on heavy chains presented the wine list, Qwilleran waved it away. "The lady will have a glass of your driest sherry, and you can bring me Squunk water with a slice of lime. That is," he added slyly to test the young man's education, "if you have a recent vintage."

With perfect aplomb and a straight face the steward said, "I happen to have a bottle dated last Thursday and labeled Export Reserve. I think you'll find it exciting, with a mellow bouquet and distinctive finish." In reference to Squunk water, "bouquet" was a flattering term.

The waitress had the breezy self-confidence of a young

woman who keeps her own horse, wins ribbons, and looks terrific in a riding habit. "I'm your waitperson," she said. "We love having you here tonight. My name is Trilby."

"May I guess the name of your horse?" Qwilleran asked.

"Brandy. He's a buckskin. No papers, but beautiful points! I'll bring you the menus."

To Polly he said, "The woman in a red dress over there is Bushy's wife, Vicki. Her escort is someone I don't know."

"Vicki's my aunt," said Trilby, presenting the menus, "and he's an officer of the riding club. They're going to open their own restaurant." She dashed away again.

In a lower voice, Qwilleran said, "The Bushlands are having marital problems."

"Oh, I'm sorry to hear that," she said. "He's such a congenial and thoughtful young man."

"Talented, too. Wait till you see his pictures of Scotland. They have nothing to do with postcard art. Arch is going to start giving him assignments."

"That's good news! The photos in the *Something* are so unimaginative."

"We use amateurs with smart cameras. What we need is a smart photographer. For starters, Bushy is going to photograph Grace Utley's teddy bears."

"Are you interested in teddy bears?" asked Trilby, who had returned to discuss the evening's specials. "We have a teddy bear club in Lockmaster."

"Good for you!" Qwilleran said. "What do you recommend this evening?"

"We have a new chef, and he's prepared some very exciting things: for an appetizer, a nice grilled duck sausage with sage polenta and green onion confit. Our soup tonight is three-mushroom velouté."

"Is your chef from Fall River, by any chance?"

"I don't think so. Our specials tonight are a lovely roasted quail with goat cheese, sun-dried tomatoes, and hickory-smoked bacon and also a pan-seared snapper with herb crust and a red pepper and artichoke relish."

"Oh, dear!" Polly said in dismay. "What do you think I would like?"

"My personal favorite," said Trilby, "is the roasted pork tenderloin with sesame fried spinach, shiitake mushrooms, and garlic chutney."

Polly decided on plain grilled swordfish, and Qwilleran ordered fillet of beef for himself. Raising his glass of Squunk water he proposed, *"Lang may your lums reek,* as they say in Scotland."

"That sounds indecent," Polly replied as she raised her glass uncertainly.

"I believe it means 'Long may your chimneys smoke.' In the old days they weren't concerned with pollution. They just wanted to keep warm and cook their oatmeal."

They talked about the Chisholm sisters' teddy bear collection (incredible!) . . . the prospect of a tag sale on Goodwinter Boulevard (deplorable!) . . . the forthcoming production of *Macbeth* (ambitious!).

Qwilleran said, "I've promised Carol I'll work in the box office next week."

"You have? There'll be a run on tickets," Polly predicted teasingly. "Everyone will want to buy a ticket from a handsome bachelor who is also a brilliant journalist and fabled philanthropist."

"You're *blethering,* as they say in Scotland," he protested modestly, although he knew she was right. He had enjoyed semicelebrityhood while writing for major newspapers Down Below, but that was nothing compared to his present status as a billionaire frog in a very small frog pond.

She said, "I hear that Derek Cuttlebrink is playing the porter, and Dwight has him telescoping his six-feet-seven into a five-foot S-curve that will probably steal the show."

"I know Derek," said Trilby swooping in with the entrées. "He's a sous chef at the Old Stone Mill."

"Very sous," Qwilleran muttered under his breath.

"I'll bring you some hot sour-dough rolls," she said as she whisked away.

"Quick!" he said to Polly. "Do you have anything private to discuss before Mata Hari brings the rolls?"

"Well . . . yes," she said, taking him seriously. "My sister-in-law does the bookkeeping at the Goodwinter Clinic, you know, and she told me in strict confidence that the staff is beginning to worry about Dr. Melinda."

"For what reason?"

"She's made at least two mistakes on prescriptions since returning from Scotland. In both cases the pharmacist caught the error—it had to do with dosage—and phoned the nurse at the clinic."

Qwilleran smoothed his moustache. "She has too many irons in the fire: worrying about the liquidation sale, rehearsing the lead in the play, running off to Scotland—"

"All the while carrying a full load of appointments," Polly reminded him.

"I thought her patients were deserting her."

"Most of Dr. Hal's male patients transferred, but women are flocking to the clinic in droves."

The hot rolls came to the table, and Qwilleran applied his attention to enjoyment of the food, but his imagination was flirting with the idea of Melinda's mistakes. Doctors are not always right, he told himself. She could have been wrong about Irma's death. Wisely, he refrained from mentioning it to Polly.

The house salad, served after the entrée, was a botanical cross section of Bibb lettuce surrounded by precise mounds of shredded radish, paper-thin carrot, and cubed tofu, drizzled with gingered rice wine vinaigrette dressing and finished with a veil of alfalfa sprouts and a sliver of Brie.

"And for dessert tonight," Trilby recited, "the chef has prepared a delicate terrine of three kinds of chocolate drenched in raspberry coulis."

"I'm fighting it," Polly said wistfully.

"I surrender," said Qwilleran.

After a demitasse that smelled like almonds and tasted like a hot fudge sundae, they drove back to Pickax in the comfortable silence of a pair of well-fed ruminants. Finally Qwilleran asked, "How was your dinner with the Hasselriches last night?"

"Rather depressing. They're going through a bad period."

"Do you know if . . . uh . . . Irma's medical records were returned to them?"

"I don't know. Is that customary?"

"I have no idea," he said, "but one would think they might be turned over to the family by the attending physician."

"Why do you ask, Qwill?"

"No particular reason. As a matter of curiosity, though, why don't you ask your sister-in-law, discreetly, what happens to the records of a deceased patient?"

"I suppose I could do that. I'll see her at church tomorrow." They had arrived at Polly's carriage house. "Will you come up for a little reading?"

"Is that all?" he asked. "I could use a large cup of real coffee."

He had brought *Memoirs of an Eighteenth Century Footman* for reading aloud. "It's a true story," he explained, "about the orphan of a Scottish gentleman, who became a veritable prince of servants, with gold lace on his livery and a silk bag on his hair."

With its Scottish background and unbowdlerized style, it proved to be more interesting than they expected, and it was late when Qwilleran returned to the barn.

The Siamese were prancing in figure eights, demanding their overdue bedtime snack, and he gave them their crunchy treat before checking his answering machine. There was a message from Nick Bamba: "Got some good news for you. Call whenever you get in. We'll be watching the late movie."

It was two o'clock when he called the Mooseville number. "Are you sure I'm not calling too late?" he asked.

Lori assured him, "With all the commercials they throw in, the movie won't be over till four. I'll let you talk to Nick."

"Hey, Qwill!" said her husband. "I saw the maroon car again tonight!"

"You did? Where was it?"

"Parked on Main Street in Mooseville. He could have been in the Shipwreck Tavern or he could have been in the Northern Lights Hotel."

"More likely the tavern."

"And that's not all. Lori went to a baby shower in Indian Village, and she saw the same car leaving the parking lot."

"What do you suppose he was doing among all those yuppies?"

"I dunno. Maybe looking for a victim . . . Sorry, I shouldn't kid about it."

"Well, there's nothing we can do until he makes an overt move," Qwilleran said. "I'll tell you one thing: I'm not letting Polly go out alone after dark!"

Nick had barely hung up when the phone rang again, and Qwilleran assumed he was calling back; no one else in Moose County would call at that hour. He picked up the receiver. "Yes, Nick."

"Nick? Who's Nick?" asked a woman's voice. "This is Melinda. Hi, lover!"

Annoyed, he said stiffly, "Isn't that epithet somewhat obsolete under present circumstances?"

"Ooh! You're in a beastly mood tonight! What can we do about that . . . huh?"

"You'll have to excuse me," he said. "I'm expecting an important call."

"Are you trying to brush me off, lover? My feelings are hurt," she said with coy petulance. "We used to be such good *friends!* Don't you remember? We were really attracted to each other. I should have trapped you three years ago—"

"Melinda," he said firmly, "I'm sorry but I must hang up and take another urgent call." And he hung up. To Koko—who was standing by as usual, with disapproval in his whiskers—he said, "That was your friend Melinda. She's over the edge!"

Twelve

It was a peaceful Sunday morning. The church bells were ringing on Park Circle as Qwilleran walked downtown to pick up the out-of-town newspapers. At the apple barn, the Siamese huddled in a window to count the leaves that were beginning to fall from the trees. Their heads raised and lowered in unison, following the downward course of each individual leaf. In another week there would be too many to count, and they would lose interest.

At noon, Polly phoned. "I forgot to tell you, Qwill. The Senior Care Facility is trying the Pets for Patients idea this afternoon. I'm taking Bootsie. Would you be willing to take Yum Yum?"

"I'll give it a try. What time?"

"Two o'clock. Report to the main lobby."

"Did you speak to your sister-in-law, Polly?"

"Yes. She said doctors usually keep the records of deceased patients for a few years—for their own protection in case of dispute."

"I see. Well, thank you. And thank her, also."

Shortly before two o'clock he brought the cat carrier out of the broom closet. "Come on, sweetheart," he said to Yum Yum. "Come and have your horizon expanded."

Koko, usually ready for an adventure, jumped uninvited into the carrying coop, but Yum Yum promptly sped away—up the ramp, around the balcony, and up the next ramp with Qwilleran in pursuit. On the second balcony he was able to grab her, but she slithered from his grasp, leaving him down on all fours. She stopped and gazed at his predicament, but as soon as he scrambled to his feet, she raced to the third balcony. He lunged at her just as she started to crawl along a horizontal beam that was forty feet above the main floor. "Not this time, baby!" he scolded.

It was no small endeavor to evict the stubborn male from the carrier with one hand and install the squirming, clutching, kicking female with the other, and they were the last to arrive at the Senior Care Facility. There was a high decibel level of vocal hubbub, barking, snarling, growling, and hissing in the lobby, which teemed with pet lovers, dogs on leashes, cats in carriers, and volunteers in yellow smocks, known as "canaries" at the facility. Lisa Compton was there with a clipboard, assigning pets to patients.

Qwilleran asked her, "Are you the new chief of volunteers?"

"I've applied for the job," she said, "but today I'm just helping out. It's our first go at this project, and there are some wrinkles to iron out. Next time we'll stagger the visitors. Who's your friend?"

"Her name is Yum Yum."

"Is she gentle? We have an emphysema patient who's requested a pet, and the doctor has okayed a cat, thinking a dog would be too frisky. Yum Yum seems quite relaxed."

Qwilleran peered into the carrier, where Yum Yum had struck the dead-cat pose she always assumed after losing an argument. "Yes, I'd say she's quite relaxed."

Lisa beckoned to a canary. "Would you take Mr. Qwilleran and Yum Yum up to 15-C for Mr. Hornbuckle? The limit is twenty minutes."

In the elevator, the volunteer remarked, "This old gentleman was caretaker for Dr. Halifax on Goodwinter Boulevard until a couple of years ago. The doctor kept him on even though he couldn't work much toward the end. Dr. Hal was a wonderful man."

The occupant of 15-C was sitting in a wheelchair when

they entered—a small, weak figure literally plugged into the wall as he received a metered supply of oxygen through a long tube, but he was waiting eagerly with bright eyes and a toothy grin.

The canary said loudly, "You have a visitor, Mr. Hornbuckle. Her name is Yum Yum." To Qwilleran she said, "I'll come back for you when the time's up."

Yum Yum was relaxed to the consistency of jelly when Qwilleran lifted her from the carrier.

"That's a *cat?*" the old man said in a strange voice. The nasal prongs made his voice unnaturally resonant, and ill-fitting dentures gave his speech a juicy sibilance.

"She's a Siamese," Qwilleran said, putting the limp bundle of fur on the patient's lap blanket.

"Purty kitty," he said, stroking her with a quivering hand. "Soft, ain't she? Blue eyes! Never seen one like this." He spoke slowly in short sentences.

Qwilleran made an attempt to entertain him with anecdotes about Siamese until he realized that the patient would rather talk than listen.

"Growed up on a farm with animules," he said. "Barn cats, hunt'n' dogs, cows, chickens . . ."

"I hear you used to work for Dr. Halifax."

"Fifty year, nigh onto. I were like family. Mighty fine man, he were. What's your name?"

"Qwilleran. Jim Qwilleran."

"Been here long?"

"Five years."

"Y'knowed Dr. Halifax? I were his caretaker. Lived over the garage. Drove 'im all over, makin' calls. Many's a time they'd call 'im middle o' the night, and I drove 'im. Saved lives, we did. Plenty of 'em."

Yum Yum sat in a contented bundle on the blanketed lap, purring gently, her forepaws folded under her breast. Occasionally an ear flicked, tickled by a spray of saliva.

"Sittin' on her brisket, she is! She's happy!" He had a happy grin of his own.

Qwilleran said, "I know Dr. Halifax worked long hours,

taking care of his patients. What did he do for relaxation? Did he have any hobbies, like fishing or golf?"

The old man looked furtive as if about to reveal some unsavory secret. "Painted pitchers, he did. Di'n't tell nobody."

"What kind of pictures?" Qwilleran asked, envisioning something anatomical.

"Pitchers of animules. Thick paint, it were. Took a long time to dry."

"What did he do with them?" Melinda had never mentioned her father's hobby; in fact, she had avoided talking about her family.

"Put 'em away. Di'n't give 'em to nobody. Warn't good enough, he said."

"What did you think of them, Mr. Hornbuckle?"

With a guilty grin he said, "Looked like pitchers in the funny papers."

"Where did he go to paint them?"

"Upstairs, 'way in the back. Nobody went there, oney me. We got along good, him and me. Never thought he'd go first, like he did."

Yum Yum was stirring, and she stretched one foreleg to touch the oxygen tube.

"No, no!" Qwilleran scolded, and she withdrew.

"Minds purty good, don't she?"

"Mr. Hornbuckle, do you know that Dr. Hal's daughter is a doctor now? She's following in her father's footsteps."

The old man nodded. "She were the smart one. Boy di'n't turn out so good."

"In what way?" Qwilleran had a sympathetic way of asking prying questions and a sincerity that could draw out confidences.

"He were into scrapes all the time. Police'd call, middle o' the night, and I'd drive the doctor to the jail. It were too bad, his ma bein' sick and all—always sick abed."

"What happened to the boy finally?"

"Went away. Doctor sent 'im away. Paid 'im money reg'lar iffen he di'n't come back."

THE CAT WHO WASN'T THERE 163

"How do you know this?"

"It were through a bank in Lockmaster. Drove down there reg'lar, I did. Took care of it for the doctor. Never told nobody."

Qwilleran asked, "Wasn't the young man eventually killed in a car accident?"

"That he were! Broke the doctor's heart. Di'n't make no difference he were a rotten apple; he were his oney son . . . Funny thing, though . . ."

"Yes?" Qwilleran said encouragingly.

"After the boy died, the doctor kep' sendin' me to the bank, reg'lar, once a month."

"Did he explain?"

"Nope."

"Didn't you wonder about it?"

"Nope. 'Twarn't none o' my business."

There was a knock on the door at that moment, and the canary entered. "Time for Yum Yum to go home, Mr. Hornbuckle. Say goodbye to your visitors."

As Qwilleran lifted the cat gently from the lap blanket, she uttered a loud, indignant "N-n-now!"

"Likes me, don't she?" said the old man, showing his unnatural dentures. "Bring 'er ag'in. Don't wait too long!" he said with a cackling laugh. "Mightn't be here!"

Downstairs in the lobby, Lisa asked for comments to chart on her clipboard.

"A good time was had by all," Qwilleran reported. "Yum Yum cuddled and purred, or *croodled,* as they say in Scotland. Is Polly Duncan here?"

"No, she and Bootsie came early. They've gone home."

Arriving at the barn, Qwilleran released Yum Yum from the carrier, and she strolled around the main floor like a prima donna, while Koko tagged after her, sniffing with disapproval. He knew she had been to some kind of medical facility.

Later, Qwilleran phoned Polly and asked, "How did the macho behemoth perform this afternoon?"

"The visit wasn't too successful, I'm afraid. We were assigned to an elderly farm woman who had lost her sight, and she complained that Bootsie didn't feel like a cat. Too sleek and silky, I imagine. She was used to barn cats."

"We had an emphysema patient, and I thought Yum Yum might turn into a fur tornado when she saw the oxygen equipment, but she played her role beautifully. She croodled. She's a professional croodler."

"Cats know when someone needs comforting," Polly said. "When Edgar Allan Poe's wife was dying in a poor cottage without heat or blankets, her only sources of warmth were her husband's overcoat and a large tortoiseshell cat."

"A touching story, if true," Qwilleran commented.

"I've read it in several books. Most cats are lovable."

"Or *loosome,* as the Scots say. By the way, I promised Mildred we'd tell her all about Scotland. How will it be if we take her to dinner at Linguini's next Sunday? We'll invite Arch Riker, too."

Polly thought it would be a nice idea. Actually, the following Sunday was her birthday, but he pretended not to know, and she pretended not to know that he knew.

The next morning he walked downtown to buy her a birthday gift, but first he had to hand in his copy at the newspaper. In the city room he picked up a Monday edition and read his Bonnie Scots cutlines to see if anyone had tampered with his carefully worded prose. Then he read the large ad on page three:

TAG SALE

Estate of Dr. Halifax Goodwinter
At the residence, 180 Goodwinter Boulevard
Sale: Saturday, 8 A.M. to 6 P.M.
Preview: Friday, 9 A.M. to 4 P.M.

Furniture, antiques, art, household equipment,
books, clothing, jewelry, linens, china, silver,
crystal, personal effects. All items tagged. All

prices firm. All sales final. No deliveries. Dealers welcome. Curb parking permitted.

Managed by:
Foxy Fred's Bid-a-Bit Auctions

"Did you see the ad for the Goodwinter sale?" Carol Lanspeak asked him when he went to the Lanspeak Department Store to buy a gift. "Melinda hasn't said a word to the Historical Society. One would think she'd give the museum first choice—or even donate certain items."

"I suppose she has a lot on her mind," Qwilleran said. "How's her Lady Macbeth progressing?"

Carol, who had been arranging a scarf display in the women's department, steered him away from the hovering staff who were eager to wait on Mr. Q. He was a regular customer, and they all knew that Polly wore size 16, liked blue and gray, preferred silver jewelry, and avoided anything that required ironing.

Before answering his question, Carol said, "This is off the record, I hope."

"Always."

"Well, Larry finds her very hard to work with. She never looks at him when they're acting together, and there's nothing worse! She acts for herself and doesn't give him anything to play against. Very bad!"

"Is Dwight aware of this?"

"Yes, he's given her notes several times. Granted we have another ten days to rehearse, but . . . I don't know about Melinda. Did you hear that she lost another patient? Wally Toddwhistle's grandmother. Perhaps you saw the obituary."

"What can you expect, Carol? She inherited all of Dr. Hal's octogenarian and nonagenarian patients with one foot in the grave."

"Well . . ." Carol said uncertainly, "our daughter got her M.D. in June and is interning in Chicago. Melinda wants her to come back and join the clinic. Naturally, Larry and I would love to have her living here rather than Down Below, but we're not sure it's the wise thing to do, considering . . ." She shrugged. "What do you think?"

"What does your daughter think?"

"She wants to stay in Chicago."

"Then let her stay there. It's her decision. Don't interfere."

"I guess you're right, Qwill," Carol admitted. "Now what can we do for you?"

"I need a birthday gift for Polly. Any ideas?"

"How about a lovely gown and robe set?" She showed him a blue one in size 16.

"Fine! Wrap it up," he said. "Nothing fancy, please." He was a brisk shopper.

"White box with blue ribbon?"

"That'll do . . . Now, what do I need to know about the box office job tomorrow?"

"Just report a few minutes early," Carol said. "I'll meet you there and explain the system."

At one-thirty the next day, Qwilleran said to the Siamese, "Well, here goes! Let's hope I don't sell the same seat twice." He had sold baseball programs at Comiskey Park and ties at Macy's, but he had never sold tickets in a box office. He walked to the theatre, through the woods and across the parking lot, where there appeared to be an unusual profusion of cars for a Tuesday afternoon. In the lobby, the ticket purchasers were milling about as if it were opening night.

"Hi, Mr. Q," several called out as he pushed through to the box office. The window was shuttered, but there was a light inside, and Carol admitted him through the side door.

"Can you believe this crowd?" she remarked. "Looks like we've got a hit show! . . . Now, here's what you do. When customers first come up to the window, ask them what date they want, and pull the seating chart for that performance. Seats already sold have been x-ed out on the chart."

The chart of the auditorium showed twelve rows of seats on the main floor and three in the balcony—twenty seats to the row, divided into left, right, and center sections.

"Next, ask them how many tickets they want and where they want to sit. All seats are the same price. Then you take the tickets out of this rack; they're in cubbyholes labeled according to row. Be sure to x-out the seats they're buying . . . Then take their money. No credit cards, but personal checks are okay. Any questions?"

"What's that other rack?"

"Those are reserved tickets waiting to be picked up. You probably won't have any pickups so early in the game, but you'll get phone orders. When you sell tickets by phone, put them in the pickup rack, and don't forget to x-out the seats on the chart." Carol pulled out a drawer under the counter. "There's the till, with enough small bills to make change. Lock it when you're through, and lock the box office when you leave."

"What do I do with the keys?"

"Put them in the bottom of the tall-case clock in the lobby. It's all very simple."

The hard part, Qwilleran discovered, was on the other side of the window. He opened the shutters and faced his public. They had formed a queue, and there were about forty in a line that snaked around the lobby.

The first at the window was a small, nervous woman with graying hair and wrinkled brow. "Do you know me?" she asked. "I'm Jennifer's mother."

"Jennifer?" he repeated.

"Jennifer Olson. She's in the play."

"No doubt you'll want tickets for opening night," he guessed, reaching for the Wednesday chart.

"Yes, ten tickets. Our whole family is going."

"Here's what's available, Mrs. Olson. Do you want them all in the same row, or a block of seats?"

"What would a block be like?"

"It could be two rows of five, one behind the other, or three shorter rows bunched together."

"I don't know. Which do you think would be best?"

"Well, it's like this," Qwilleran explained. "If you take a block, it can be closer to the stage. To get a full row you'll have to sit farther back."

"Why is that?"

"Because," he said patiently, "tickets have already been sold in various rows at the front of the auditorium, as you can see by this chart." He pushed the seating plan closer to the glass and waited for Mrs. Olson to find her reading glasses.

Frowning at the chart, she said, "Which is the front?"

"Here's the stage. As you can see, the entire front row is still available, if you don't mind sitting that close."

"No, I don't think we should sit in the front row. It might make Jennifer nervous."

"In that case, the next full row available is H. That's the eighth row."

"I wonder if Grandma Olson will be able to hear from the eighth row."

"The acoustics are very good," he assured her.

"What are those?" Mrs. Olson asked.

The customers standing in line were getting restless. The man behind her kept looking at his watch with exaggerated gestures. A young woman had a child in a stroller whose fretting had escalated to screams. An older woman leaning on a quad-cane was volubly indignant. And the front doors opened and closed constantly as frustrated ticket purchasers left and new ones arrived.

Qwilleran said, "Mrs. Olson, why don't you walk down into the auditorium and try sitting in the various rows to see how you like the location? Meanwhile, I can take care of these other customers . . . Take your time, so that you're sure."

There was a groan of relief as she left, and Qwilleran was able to serve the entire lineup by the time she returned.

The selection had dwindled considerably, but he could offer her an irregular block of seats in the center section.

"But we need three aisle seats," she said. "My husband is with the volunteer fire department and will have to leave if his beeper goes off. My sister has anxiety attacks and sometimes has to rush out in a hurry. And Grandpa Olson has a bad leg from the war and has to stretch it in the aisle."

"Left leg or right leg?" Qwilleran asked.

"It's his left leg. He took shrapnel."

"Then you'll have to take the left of the center section or the left of the right section."

"Oh, dearie me! It's so confusing. There are so many people to please."

Helpfully Qwilleran suggested, "Why not let me select a block of tickets for you, and if your family decides they're not right, bring them back for exchange."

"That's a wonderful idea!" she cried gratefully. "Thank you, Mr. Q. You have been so helpful. And I must tell you how much I enjoy your column in the paper."

"Thank you," he said. "That will be sixty dollars."

"And now I need eight more for Saturday night," she said. "They're for Jennifer's godparents and her boyfriend's family."

It crossed Qwilleran's mind that Jennifer probably had two lines to speak, but diplomatically he asked, "Is your daughter playing Lady Macbeth?"

"Oh! How strange you should mention that!" Mrs. Olson seemed flustered. "She's really doing Lady Macduff, but . . ."

"That's a good role. I'm sure you'll be proud of her."

The woman scanned the lobby and then said confidentially, "Jennifer has learned all of Lady Macbeth's lines— just in case."

"Was that her own idea?" Qwilleran was aware that understudies were a luxury the Theatre Club had never enjoyed.

In a near-whisper she said, "Mr. Somers, the director,

asked her to do it and not tell anyone. You won't mention this, will you?"

"I wouldn't think of it," he said.

When Jennifer's mother had left, he thought, So! Dwight is doubting Melinda's capability to play the lead! And she's already making errors in prescriptions! What is happening to her?

Despite Qwilleran's desire to be rid of Melinda, he could hardly ignore her plight. They had been good friends once. Quite apart from that, he had a newsman's curiosity about the story behind the story.

The towering clock in the theatre lobby finally bonged four, and he counted the money, balanced it against the number of tickets sold, locked up, hid the keys, and walked home slowly. Ambling through the cool woods he began to think about Bushy's photographs, particularly three Highland scenes.

There was a lonely moor without a tree or a boulder or a lost sheep—totally empty and isolated except for a telephone booth in the middle of nowhere, and Bushy had added a woman digging for a coin in the depths of her shoulder bag.

One was a haunting scene of a silvery loch in which floated an uninhabited island with a ruined castle reflected in the still water. In the background a gray, mysterious mountain rose steeply from the loch, and in the foreground a woman sat on a stone wall reading a paperback with her back to the view.

Then there was a riot of flowers behind a rustic fence and garden gate, on which hung the sign:

> *Be ye mon or be ye wumin,*
> *Be ye gaun or be ye cumin,*
> *Be ye early, be ye late,*
> *Dinna fergit tae* SHUT THE GATE!

In Bushy's picture there was a woman in the garden, and the gate stood open.

The series ought to be titled "Tourism," Qwilleran thought, and as soon as he reached the barn he hunted up Bushy's yellow boxes and pulled out the three photos. Each one had its surface defaced by Koko's rough tongue, and in each photo the woman was Melinda.

Thirteen

That was the week that Moose County was discovered by the media. Overnight it became the Teddy Bear Capital of the nation. Qwilleran's story and Bushy's photographs ran in the *Moose County Something* with a teaser on the front page and the full treatment on the back page. It was picked up by the wire services and published in several major newspapers around the country, and a television crew flew up from Down Below on Thursday to film the collection and interview the collectors.

During the week there was also a series of break-ins in the affluent Purple Point area, but this untimely happening was played down while the TV people were around. It was also the week of the Goodwinter tag sale, and on Friday afternoon Qwilleran attended the preview.

Goodwinter Boulevard was a broad, quiet avenue off Main Street with two stone pylons at the entrance to give it an air of exclusivity. A cul-de-sac with a landscaped median and old-fashioned street lights, it extended the equivalent of three blocks, ending at a vest-pocket park with an impressive monument. The granite monolith rose about twelve feet and bore a bronze plaque commemorating the four Goodwinter brothers who founded the city. Their mansions—and those of other tycoons who had made fortunes in mining and lumbering—lined both sides of the boulevard. Qwilleran usually found it a pleasant place for a walk, having interesting architecture and virtually no traffic—only an occasional car turning into a side drive and disappearing into a garage at the rear.

Friday afternoon was different. The ban on curb parking was lifted, and both sides of the streets were lined with parked cars bumper-to-bumper, while other vehicles cruised hopefully and continually, waiting for someone to leave. Many had to give up and park on Main Street. As for the sidewalks, they teemed with individuals going to and from the preview, with a large group gathered in front of No. 180.

Qwilleran approached a woman on the fringe of the crowd and asked her what was happening.

She squealed in delight at recognizing his moustache and said, "Oh, you're Mr. Q! They won't let us in until some of the others come out. I've been out here since eleven. Wish I'd brought my lunch."

No one showed impatience. They chatted sociably as they edged closer to the entrance of the mansion. Qwilleran slipped around to the rear and used his press card for admittance, although the well-known overgrown moustache would have accomplished the same end.

He entered a kitchen large enough to accommodate three cooks, where a Bid-a-Bit employee at the coffee urn offered him a cup. He accepted and sat down on a kitchen chair just as Foxy Fred walked in from the front of the house, wearing a red jacket and his usual western hat. Qwilleran, turning on his tape recorder, asked him, "How do you size up this collection?"

"Four generations of treasures going at give-away prices!" said the auctioneer, who was not known for understatement. "Most prestigious sale in the history of Moose County! Fifty or seventy-five years from now, our grandkids will be proud to say they own a drinking mug or a pair of nail clippers that belonged to a great twentieth-century humanitarian!"

"But Fred, this kind of sale raises havoc with a quiet

neighborhood," Qwilleran said. "Why didn't you cart the goods away and hold an auction in a tent out in the country?"

"The customer requested a tag sale, and the customer is always right," said Foxy Fred, gulping down a cup of coffee. "Well, I gotta get back where the action is."

In the large rooms on the main floor the ponderous heirloom furniture had been pushed back and rugs had been rolled up. Long folding tables were loaded with china, crystal, silver, linens, and bric-a-brac. The interior had the sadness of a house that had not seen a formal dinner, afternoon tea, or cocktail party for twenty-five years, the span of Mrs. Goodwinter's illness.

Curious crowds moved up and down the aisles, examining the items, checking the prices and muttering comments, while red-jacketed attendants announced repeatedly, "Keep moving, folks! Lots more waiting to get in." There were also three roving security guards, making themselves highly visible and looking seriously watchful.

Qwilleran dodged from aisle to aisle, asking viewers, "Why are you here? . . . See anything you like? . . . How are the prices? . . . Will you come back tomorrow to buy? . . . Did you know the Goodwinter family?" He himself spotted a silver pocketknife he wouldn't mind buying; engraved with the doctor's initials, it was priced at $150.

Upstairs, the crowds were less dense. Chests and dressers and disassembled beds were pushed back, and long tables were piled with blankets, towels and such. Clothing filled portable racks. One room, which was empty, had obviously been Melinda's; she had removed her furnishings to her apartment, but her distinctive fragrance lingered.

At the rear of the second floor there was a large room that no one entered, although an occasional viewer would poke a head through the doorway and back away quickly. It was two stories high and had three large north windows. This had been Dr. Hal's studio. Hanging in every wall space and filed on floor-to-ceiling shelves like books were brightly

colored paintings on stretched canvas or rectangles of wall-
board, and hundreds more were stacked on the Bid-a-Bit
tables. It was the output, Qwilleran surmised, of twenty-
five lonely years. None was bigger than an ordinary book.
All were flat, two-dimensional depictions of animals against
unrealistic landscapes of kelly green and cobalt blue. Red
cats and turquoise dogs stood on hind legs and danced together. Orange ducks with purple beaks faced each other
and quacked sociably. Tigers and kangaroos flew overhead
like airplanes. These were the "animules" that had caused
old Mr. Hornbuckle both wonderment and amusement.

A sign saying "Pictures $1.00" prompted Qwilleran to
run downstairs to the kitchen and phone the high school
where Mildred Hanstable taught art as well as home ec.

"She's in class at this hour," said an anonymous voice in
the school office.

"This is urgent! Jim Qwilleran calling! Get her on the
phone!" He was willing to throw his name around when it
served a good purpose.

"Just a minute, Mr. Q."

A breathless art teacher came on the line.

"Mildred, this is Qwill," he said. "I'm at the Goodwinter
house previewing the tag sale, and there's something here
that you must definitely see! How fast can you make it over
here?"

"I'm free next hour, but the period's just started."

"Cut class! Get here on the double! You'll be back before
anyone misses you. Come in the back way. Use my name."
Meanwhile he went upstairs and closed the door to Dr.
Hal's studio.

When Mildred arrived, they climbed the servants' stairs
from the kitchen, Qwilleran explaining, "Dr. Hal had a
secret hobby. He painted pictures."

"My God!" Mildred gasped when she saw them.

"My words exactly! They're marked a dollar apiece, and
no one is interested. A hundred dollars would be more appropriate. They might sell for a thousand in the right gal-

lery. I don't know anything about art, but I've seen crazier stuff than this in museums."

"It's contemporary folk art," she said. "They're charming! They're unique! Wait till the art magazines get hold of these!"

"Wait till the psychologists get their claws into them! It's the Noah's Ark of a madman."

"I'm weak," Mildred said. "I don't know what to say."

"Go back to your class. I simply wanted an opinion to corroborate my own hunch."

"What are you going to do about it, Qwill?"

"First, take the decimal point out of that sign. Then notify the K Foundation."

Reluctantly the art teacher tore herself away from the bizarre collection, and Qwilleran went back to asking questions downstairs: "Do you collect antiques? . . . Are you a dealer? . . . Have you ever seen a sale to equal this? . . . What do you plan to buy?"

It was while taping their uninspired answers that he caught a glimpse of a bushy-haired, bushy-bearded young man in jeans and faded sweatshirt, wearing a fanny pack. He was browsing among odds and ends on a table toward the rear of the main floor.

Qwilleran's moustache bristled; he remembered that shaggy head from the reading room at the public library. It had been three months before, but he was sure this was the person who drove away in a maroon car with a Massachusetts plate and who was later identified as Charles Edward Martin. The man was reading labels on old LP records and fingering household tools. He examined the initials on the silver pocketknife. He picked up a cast-iron piggy bank and shook it; there was no rattle.

Sidling up to him, Qwilleran asked in a friendly way, "Quite a bunch of junk, isn't it?"

"Yeah," said the fellow.

"Find anything worth buying?"

"Nah."

"What do you think of the prices? Aren't they a bit high?"

The young man shrugged.

Hoping to hear him say a few words with an eastern accent, Qwilleran remarked, "I have a feeling we've met somewhere. Ever go to the Shipwreck Tavern in Mooseville?"

"Yeah."

"That's where I've met you! You're Ronald Frobnitz!" Qwilleran said.

The subject was supposed to say, "No, I'm Charles Martin," or better yet, "Chahles Mahtin." Instead he shook his head and scuttled away.

Noting that the silver pocketknife had scuttled at the same time, Qwilleran followed him to the front door, hindered by the crowds. The man was moving fast enough to make good time but not fast enough to arouse the suspicion of the security guards. Qwilleran thought, That Chahles Mahtin is smaht! He followed him through the milling hordes on the sidewalk—all the way to Main Street, where the suspect drove off in a maroon car with a Massachusetts plate.

Qwilleran, who was without his car at the moment, jogged to the police station, hoping to catch Brodie in the office, but the chief was striding out of the building. "Do you have a minute, Andy?" Qwilleran asked urgently.

"Make it half a minute."

"Okay. I attended the preview of the Goodwinter sale and saw someone who is undoubtedly Charles Edward Martin."

"Who?"

"The guy I suspect of being the Boulevard Prowler. I tried to get him into conversation, but he was close-mouthed. When Polly was threatened three months ago, you checked the registration and came up with the name of Charles Edward Martin. The same car has been spotted three times in the last few days: headed for Shantytown, parked near the Shipwreck Tavern, and pulling out of the parking lot at Indian Village."

"Probably selling cemetery lots," Brodie quipped as he

edged toward the curb. "I can't pick him up for driving around with a foreign license plate. Has Polly been threatened again? Has he been hanging around the boulevard after dark?"

"No," Qwilleran had to admit, although he pounded his moustache with his fist. How could he explain? Brodie might accept the idea of a psychic cat, but he'd balk at a moustache that telegraphed hunches.

"Tell you what to do, Qwill. Get your mind off those damned license plates. Come to the lodge hall for dinner tonight. It's Scottish Night. Six o'clock. Tell 'em at the door you're my guest." Brodie jumped into a police car without waiting for an answer.

Qwilleran went for a long walk. While he walked, he assessed his apprehensions in connection with the Boulevard Prowler. As a crime reporter and war correspondent he had faced frequent danger without a moment's fear. Now, for the first time in his life, he was experiencing that heart-sinking sensation—fear for the safety of another. For the first time in his life, he had someone close enough to make him vulnerable. It was a realization that warmed his blood and chilled it at the same time.

As for Brodie's patronizing invitation, he was inclined to ignore it. He knew many of the lodge members, and he had passed the hall hundreds of times—a three-story stone building like a miniature French Bastille—but he had never stepped inside the door. True, he had a certain amount of curiosity about Scottish Night, but he decided against it. Brodie's cheeky attitude annoyed him. And how good could the food be at a lodge hall?

In that frame of mind he returned to the apple barn, expecting to thaw some sort of meal out of the freezer. The Siamese met him at the door as usual and marched to the feeding station, where they sat confidently staring at the empty plate. Well aware of priorities in that household, Qwilleran opened a can of boned chicken for the cats before checking his answering machine and going up the ramp to change into a warmup suit. And then it happened again!

He was halfway to the balcony when Koko rushed him. This time he heard the thundering paws on the ramp and braced himself before the muscular body crashed into his legs.

"What the devil are you trying to tell me?" he demanded as Koko picked himself up, shook his head, and licked his left shoulder.

In the past Koko had thrown irrational catfits when Qwilleran was making the wrong decision or following the wrong scent. Whatever his present motive, his violence put Brodie's invitation in another light, and Qwilleran continued up the ramp—not to change into a warmup suit but to shower and dress for Scottish Night.

He drove to the lodge hall on Main Street, and as he parked the car he saw men in kilts and tartan trews converging from all directions. At the door he was greeted by Whannell MacWhannell, the portly accountant from the Bonnie Scots Tour, who looked even bigger in his pleated kilt, Argyle jacket, leather sporran, tasseled garters, and ghillie brogies.

"Andy told me to watch for you," said Big Mac. "He's upstairs, tuning up the doodlesack, but don't tell him I called it that."

Most of the men gathering in the lounge were in full Highland kit, making Qwilleran feel conspicuous in a suit and tie. As a public figure in Pickax he was greeted heartily by all. "Are you a Scot?" they asked. "Where did you get the W in your name?"

"My mother was a Mackintosh," he explained, "and I believe my father's family came from the Northern Isles. There's a Danish connection somewhere—way back, no doubt."

The walls of the lounge were hung with colorful clan banners—reproductions, MacWhannell explained, of the battle standards that were systematically burned after the defeat at Culloden.

"What tartan are you wearing?" Qwilleran asked him.

"Macdonald of Sleat. The MacWhannells are connected

with that clan, somewhere along the line, and Glenda liked this tartan because it's red. Why don't you order a Mackintosh kilt, Qwill?"

"I'm not ready for that yet, but I've been boning up on Mackintosh history—twelve centuries of political brawls, feuds, raids, battles, betrayals, poisonings, hangings, assassinations, and violent acts of revenge. It's amazing that we have any Mackintoshes left."

At a given signal the party trooped upstairs to the great hall, a lofty room decorated wall-to-wall with weaponry. Six round tables were set for dinner, each seating ten. At each place a souvenir program listed the events of the evening and the bill of fare: haggis, tatties and neeps, Forfar bridies, Pitlochry salad, tea, shortbread, and a "wee dram" for toasting.

"We'll sit here and save a seat for Andy," said Big Mac, leaning a chair against a table. "He has to pipe in the haggis before he can sit down."

Looking around at the ancient weapons on the walls, Qwilleran remarked, "Does the FBI know about the arsenal you have up here? You could start a war with Lockmaster."

"It's our private museum," said his host. "I'm the registrar. We have 27 broadswords, 45 dirks, 12 claymores, 7 basket hilts, 14 leather bucklers, 12 pistols, 21 muskets, and 30 bayonets, all properly catalogued."

Politely Qwilleran inquired about Glenda's health. "Has she recovered from the stress of the tour?"

"Frankly, she should have stayed in Pickax. She doesn't like to travel," her husband explained. "She'd rather watch video travelogues. I took eight hundred pictures on this trip just for her. She gets a kick out of putting them in albums and labeling them. How about you? Did you stick it out to the end?"

"All except Edinburgh, but I'd like to go back there with Polly someday."

"We spent a couple of days in Auld Reekie before catching our plane. I left Glenda in the hotel and went out taking pictures. You can get some good bird's-eye views in Edinburgh. I climbed 287 steps to the top of a monument. The castle rock is 400 feet high. Arthur's Seat is 822 feet. Funny name for a hill, but the Scots have some funny words. How about 'mixty-maxty' and 'whittie-whattie'? Don't ask me what they mean."

Big Mac was more talkative than he had been with the nervous Glenda in tow, and he had statistics for everything: where 300 witches were burned and who died from 56 dagger wounds. He was interrupted by the plaintive wail of a bagpipe.

The rumble of male voices faded away. The double doors burst open, and a solemn procession entered and circled the room, led by Chief Brodie. Normally a big man with proud carriage, he was a formidable giant in full kit with towering feather "bonnet," scarlet doublet, fur sporran, and white spats. With the bag beneath his arm and the drones over his shoulder, he swaggered to the slow heroic rhythm of "Scotland the Brave," the pleated kilt swaying and the bagpipe filling the room with skirling that stirred Qwilleran's Mackintosh blood. Behind the piper marched a snare drummer, followed by seven young men in kilts and white shirts, each carrying a tray. On the first was a smooth gray lump; that was the haggis. On each of the other six trays was a bottle of Scotch. They circled the room twice. Then a bottle was placed on each table, and the master of ceremonies—in the words of Robert Burns—addressed the "great chieftain o' the puddin' race," after which the assembly drank a toast to the haggis. It was cut and served, and the marchers made one more turn about the room before filing out through the double doors to the lively rhythm of a strathspey.

Brodie returned without bagpipe and bonnet to join them at the table.

"Weel done, laddie," Qwilleran said to him. "When a Brodie plays the pipe, even a Mackintosh gets goosebumps. That's an impressive instrument you have."

"The chanter's an old one, with silver and real ivory. You can't get 'em like that any more," Brodie said. "I'm a seventh-generation piper. It used to be a noble vocation in the Highlands. Every chief had his personal piper who went everywhere with him, even into battle. The screaming of the pipes drove the clans to attack and unnerved the enemy. At least, that was the idea."

When dinner was served, Big Mac leaned over and asked the chief, "Are you related to the master criminal of Edinburgh, Andy? I saw the place where he was hanged in 1788."

"Deacon Brodie? Well, I admit I've got his sense of humor and steel nerves, but he wasn't a piper."

Qwilleran said, "We've had a lot of excitement on Goodwinter Boulevard this week, with the TV coverage and the mob that turned out for the preview."

"It'll be worse tomorrow," Brodie said with a dour look.

"Why is the sale being held at the house?"

"Too many ways to cheat when it's trucked away for an auction. I'm not saying Foxy Fred is a crook, you understand, but Dr. Melinda's a sharpie. Never underestimate that lassie!"

"Tell me something, Andy—about those break-ins on Purple Point. We never had break-ins when I first came here, but since they've started promoting tourism, the picture is changing."

"You can't blame the tourists for Purple Point; that was done by locals—young kids, most likely—who knew when to hit. They knew the cottages are vacant in September except on weekends. Besides, they took small stuff. An operator from Down Below would back a truck up to the cottage and clean it out."

"What kind of thing did they take?"

"Electronic stuff, cameras, binoculars. It was kids."

The emcee rapped for attention and announced the serious business of drinking toasts. Tribute was paid to William Wallace, guerrilla fighter and the first hero of Scotland's struggle for independence.

MacWhannell said to Qwilleran, "He was a huge man. His claymore was five feet four inches long."

Then the diners toasted the memory of Robert the Bruce, Mary Queen of Scots, Bonnie Prince Charlie, Flora Macdonald, Robert Burns, Sir Walter Scott, and Robert Louis Stevenson, the response becoming more boisterous with each ovation. Qwilleran was toasting with cold tea, but the others were sipping usquebaugh.

The evening ended with the reading of Robert Burns's poetry by the proprietor of Scottie's Men's Store and the singing of "Katie Bairdie Had a Coo" by the entire assembly with loud and lusty voices, thanks to the usquebaugh. That was followed by a surprisingly sober "Auld Lang Syne," after which Brodie said to Qwilleran, "Come to the kitchen. I told the catering guy to save some haggis for that smart cat of yours."

Many of the members lingered in the lounge, but Qwilleran thanked his host and drove home with his foil-wrapped trophy. When he reached the barn the electronic timer had illuminated the premises indoors and out. "Treat!" he shouted as he entered through the back door, his voice reverberating around the balconies and catwalks. The cats came running from opposite directions and collided head-on at a blind corner. They shook themselves and followed him to the feeding station for their first taste of haggis.

As Qwilleran watched their heads bobbing with approval and their tails waving in rapture, an infuriating thought occurred to him: Is this why Koko wanted me to go to the lodge hall? The notion was too farfetched even for Qwilleran to entertain. And yet, he realized Koko was trying to communicate.

Qwilleran wondered, Am I barking up the wrong tree? . . . Am I suspecting the wrong person? . . . Are my suspicions totally unfounded? And then he wondered, Am I working on the wrong case?

He considered Koko's reaction to Melinda's voice on the tapes . . . the licking of photographs in which she appeared . . . the whisker-bristling when she called on the phone . . . his hostile attitude after Qwilleran had spent a mere two minutes with her at the rehearsal. It could be Koko's old animosity, remembered through sounds and smells. It could be a campaign to expose something reprehensible: a lie, a lurking danger, a guilty secret, a gross error.

That was when Qwilleran dared to wonder, Did Melinda make a mistake in Irma's medication? Could it be that she—not the bus driver—was responsible for Irma's fatal attack?

Fourteen

On Saturday morning, in the hours between midnight and dawn, residents of Goodwinter Boulevard sleeping in bedrooms insulated by foot-thick stone walls became aware of a constant rumbling, like an approaching storm. If they looked out the window, they saw a string of headlights moving down the boulevard. Several of the residents called the police, and the lone night patrol that responded found scores of cars, vans, and pickups parked at the curb, leaving a single lane for moving traffic. The occupants of these vehicles had brought pillows, blankets, and thermos jugs; some had brought children and dogs. The more aggressive were on the front porch of the Goodwinter mansion, lined up on the stone floor in sleeping bags.

When the officer ordered the motorists to move on, they were unable to comply, being trapped at the curb by incoming bumper-to-bumper traffic. Both eastbound and westbound lanes were clogged with the constant stream of new arrivals, and when the curb space was all occupied, they pulled into private drives and onto the landscaped median. The patrol car itself was unable to move after a while, and the officer radioed for help.

Immediately the state police and sheriff's cars arrived, only to be faced with a vehicular impasse. Not a car could move. By this time lights were turned on in all the houses, and influential residents were calling the police chief, the mayor, and Foxy Fred at their homes, routing them out of bed and into the chill of a late September morning.

First, the police blockaded the entrance to the westbound lane and started prying vehicles from the eastbound lane until the traffic flow was restored. Motorists who had parked in private drives or on the grassy median were ticketed and evicted.

By that time, dawn was breaking, and legal parkers were allowed to stay, since the city had lifted the ban on curb parking for the duration of the tag sale. As for the evicted vehicles, they now lined both sides of Main Street, while more traffic poured into the city from all directions.

Qwilleran heard about the tie-up on the WPKX newscast and called Polly. "How are you going to get out to go to work?" he asked.

"Fortunately it's my day off, and I'm not leaving my apartment for anything less than an earthquake. Besides, my car is at Gippel's garage . . . You can imagine that Bootsie is quite upset by the commotion."

"What's wrong with your car?"

"It's the carburetor, and the mechanic is sending away for a rebuilt one. It won't be ready until Tuesday. But that's no problem; I can walk to and from the library."

"I don't want you walking alone," he said.

"But . . . in broad daylight?" she protested.

"I don't want you walking alone, Polly! I'll provide the transportation. Is there anything I can do for you today? Need anything from the store?"

"Not a thing, thank you. I plan to spend the day cleaning out closets."

"Then I'll pick you up at six-thirty tomorrow night," he said. "We have a seven o'clock reservation at Linguini's."

Qwilleran lost no time in hiking to the tag sale. It was his professional instinct to follow the action. The action was, in fact, all over town. The overflow from Goodwinter Boulevard and Main Street now filled the parking lots at the courthouse, library, theatre, and two churches, as well as the parking space that business firms provided for customers only.

On the boulevard excited pedestrians who had parked half a mile away were swarming toward No. 180, while others were leaving the area with triumphant smiles, carrying articles like bed pillows, boxes of pots and pans, and window shades. Foxy Fred had organized the crowd in queues, admitting only a few at a time, and the lineup extended the length of the westbound sidewalk and doubled back on itself before doing the same on the eastbound sidewalk. Persons with forethought had brought folding camp stools, food, and beverages.

Across from the doctor's residence there was another stone mansion that Amanda Goodwinter had inherited from her branch of the family, and when Qwilleran arrived on the scene she was standing on her porch with hands on hips, glaring at the mob.

"The city council will act on this at our next meeting!" she declared when she saw him. "We'll pass an ordinance against disrupting peaceful neighborhoods with commercial activities! I don't care that she's my cousin *and* a doctor *and* an orphan! This can't be allowed! She's a selfish brat and always has been!" Amanda looked fiercely up and down the street. "The first person who parks in my drive or on my lawn is going to get a blast of buckshot!"

Qwilleran pushed his way through the crowd and around to the back door, flashing his press card, and entered through the kitchen, where he scrounged a cup of coffee. In the front of the house Foxy Fred's red-coated helpers were expediting sales and handling will-calls. Portable items were carried to the row of cashiers in the foyer, and purchasers of furniture and other large items were instructed to haul them away on Monday, or Tuesday—no later.

The Comptons were there, and Lyle said to Qwilleran, "If you think this is a mess, wait till the trucks start coming to pick up the big stuff next week."

"We've got a will-call on that black walnut breakfront,"

Lisa said. "I'd love to have the silver tea set." She glanced at her husband hopefully.

"At that price we don't need it," he said. "There are no bargains here. Melinda's going to make out like gangbusters on this sale. I saw a lot of vans and station wagons with out-of-county plates, probably dealers willing to pay the prices she's asking."

Lisa said, "I loved your story on the teddy bears, Qwill, and we saw Grace Utley on television. I wonder what she thinks of this madhouse."

"She was smart enough to leave town on the eve of the preview."

"Any news about the jewel theft?"

"Not to my knowledge."

Lyle said, "I'll bet she wanted them stolen so she could spend the insurance money on those damned teddy bears!"

On the way home Qwilleran caught up with Dwight Somers, walking empty-handed toward Main Street. "I'm getting out of here," said the director. "The line is the equivalent of twelve blocks long!"

"Would you like to come over to the barn for a drink or a cup of coffee?"

"I'd sure like to see your barn. I'm parked in the theatre lot."

After he picked up his tin whistle from his car, they started out on foot through the woods. "A hundred years ago," Qwilleran explained, "this barn serviced a large apple orchard."

"Larry told me about the murder in the orchard following a Theatre Club party. That was quite a story!"

"That was quite a party! Have you been lucky enough to plug into the Pickax grapevine?"

"I'm not a full subscriber yet. I think I'm on probation."

"The barn was used for storing apples and pressing cider originally, and even after it was renovated we could smell apples in certain weather. The orchard suffered a blight at one time, and the dead wood has been removed, but when the wind blows through the remaining trees, it sounds like a harmonica and frightens the cats."

"How many do you have?" Dwight asked.

"Two cats. Forty-seven trees."

Dwight was properly impressed by the octagonal shape of the barn and the interior system of ramps and balconies surrounding the central fireplace cube. The Siamese, who usually disappeared when a stranger entered, did him the honor of approaching within ten feet, and Koko struck a pose like an Egyptian bronze.

"Beautiful animals," said the visitor. "I used to have a Siamese—when I was married. Why is the little one staring at me like that?"

"She's fascinated by your beard. She likes beards, moustaches, toothbrushes, hair brushes—" Qwilleran said. "What'll you have to drink?"

"It's early. Make it coffee."

While they waited for the promising gurgle of the computerized coffeemaker, Qwilleran asked, "What brought you to Moose County, Dwight? Most people don't even know it exists."

"To tell the truth, I'd never heard of it until the placement agency sent me up here. The company I worked for in Des Moines merged with another, and I was outsourced. XYZ Enterprises was looking for a PR rep who could contribute to the community in some useful way and improve their corporate image, which is pretty grim right now."

"I know. Developers frighten people. The general public doesn't like to see changes in the landscape, for better or worse."

"That's the truth! My chief asset was that I'd acted and directed in community theatre, so here I am, and I like it! Never thought I'd like living in a small town."

"This is not your average small town," Qwilleran pointed out as he served the coffee.

"I can see that! Our basic idea is to make our presence felt in a positive way through participation. For example, we're collaborating with the hospital auxiliary on the first annual Distinguished Women Awards next Friday. A couple of your friends are on the list."

"How's the play shaping up?"

"On the whole I'm pleased with it. Wally Toddwhistle built some fabulous sets out of junk. Fran Brodie designed the costumes, and Wally's mother is making them. Fran is codirector—a very talented girl! Attractive, too—with those race-horse legs! Has she ever been married?"

"I don't think so. Do you know she designed the interior of this barn?"

Dwight glanced at the square-cut contemporary furniture, the Moroccan rugs, the large-scale tapestries. "She did a great job! She did Melinda's apartment, too. That girl must have spent a mint on it!"

"Melinda has expensive tastes."

Dwight had put his tin whistle on the coffee table, and Yum Yum was stalking it. With her body close to the floor she was creeping in slow motion toward the shiny black tube. Just before she pounced, Qwilleran shouted a sharp "No!" and she slunk away backwards as slowly as she had advanced. "She'll steal anything that weighs less than two ounces," he explained.

Dwight said, "I brought the whistle to get your opinion, Qwill. I'm going to tape some weird tunes to play during the witches' scenes." He picked up the whistle and tootled some wild, shrill notes that sent Koko and Yum Yum hurtling up the ramp and out of sight, with their ears back and their tails bushed.

"I think you've hit it right," Qwilleran said. "Even the cats' hair is standing on end . . . How did your Macduff turn out?"

"Better than I expected, especially in his scene with Macbeth. When he has Larry to bounce off, he's really with it. Larry is a superb actor."

"And Lady Macbeth?"

"Well . . ." the director said with hesitation. "I have to

tell you her performance is erratic. At one rehearsal she really gets inside the character, and the next night she seems diffused. Frankly, I'm disappointed. She says she hasn't been sleeping well."

"Do you think she's worrying about something?" Qwilleran asked, smoothing his moustache.

"I don't know. Another thing. She doesn't take direction very well," Dwight complained. "Is that because she's a doctor? You can't tell them anything, you know. Was she difficult when she lived here before?"

"No, she was fun to be with, and she had a great zest for life. When I inherited the Klingenschoen mansion, she staged a formal dinner party for me—with a butler, footmen, two cooks, musicians, sixteen candles on the table, and a truckload of flowers. She had unbounded energy and enthusiasm then. Something must have happened to her in Boston."

"I hate to mention this, Qwill, but I wonder if she's on drugs. I know there are hard-driving physicians who take diet pills to keep going, then downers so they can unwind. They become addicted."

Qwilleran recalled the new strangeness in Melinda's eyes. "You could be right. One reads about health-care professionals becoming chemically dependent, as they say."

"What can anyone do about it? She might get into serious trouble."

"There are treatment centers, of course, but how would one convince her to get help? Assuming that's really her problem."

The director said, "I'm concerned enough that I've coached someone to do Lady Macbeth in case Melinda doesn't make it on Wednesday night. Keep your fingers crossed!" He pocketed his tin whistle and stood up. "This is all between you and me, of course. Thanks for the coffee. You've got a fabulous barn."

After he had left, the Siamese ambled down the ramp cautiously, and Yum Yum looked in vain for the tin whistle. Koko alarmed Qwilleran, however, by sniffing one of the light Moroccan rugs. With his nose to the pile, he traced a meandering course as if following the path of a spider. Qwilleran dropped down on hands and knees to intercept it, but there was nothing but an infinitesimal spot on the rug. Koko sniffed it, pawed it, nuzzled it.

"You and your damned spots!" Qwilleran rebuked him. "You just like to see me crawling around! This is the last time I'm going to fall for it!"

The next day, when Qwilleran went out for the Sunday papers, he walked past the entrance to Goodwinter Boulevard and was appalled at the condition of the exclusive enclave. Food wrappers and beverage containers littered the pavement and sidewalks. Lawns had been trampled and the landscaped median was gouged by tires. Melinda had made no friends among her neighbors. It would be Monday before the city equipment could undertake the cleanup, and the cartage trucks were yet to come.

When Qwilleran picked up Polly for their dinner date that evening, she said, "For two days trucks will be backing into the Goodwinter driveway, running over curbs, ruining bushes, and knocking down stone planters."

"Why did the city let them do it?" he asked.

"In the first place, no one asked permission, I suppose, and even if they did, who would speak up against the estate of the revered Dr. Halifax? This is a small town, Qwill."

To reach Linguini's restaurant they drove north toward Mooseville, and Qwilleran was describing Scottish Night at Brodie's lodge when his voice trailed off in mid-sentence. They were passing the Dimsdale Diner, and he spotted a maroon car with a light-colored license plate in the parking lot.

"You were saying . . ." Polly prompted him.

"About the haggis . . . yes . . . It's not bad. In fact, it's pretty good if you like spicy concoctions. Even the cats liked it!"

The Italian trattoria in Mooseville was one of the county's few ethnic restaurants—a small mama-and-papa estab-
lishment in a storefront with a homemade sign. Mr.
Linguini cooked, and Mrs. Linguini waited on tables. There
were no murals of Capri or Venice, no strings of Italian
lights, no red-and-white checked tablecloths or candles
stuck in antique chianti bottles, no romantic mandolins on
the sound system—just good food, moderate prices, and
operatic recordings. Mr. Linguini had made the tables
from driftwood found on the beach, and they were covered
with serviceable plastic, but the napkins were cloth, and
diners could have an extra one to tie around the neck.
Qwilleran had chosen Linguini's because . . . well, that was
the surprise.

Mildred Hanstable was still living at her cottage on the
beach, so they stopped to pick her up, Arch Riker choosing
to meet them at the restaurant. There was a reason why he
wanted to drive his own car, Qwilleran suspected; they had
not been lifelong friends without developing a certain trans-
parency. The paunchy, ruddy-faced publisher was Mildred's
boss at the *Moose County Something,* for which she wrote
the food column, and when the three of them arrived, he
was already sitting at the four-stool bar sipping a tumbler
of Italian red. The opera of the evening was *Lucia di Lammermoor.*

Mrs. Linguini gave them the best of the eleven tables and
then stood staring at the four of them with one fist on her
hip. That was Linguini body language for "What do you
want from the bar?"

"What are you drinking tonight?" Qwilleran asked
Mildred.

"Whatever you're having," she said.

"One dry sherry, two white grape juice," he told Mrs.
Linguini, "and another of those for the gentleman."

Mildred said, "Dr. Melinda wants me to lose weight, so
I'm off alcohol for a while, and I'd like to ask you a personal question, Qwill, if you don't mind. When you first

went on the wagon, how did you feel about going to parties?"

"Well, all my partying was done at press clubs around the country—"

"And Qwill was a hell-raiser when he was young," Riker interrupted.

"When I first stopped drinking, I stayed away from press clubs and felt sorry for myself. That was phase one. In phase two, I found I could go to parties, drink club soda, and have a nice time. *Not a good time,* but a nice time . . . Now I realize that a good time depends on the company, the conversation, and the occasion—not a superficial high induced by a controlled substance."

"I'll drink to that!" said Riker.

There were no menu cards, and everyone in the restaurant had to eat what Mr. Linguini felt like cooking on that particular evening. Accordingly, when Mrs. Linguini brought the drinks, she also plumped down four baskets of raw vegetables and a dish of bubbling sauce kept hot over a burner. *"Bagna cauda!"* she announced. "You dip it. Verra nice."

Riker, a meat-and-potatoes man, looked askance at the vegetables, but when he tasted the anchovy and garlic sauce, he ate his whole basketful and some of Mildred's.

"Zuppa di fagioli!" Mrs. Linguini said when she brought the soup course. "Verra nice."

"Looks like bean," he observed.

"And now tell me about Scotland," Mildred requested. "Were you pleased with the tour?"

"Scotland is haunting and ingratiating," Qwilleran replied, "but when a tour guide is telling me what to look at, I don't absorb the scene as much as I do when I make my own discoveries."

"Hear! Hear!" said Riker.

"The four of us should go back there next year, rent a car, stay at bed-and-breakfasts, meet some Scots, and discover Scotland for ourselves. Of course, it's more work that way, and takes more time, and requires research."

The soup bowls having been removed, the pasta course appeared. Mrs. Linguini could hardly be said to serve; she delivered, banging the food on the table without ceremony. *"Tortellini quattro formaggi.* Verra nice."

"Four cheeses! There goes my diet," Polly complained.

"I adore tortellini," said Mildred, "even though they're known as bellybuttons. The legend is that they were inspired by Venus's navel."

"If you like legends," Polly told her, "you'll love Scotland! They have kelpies living in the lochs, ogres in haunted graveyards, and tiny fairies dressed in moss and seaweed who weave tartans from spiderwebs."

"We didn't see any," Riker said. "Probably went at the wrong time of year."

"How do you like tonight's pasta?" Qwilleran asked.

"Verra nice!" they chorused in three-part harmony.

Then Mildred wanted to know about the jewel theft, and they all pieced together the story, with Qwilleran concluding, "Scotland Yard is looking for the bus driver."

"Does anyone know why it's called Scotland Yard?"

No one knew, so Polly promised to look it up at the library the next day. Next they talked about the tag sale and Dr. Hal's secret hobby.

Riker said, "We're breaking the story on Monday's front page. The K Foundation is buying the whole collection for $100,000."

"Wonderful!" said Mildred. "Melinda needs the money."

"I wouldn't say she's hurting. I see her $45,000 car parked on the lot at Indian Village."

Qwilleran mused over his spaghetti as Mildred extolled the paintings. He wondered if the saintly Dr. Halifax had yet another secret in his life. Perhaps his monthly payments through a Lockmaster bank had not gone to his profligate son, else why would they continue after the young man's death? "Did either of you know the doctor's son?" he asked the two women.

"He never came into the library," Polly said.

"He wasn't in any of my classes," said Mildred, "but I

know he was a problem at school and a worry to his parents."

"And yet I suppose they gave him a big funeral and pulled out all the stops."

"No, just a memorial service in the home for the immediate family. His mother was bedridden, you know."

Skeptical as always, Qwilleran thought, Perhaps the car crash was no accident; it could have been planned. He remembered another such scandal in Pickax, involving a "good family." If such were the case, the doctor's payments were extortion money, going to a hired killer.

"Here she comes again," Riker mumbled.

The entrée was delivered. *"Polpettone alla bolognese!* Verra nice."

"It's meat loaf," he said after tasting it.

"But delicious! I'd love to take some home to Bootsie," Polly said.

That prompted Qwilleran to describe Koko's reaction to the Scottish tapes—how he responded to certain voices and certain sounds. Then Polly told how she liked to tease Bootsie when he was on her lap by reciting "Pickin' up paw paws, puttin' 'em in a basket." She said, "The implosive *P* tickles the sensitive hairs in his ears, and he protests."

"Now I'll tell one," Qwilleran said. "On one of my tapes, Lyle Compton tells about the Scottish psychopath who poisoned prostitutes in three countries. As soon as he mentions 'pink pills for pale prostitutes,' Koko protests forcibly, although the implosive *P* is coming from a recorder and can't possibly tickle his ears!"

"We all know that Koko is an extraordinary animal," Riker said mockingly. "He gives new meaning to the word 'cat' . . . Ye gods! Here comes dessert!"

"Zuccotto! Verra nice," said Mrs. Linguini.

As the overstuffed diners gazed at the concoction of cream, chocolate, and nuts, the coloratura aria coming from the speakers was the Mad Scene from *Lucia.*

"How appropriate!" Polly remarked.

Abruptly the music stopped, and diners at all the tables looked up as Mr. Linguini in long apron and floppy white hat burst through the kitchen door. Going down on one knee alongside Polly, he flung his arms wide and sang in a rich operatic baritone:

> "Hoppy borrrthday to you,
> "Hoppy borrrthday to you,
> "Hoppy borrrthday, cara mia,
> "Hoppy borrrthday to you!"

Everyone in the room applauded. Polly clasped her hands in delight and looked fondly at Qwilleran, and *Lucia di Lammermoor* resumed.

Mildred said, "No one told me it was your birthday, Polly. You must be a Virgo. That's why you're so modest and efficient and serene."

The evening ended with espresso, and with difficulty the party pushed themselves away from the table. Riker volunteered to drop Mildred off at her cottage, since it was right on his way to Indian Village. Uh-huh, Qwilleran mused; just what I expected.

He and Polly drove home in silence. She was a happy woman who had had too much food; he was purposely holding his tongue. He wanted to say, I still think your friend didn't die of natural causes; I suspect Melinda made an error in Irma's medication. But it was Polly's birthday, and he refrained from spoiling it with another conjecture. One should be able to say anything to a close friend, he reflected, and yet part of friendship was knowing what not to say and when not to say it, a bit of philosophy he had learned from recent experience.

When they turned into Goodwinter Boulevard, the old-fashioned streetlamps were shedding a ghastly light on the scene of Saturday's nightmare, and their car headlights exposed piles of litter in the gutter. As they approached the

Gage mansion and slowed to turn into the side drive, their headlights picked up something else that should not have been there: a car parked the wrong way, with a bearded man at the wheel.

"There he is again!" Polly screamed.

Fifteen

When Polly screamed, Qwilleran opened his car door and stepped out, facing the parked car.

"Don't!" she cried. "He may be dangerous!"

Immediately the other car went into reverse, then gunned forward, swerving around Qwilleran and narrowly missing his elbow. It headed for Main Street, traveling the wrong way in the westbound lane, traveling without lights.

"Let's get to the phone," Qwilleran said as he jumped back in the car and turned up the drive to the carriage house.

The patrol car responded at once, followed by the police chief himself, wrenched away from his Sunday night TV programs.

Qwilleran told Brodie, "This is the same prowler who was hanging around last June—the same M.O., the same beard—although he pulled the visor down when he found himself spotlighted. Last June you ran a check. He's Charles Edward Martin of Charlestown, Massachusetts."

"Did you get the number tonight?" Brodie asked.

"He drove away fast without lights, although I'd guess it was a light-colored plate—the kind we've seen before. His taillights didn't go on until he reached Main Street and turned right . . . I told you the car had been seen in Dimsdale, Mooseville, and Indian Village, and you made some quip about selling cemetery lots."

The chief's grunt was half recollection and half apology.
"Since we pried you out of your comfortable recliner,
Andy, would you take a cup of coffee? . . . Polly, do you
feel like brewing a pot?"

She was sitting on the sofa, hugging her cat and looking
upset. "Certainly," she said weakly and left the room.

In a lower voice Qwilleran said, "Why does this guy lie
in wait for Polly? I've told you my suspicions. Whoever this
creep is, he knows her connection with me, and he's plotting abduction. Believe me!" He massaged his moustache
vigorously. "Incidentally, he's the same guy I saw shoplift-
ing at the Goodwinter sale."

Brodie was not interested in coffee, but he gulped it,
promised full cooperation, and went home to catch the
eleven o'clock news.

Polly paced the floor nervously. "Why does he loiter
around here, Qwill?" She had the intelligence to know the
answer, and Qwilleran knew she was aware of the reason,
yet neither of them wanted to put it into words. Instead,
he assured her that three police agencies would be working
on it.

"But it will call for intensive vigilance on your part, Polly.
I don't want you going anywhere alone! I'll drive you to
and from work, take you shopping, deliver you to evening
meetings. It will be a bore for you, but it won't last long.
The police know exactly what they're looking for, and
they'll soon pick him up for questioning."

Qwilleran refused to abandon her until her equanimity
was restored, so it was late when he left the carriage house.
He almost forgot the birthday gift in the trunk of the car.
The sight of the blue gown and robe ensemble did much to
cheer her—or so she made it seem. It was unclear who was
trying to reassure whom.

The next morning, after driving Polly to the library, he
took his white car to Gippel's garage. "Give this crate the
once-over, will you?" he asked the head mechanic. "And
let me have a loaner for the day."

Gippel's loaners had decent engines, but the paint was dull, the fenders were bent, the springs were worn out, the interior was dirty, and the upholstery was torn—exactly the kind of vehicle Qwilleran wanted for a tour of Moose County. His first destination was Dimsdale, where his loaner looked quite normal in Shantytown. There was no maroon car there. Next he drove to Mooseville and checked the Shipwreck Tavern, the eatery called the Foo, and the shabby waterfront where he had once made the mistake of chartering a boat. From there he proceeded east along the lakeshore to the affluent resort area called Purple Point, which was completely deserted on a September Monday. Next came the village of Brrr, coldest spot in the county. Already it was in the throes of November winds from the northeast, and the scene was bleak. Even the parking lot of the Hotel Booze was empty, but Qwilleran went into the Black Bear Café to see Gary Pratt, the proprietor. With his shaggy hair and beard he resembled the mounted black bear at the entrance. Gary was puttering behind the bar.

"Where's everybody?" Qwilleran asked.

"It's early. They'll be in for burgers at noon. What brings you up here?" Automatically he poured a glass of Squunk water on the rocks.

"Just moseying around before snow falls. What kind of winter do you expect?"

"Lots of snow but an early thaw. I see by the paper that you went to Scotland. How'd you like it?"

"Nice country. Reminds me of Brrr. Did you do much sailing this summer?"

"Not as much as I'd like to. Business was too good."

"If you guys are going to promote tourism," Qwilleran said, "you can kiss your summer loafing goodbye . . . but then you can afford to go to Florida in the winter."

"That's not for me. I like winters up here. I'm into dog-sledding."

"Are you getting more out-of-state customers these days?"

"Yeah, quite a few."

"Have you run into a guy from Massachusetts called Charles Martin? Wears a beard like yours. Drives a maroon car."

"There was a bearded guy in here, trying to sell cameras and watches to my customers—obviously hot. I threw him out," Gary said.

Two other bartenders reported similar incidents. Otherwise, no one knew a Charles Martin. Qwilleran visited Sawdust City, North Kennebeck, Chipmunk, Trawnto, and Wildcat and drank a lot of Squunk water that day.

After returning the loaner he picked up Polly at the library and took her to dinner. Eight hours in the real world of the Dewey decimal system had helped her recover from the fright of the night before, but not from the dinner of the night before. All she wanted to eat, she said, was a simple salad and a bran muffin.

"What did you do all day?" she asked, as they settled in a booth at Lois's Luncheonette.

"Just cruised around, looking for ideas for my column. It was a good day to get out of the house because Mrs. Fulgrove was coming to clean and complain about cathair. I pay her extra for cathair, but she complains just the same."

Polly said, "I looked up the origin of Scotland Yard. It was an area in London with a palace for visiting Scottish kings in the twelfth century. It later became headquarters for the CID."

"Polly, you're the only person I know who follows through."

"That's what libraries are all about," she said with professional pride. "By the way, Gippel called to say the supplier sent the wrong part, so I won't have my car until Friday."

"You have a full-time volunteer chauffeur, so that's no problem," he said. At the same time he was thinking, If no car is parked at her carriage house, the prowler will wait for her to drive in; the police can set a trap. He made a mental note to pass this information along to Brodie.

Driving Polly home, he noted that the trucks were still carting purchases away from the Goodwinter mansion, and he pointed out the breakfront that the Comptons had bought. At her apartment he stayed just long enough for a piece of pie and then went home to feed the Siamese. The conscientious Mrs. Fulgrove was driving away as he pulled into the barnyard, and he waved to her; the woman's scowl indicated that she had worked overtime because of the vast amount of cathair *everywhere.*

He unlocked the back door, expecting to be welcomed by the usual clamor and waving tails, but the cats surprised him by their absence, and when he went to the kitchen to stow his car keys in the drawer, he was surprised to find it open—just enough for an adroit paw to reach in and hook a claw around a small brown velvet teddy bear.

"Oh-oh!" he said and went looking for Tiny Tim. All he found was a pair of debilitated animals lying on the rug in front of the sofa, apparently too weak to jump on the cushioned seat. They were stretched out on their sides, their eyes open but glazed, their tails flat on the floor. He felt them, and their noses were hot! Their fur was hot!

He rushed to the telephone and called the animal clinic, but it was closed. Anxiously he called Lori Bamba, who was so knowledgeable about cats.

"What's the trouble, Qwill?" she asked, responding to the alarm in his voice.

"The cats are sick! I think they've eaten foreign matter. What can I do? The vet's office is closed. Shouldn't they have their stomachs pumped out?"

"Do you know what they ate?"

"A stuffed toy, not much larger than a mouse. It was in a kitchen drawer, and I think Mrs. Fulgrove left it open."

"Was it catnip?"

"No, a miniature teddy bear. They act as if they're doped. Their fur is red hot!"

"Don't panic, Qwill," she said. "Did Mrs. Fulgrove use the laundry equipment?"

"She always puts sheets and towels through the washer."

"Well, the cats probably slept on top of the dryer until they were half-cooked. Our cats do that all the time—all five of them—and the house smells like hot fur."

"You don't think they would have eaten the teddy bear?"

"They may have chewed some of it, in which case they'll throw it up. I wouldn't worry if I were you."

"Thanks, Lori. You're a great comfort. Is Nick there? I'd like to have a word with him."

When her husband came on the line, Qwilleran reported the return of the Boulevard Prowler and his own scouting expedition around the county, adding, "None of the bartenders had heard of Charles Martin, so he might not be giving his right name—that is, if he gives any name at all. He's an unsociable cuss. Anyway, it would be interesting to know where he's holing up."

"I'll still put my money on Shantytown," Nick said. "Anyone can shack up there. Or if he thinks the police are after him, he could hide out in one of the abandoned mines. He could drive his car right into the shafthouse, and no one would ever know."

"Okay, we'll keep in touch. Would you and Lori like to see *Macbeth* on opening night? I'll leave a pair of tickets at the box office in your name."

"I know Lori would like it. I don't know much about Shakespeare, but I'm willing to give it a try."

"You'll like *Macbeth*, Nick. It has lots of violence."

"Don't tell me about violence! I get enough of that at work!"

Next, Qwilleran called Junior Goodwinter at home and said, "You left a message on my machine. What's on your mind?"

"I have news for you, Qwill. Grandma Gage is here from Florida to sign the house over to me. Are you still interested in renting?"

"Definitely." Now Qwilleran was even more eager to live on the property where Polly had her carriage house.

"It has a subterranean ballroom," Junior said to sweeten the deal.

"Just what I need! Can I move in before snow falls?"

"As soon as I have the title."

"Okay, Junior. Are you and Jody going to opening night?"

"Wouldn't miss it!"

By the time Qwilleran had changed into a warmup suit and had read a newsmagazine, the Siamese started coming back to life—yawning, stretching, grooming themselves, grooming each other, and making hungry noises.

"You scoundrels!" he said. "You gave me a fright! What did you do with Tiny Tim?"

Ignoring him, they walked to the feeding station and stared at the empty plate, as if to say, "Where's our grub?"

While Qwilleran was preparing their food, a loud and hostile yowl came from Koko's throat, and he jumped to the kitchen counter, where he could look out the window and stare into the blackness of the woods. Standing on his hind legs he was a long lean stretch of muscle and fur, with ears perked and tail stiffened into a question mark.

"What is it, old boy? What do you see out there?" Qwilleran asked.

There were lights bobbing between the trees—headlights coming slowly along the bumpy trail from the theatre parking lot. He checked his watch. It was the hour when the rehearsal would be over and Dwight would be dropping in for another confidential chat about his problem with Melinda. But why was Koko so unfriendly? He had shown no objection to Dwight on the previous visit, and it was not the first time he had seen mysterious, weaving lights in the woods. Qwilleran turned on the exterior lights.

"Oh, no!" he said. "You were right, Koko."

The floodlights illuminated a sleek, silvery sportscar, and Melinda was stepping out. He went to meet her—not to express hospitality but to steer her around to the front entrance. If she insisted on intruding, he wanted to keep it formal. He approached her and waited for her to speak, bracing himself for the usual brash salutation.

She surprised him. "Hello, Qwill," she said pleasantly.

"We just finished our first dress rehearsal. Dwight told me about your barn, and I couldn't wait another minute to see it."

"Come around to the front and make a grand entrance," he said coolly. It was the barn that was grand—not his visitor. She wore typical rehearsal clothes: tattered jeans and faded sweatshirt, with the arms of a shabby sweater tied about her shoulders. Her familiar scent perfumed the night air.

"I remember this orchard when we were kids," she said. "My brother and I used to ride up that trail on our bikes, looking for apples, but they were always wormy. Dad told us never to go into the barn; it was full of bats and rodents."

Opening the front door, he reached in and pressed a single switch that illuminated the entire interior with uplights and downlights, dramatizing balconies, catwalks, and beams.

"Oooooooh!" she exclaimed, which was what visitors usually said.

Qwilleran was aware that the Siamese had scampered up the ramps and disappeared without even waiting for their food.

"You could give great parties here," she said.

"I'm not much of a party giver; I simply like space, and the cats enjoy racing around overhead." He was trying to sound dull and uninteresting.

"Where are the little dears?"

"Probably on one of the balconies." He made no move to take her up the ramps for sightseeing.

Melinda was being unnaturally polite instead of wittily impudent. "The tapestries are gorgeous. Were they your idea?"

"No. Fran Brodie did all the furnishings . . . Would you care for . . . a glass of apple cider?"

"Sounds good." She dropped her shoulder bag on the floor and her sweater on a chair and curled up on a sofa.

When he brought the tray, she said, "Qwill, I want to thank you for buying my dad's paintings."

"Don't thank me. The K Foundation purchased them for exhibition."

"But you must have instigated the deal. At a hundred dollars apiece it came to $101,500. Foxy Fred would have sold them for a thousand dollars."

"It was Mildred Hanstable's idea. Being an artist, she saw their merit."

The conversation limped along. He could have sparked it with questions about the play, the tag sale, the clinic, and her life in Boston. He could have turned on a degree of affability, but that would only prolong the visit, and he hoped she would leave after a single glass of cider. She was being too nice, and he suspected her motive.

Melinda said, "I'm sorry I was a nuisance on the telephone last week, Qwill. I guess I was sloshed. Forgive me."

"Of course," he said. What else could he say?

"Do you ever think of the good times we had together? I remember that crazy dinner at Otto's Tasty Eats . . . and the picnic on the floor of my apartment when the only furniture I had was a bed . . . and the formal dinner with a butler and musicians. Whatever became of that pleasant Mrs. Cobb?"

"She died."

"Knowing you, Qwill, was the highlight of my entire life. Honestly! Too bad it had to be so short." She looked at him intently. "I thought you were the perfect man for me, and I still do."

Qwilleran's naturally mournful expression was noncommittal as he recalled his mother's sage advice: When there's nothing to say, don't say it. During his calculated silence Melinda gazed into her glass of cider, and he studied the framed zoological prints on the wall. At the end of the wordless hiatus he asked, "How did the dress rehearsal go tonight?"

She roused from her reverie. "Dwight said it was bad

enough to guarantee a good performance on opening night. Will you be there?"

"Yes, I always take a group of friends on opening night."

"Will you come backstage after the show?"

"Unfortunately," he said, "I'm reviewing it for the paper, and I'll have to rush home to my typewriter."

She glanced around the barn. "Why don't the cats come around? I'd love to see them before I go. I always adored little Yum Yum." As Qwilleran recalled, the two females ignored each other. "And I thought Koko was really smart, although I don't think he liked me."

Gratefully Qwilleran sensed that the end of her visit was in view, and to speed the departing guest he summoned the Siamese. "Treat!" he shouted toward the upper regions of the barn. The rumble of eight pounding paws was heard, and two furry bodies swooped neck-and-neck down the ramp to the kitchen. He explained to Melinda, "The T word always works, but I'm honor-bound to deliver, or the strategy loses its effectiveness. Excuse me a moment."

She took the opportunity to browse around, asking about the antique typecase that hung over his desk and remarking about the collection of Scottish tapes, labeled Day One, Day Two, etc. "I'd love to hear them sometime, and your kitchen is so grand, Qwill! Have you learned to cook?"

"No," he said without explanation or apology.

"I've become a pretty good cook. My specialty is Szechuan stir fry with cashews."

Koko polished off his five-eighths of the treat and left the room with purposeful step as if he knew exactly where he was going—and why. Yum Yum lingered, however, and allowed herself to be picked up and cuddled in Melinda's arms.

"Look at her gorgeous eyes! Isn't she a darling?"

"Yes, she's a nice cat."

"Well, I guess I'd better head for home. I have appointments all day tomorrow, starting at seven o'clock at the hospital. And then tomorrow night is the final dress rehearsal."

"Drive carefully," he said.

She picked up her shoulder bag and looked for her sweater. *"What's that?"* Her face wrinkled with disgust. Alongside her sweater was something brown and slimy.

"Sorry about that," Qwilleran said, gingerly removing the chewed remains of Tiny Tim. "Koko was presenting you with a parting gift—his favorite toy." Courteously he walked his uninvited guest to her car and said, "Break a leg Wednesday night!"

He watched the silver bullet wind through the woods and then returned to the barn. Koko was sitting on the coffee table, looking proud of himself; there were times when his whiskers seemed to be smiling. "You're an impertinent rascal," Qwilleran told him with admiration. "Now tell me why she came here tonight."

"Yow," said Koko.

Qwilleran tugged at his moustache. "It was not to see the barn . . . not to see you . . . not to talk about old times . . . What was her real motive?"

Sixteen

:::

The morning after the impromptu visit from Melinda, Qwilleran drove Polly to work. She said, "The trucks were still hauling things away until late last night, but thank goodness they're required to have everything out by tonight. It's been nerve-wracking. Bootsie is very unhappy."

After dropping her at the library, Qwilleran continued on to the police station to see if they had picked up a prowler suspect, but the normally quiet headquarters bristled with activity. Phones were busy; the computer was working overtime; officers were bustling in and out. Brodie, between phone calls, waved Qwilleran away and said, "Talk to you later."

Mystified by the unusual dismissal, Qwilleran backed out of the station and went to the office of the *Moose County Something*. Even the unflappable city room reflected the excitement of breaking news.

"What's happening at the police station?" he asked the managing editor.

"This'll floor you, Qwill," said Junior. "Roger just came from headquarters. You know all those trucks hauling stuff from the Goodwinter sale? One of them backed up to the Utley house last night and cleaned out all the teddy bears! They used the tag sale as a cover. Sounds like professionals from Down Below. By now the stuff is probably on a plane headed for California."

"Where were the women?"

"Still in Minneapolis."

"They had a watchman. Where was he?"

"Threatened at gunpoint and then tied up. His wife was visiting relatives in Kennebeck, came home late and found him bound and gagged."

Qwilleran said, "It would be interesting to know how they transported 1,862 teddy bears."

"They bagged them in leaf bags—those large black plastic ones. That's according to the caretaker."

"I wonder if they got Theodore. He was worth $80,000. No doubt the women had Ulysses and Ignace with them in Minneapolis. Doesn't it sound like an inside job, Junior? I'd question the caretaker. I'd find out if the local supermarkets had a run on black plastic leaf bags in the last few days. Have you talked to Grace Utley?"

"Roger tracked her down in Minneapolis. She's furious, and her sister is under a doctor's care. They're not coming back. They're going to live down there and sell their house, so we'll have one more haunted house on the street. They should change the name to Halloween Boulevard."

A brief bulletin about the theft appeared in the Tuesday paper, ending with the usual statement: "Police are investigating."

Qwilleran spent Tuesday and Wednesday writing copy for his column, when not chauffeuring Polly or helping out at the box office. The house was sold out for opening night, and there was a great ferment of anticipation in Pickax; everyone who was not in the cast knew someone who was. Comments from ticket purchasers were varied: "Dr. Melinda is playing the female lead . . . The director is a new man in town, unmarried . . . That funny Derek Cuttlebrink is in the show."

As Qwilleran and Polly drove to the theatre on opening night, he said, "I think we'll like what Dwight has done with this play. For one thing, he's cut out Hecate's long, boring scene."

"Good decision," she agreed. "It wasn't written by Shakespeare anyway."

Excited and well-attired townfolk were gathering under the marquee of the theatre and milling about the lobby, where the Bonnie Scots photographs were on exhibit. It was a big occasion in a small town, an occasion for dressing up. Polly wore her dinner dress and pearls; Qwilleran wore his suit. When they took their seats in row five on the aisle, Jennifer Olson's family was already there—all ten of them—and Grandma Olson kept waving her program at occupants of surrounding seats and saying, "My granddaughter is in the play!"

The house lights dimmed, and after a moment of breathless silence the haunting notes of a tin whistle filled the theatre—no melody, just sounds from another world.

Polly whispered, "It gives me shivers."

There were rumblings of thunder and flashes of lightning, and three shadowy, gray, ugly creatures whished onto the dimly lighted stage, their bodies bent in half, their voices cackling, *"When shall we three meet again?"* One looked like a cat, another like a toad. *"Fair is foul, and foul is fair!"*

The mood was set, and the story unfolded with the entrance of the king and his sons, the report from the bleeding captain, and praise for brave Macbeth. Then the tin whistle again chilled the audience, and the three witches sidled on stage to celebrate their evil achievements, dancing in an unholy circle as drumbeats were heard off stage. *"A drum, a drum! Macbeth doth come!"*

A murmur rippled through the audience when Larry made his entrance, proclaiming in his great voice, *"So foul and fair a day I have not seen."* Two scenes later, when Melinda entered as Lady Macbeth, the audience gasped at her costume—sweeping robes of what looked like fur, and a jeweled wimple. When she began her monologue, however, Qwilleran and Polly exchanged brief glances; her delivery lacked energy. Still, act one kept the audience on the edge of their seats: the king murdered by Macbeth . . . the two grooms murdered as a cover-up . . . alarm bells and bloody daggers. There was a moment's comic relief when Derek Cuttlebrink telescoped his youth and height into the arthritic shape of an ancient porter. *"Knock, knock, knock! Who's there?"* At intermission it was the French fry chef from the Old Stone Mill who was the topic of conversation in the lobby.

When Qwilleran spoke to the Comptons, Lyle said, "I think *Macbeth* was written for bumper stickers: *What's done is done! . . . Out, out, brief candle . . . Lay on, Macduff!*"

Lisa said, "Qwill, how do you like Melinda. I think she's dragging."

Her husband agreed. "The sleepwalking scene is supposed to come in act two. She played it in act one."

Most of the audience, while waiting for flashing lights to signal them back into their seats, spoke of other things, as small-town audiences do: "Hey, what did you think about the teddy bear heist?" . . . "Everybody on Goodwinter Boulevard is blowing their stack after that sale!"

Nick and Lori Bamba were there, and Nick whispered something in Qwilleran's ear that he remembered later.

In the second act the weird music accompanied the witches' dance around the cauldron. *"Thrice the brinded cat hath mew'd!"* Macbeth, suffering from strange diseases and seeing ghosts, was going mad. Lady Macbeth walked in her sleep, plagued by visions of bloody hands. *"Out, damned spot! Out, I say!"* To make matters worse, their castle was besieged by an army of ten thousand soldiers.

While waiting for his favorite line—*Tomorrow, and tomorrow, and tomorrow, creeps in this petty pace from day to day*—Qwilleran began to feel uncomfortable. He found himself staring at the stage without seeing it. Then a chilling shriek of women's voices came from the wings. He

214 *Lilian Jackson Braun*

clapped his hand to his moustache and half rose from his seat, whispering to Polly. "Tell Arch to drive you home!" A second later he was walking quickly up the aisle.

On the stage, Macbeth was saying, *"Wherefore was that cry?"* And an attendant replied, *"The Queen, my lord, is dead!"*

Neither line was heard by Qwilleran. He was running across the theatre parking lot to his car. He drove through the woods at the rear, and as he approached the barn, he could see the long orchard trail and red taillights receding at the far end of it.

The barn's automatic lights were on, indoors and out, but he beamed his headlights on the rear entrance and found the glass panel in the door shattered. Jumping out of his car he hurried into the kitchen. The first thing he saw was blood on the earthen tile floor. "Koko!" he shouted.

The cat was sitting on top of the refrigerator, methodically licking his paws with toes spread wide and claws extended. For one moment, Qwilleran thought he had attacked the intruder and driven him away. Yet, there was too much blood for ordinary cat scratches. More likely the housebreaker suffered gashes from broken glass. He phoned the police from the kitchen, and the patrol car reported immediately, with the state police not far behind. A B&E at the Qwilleran barn had top priority.

By the time they arrived, he had assessed the damage: "Broken window, forced entry, two items missing," he reported. "One is a combination radio and cassette player. The other is a carrying case of cassettes—all spoken tapes from my trip to Scotland plus interviews conducted around Moose County. The tapes would be of no value to anyone, unless he wanted to suppress the material contained, and that's highly unlikely."

Or is it? he wondered, almost at the same moment.

One of the officers said, "They thought it was country music or rock. Cassettes are like candy to the kids."

"You think it was a juvenile break-in?" Qwilleran asked. "It happened just before I arrived home. I saw a car leaving through the orchard and turning right on Trevelyan. Either I interrupted them, or they had taken what they came for. The equipment was on my desk, visible through the windows. The interior lights came on automatically at dusk."

"You should keep the shades pulled when you go out," the officer advised. "Lotta nice stuff here."

"I guess you're right. What's happening to Pickax? Petty thieves . . . master burglars . . . prowlers . . ."

"The town's growing. New people coming in. We were on TV last week."

Koko was watching the police stoically from the top of the refrigerator, and one of them, feeling eyes boring into the back of his head, turned suddenly and asked, "Is that the cat Brodie talks about?"

As soon as they were off the premises, however, Koko's cool behavior changed. He uttered a loud wail from the pit of his stomach, ending in a falsetto shriek.

"For God's sake! What's that about?" Qwilleran gasped. And then he shouted in alarm, *"Where's Yum Yum?"*

She had a dozen secret hiding places and was known to evaporate when strangers came to the house.

"TREAT!" Qwilleran shouted and then listened for the soft thumps meaning a cat had jumped down from a perch. There was a hollow silence.

"TREAT!" His voice reverberated among the beams and balconies, but there was no soft patter of bounding feet. Even Koko was ignoring the irresistible T word; he sat on the refrigerator as if petrified.

Qwilleran peeled off his coat and tie, grabbed a high-powered flashlight from the broom closet, and raced to the upper level to begin a frantic search of every known hiding place, every crevice in the radiating beams, under and over every piece of furniture, inside every drawer and closet . . . all the while calling her name.

He didn't see the headlights approaching the barn

through the woods, but he heard the pounding on what remained of the back door. Looking over the balcony railing, he saw Nick and Lori Bamba wandering inquisitively into the kitchen.

"Is this blood on the floor?" Nick was asking.

"What's wrong with Koko?" Lori was saying.

As Qwilleran walked down the ramp, flashlight in hand, Nick called up to him, "I picked up the B&E on my police band when we left the theatre. How bad is it?"

Qwilleran could hardly force himself to say what he was thinking. "It looks . . . as if . . . they've stolen Yum Yum."

"Stolen Yum Yum!" they echoed in shocked unison.

"The police were here, and I reported the theft of a radio and cassettes. I didn't know then that she was missing. I've searched everywhere. I'm convinced she's gone. There's an emptiness when she's not here." He stooped and picked up a stray emery board and snapped it in two. "Koko knows something's radically wrong. He knows she's gone."

"Why would they take her?" Lori wondered.

That was something Qwilleran preferred not to contemplate. He walked aimlessly back and forth, pounding his moustache.

Nick headed for the phone. "I'm going to call the police again."

Qwilleran and the cat on the refrigerator had been staring at each other. "One minute, Nick!" he said. "At the theatre you mentioned you'd seen the prowler again."

"Yes, today. His car was parked outside the Dimsdale Diner, so I went in and sat at the counter next to this bearded guy. The cook called him Chuck. I talked about fishing and baseball, but he didn't respond. I got the impression he wasn't tightly wound, or else he was stoned. I'm sure he hangs out in Shantytown."

"Let's go out there," Qwilleran said impulsively, reaching for a jacket.

"D'you think he's the one who broke in?"

"I'm getting ideas. Everything's beginning to mesh." He combed his moustache vigorously with his fingertips.

"Okay. We'll take my car. It's got everything we need."

Qwilleran said, "Lori, talk to Koko. He's acting like a zombie."

The road north from Pickax ran straight, and Nick drove fast. At Ittibittiwassee Road he turned left into the wooded slum, the car bouncing slowly along the rutted road between the trees, the headlights picking up glimpses of shacks and junk vehicles.

"If his car isn't here," Nick said, "we'll try the site of the old mine."

At the mention of the abandoned mine, and all it implied, Qwilleran felt nausea in the pit of his stomach. "There it is! That's the car!" he said.

Nick turned off his lights and parked in a patch of weeds behind a junk truck. "If he's the right one, I can radio the police."

"How shall we work this?"

"I'll get him to open up. You stand back out of sight, Qwill, until I get my foot in the door."

"Let me go first."

"No. Your moustache is too well known. Hand me the gun from the glove compartment, in case he gives us any trouble."

"Easy with the car door," Qwilleran said, as they stepped out into the weeds.

The maroon car was pulled up to a ramshackle travel trailer with a dim light showing through the small window. A radio was playing. By approaching the window obliquely, the two men could see parts of the interior while avoiding the meagre spill of light into the yard. They saw a heavily bearded man lying on a cot, fully clothed, taking swigs from a pint bottle. Although the face was hairy, red gashes could be seen on the forehead. Another gash crusted with dried blood trailed from the corner of one eye, which was swollen shut.

Qwilleran thought, To get those wounds from glass, he'd have to go through the door headfirst; he was clawed! He whispered to Nick, "I can see my radio and cassettes in there."

They crept forward. Then Nick banged on the door and called out in a friendly voice, "Hey, Chuck! I've got some burgers and beer from the diner!" After a slight delay, the door opened cautiously. It opened outward, and Nick yanked it all the way. "Jeez, man! Wha' happened? You been in a fight—or what?"

"Who're you?" the bearded man mumbled.

"You know me—Harry from the diner." Both men barged through the door as the fellow stepped back uncertainly.

"You're cops!"

"Hell, no! I'm Harry, don't you remember? This is my uncle Bob."

There was a foul odor in the littered trailer, also a large collection of electronic equipment, also a silver pocketknife alongside a small sink.

"Wotcha doin' here?"

"Just wanna warn you, Chuck. The cops are on your tail. You gotta get out of here."

"Where's the beer?"

Qwilleran said with avuncular concern, "Forget the beer, son. You need a doctor . . . Harry, can we take him to a doctor? . . . Yes, son, you could lose an eye if you don't have it taken care of fast. Where'd you get those bloody gashes?"

"Uh . . . in the woods," was his fuzzy-minded reply.

"You must have been attacked by a wildcat! You can get blood poisoning from something like that. We've got to get you to the hospital for a shot, son, or you're dead! Was it a wildcat? . . . *Or was it a housecat?*" Qwilleran gave it a threatening emphasis.

The wounded man looked at him suspiciously.

Qwilleran, who had been sniffing the fetid air of the trailer like a connoisseur, suddenly bellowed, "TREAT!"

"NOW!" came a piercing shriek from behind a small closed door.

He yanked it open. It was a closet-size toilet, and Yum Yum was perched precariously on the rim. She was wet. She had slipped into the rusty bowl.

Ripping off his jacket, he wrapped it around her, crooning reassurances in her ear. "Take her to the car," he said to Nick, "and stay with her. You know what to do. I want to talk to Chuck for a minute."

Yum Yum knew Nick, and she was purring as he carried her from the trailer. As an afterthought, he took the gun from his pocket and laid it on the sink.

Casually picking it up, Qwilleran said, "Sit down, son. You look sick. The poison's getting into your bloodstream. I want to give you some advice before the police get here. They're going to ask a lot of questions, and you'd better be ready with some good answers."

The fellow sat down on the cot, looking bewildered.

"Where did you get all these radios and cameras?" Qwilleran began. "Where did you get that pocketknife? What brought you here from Massachusetts? Do you know someone in Pickax? Do you have a partner here? Why did you break into my barn and take my cat? Did you think I'd pay a lot of money to get her back? Who told you I had a valuable cat? Was it your partner's idea? What was your name before you changed it to Charles Edward Martin?"

Headlights and flashing blue lights were approaching through the woods.

"Here comes the popcorn machine! Better tell the police the whole truth, or you'll be in bad trouble. And tell them the name of your partner, or they'll throw the book at you, and your partner will go scot-free . . . Here they are! And now, if you don't mind, I'll take my radio and cassettes."

On the way back to town, Qwilleran held Yum Yum tightly. Only her nose projected from the enfolding jacket as she looked up with trusting eyes and contemplated his moustache. He said, "That guy's not very sharp. He has the instincts of a criminal, I think, but not the capabilities."

"He's punch-drunk," Nick said, "from booze or drugs or both. I've seen a lot of 'em. What I don't understand—how did he manage to grab Yum Yum? She's always leery of strangers."

Qwilleran was not ready to tell the whole story as he perceived it, not even to Nick. He said, "She likes beards. She's a pushover for anything resembling a brush. I think he broke in primarily to abduct one of the cats for ransom. After he had grabbed her and taken her out to the car, he came back for the radio he'd seen on my desk. That's when Koko sprang on his head from the top of the refrigerator and drew blood."

"Mmmmmmmmmm," Yum Yum murmured.

"Yes, sweetheart, we'll soon be home, and you can have a bath."

Nick said, "How did you know she was in that john?"

"The pervading stink in that place had a distinct overtone of cat—nervous cat! I know it well! And there were cat hairs everywhere. I can imagine her flying around that trailer, shedding hair like a snowstorm and finally seeking refuge in that foul closet. My poor little sweetheart!"

Before the Bambas left the apple barn that night, Lori gave Yum Yum a bath, and Qwilleran supplied warm towels, while Nick nailed something over the broken window in the door.

"I feel guilty about keeping you people out so late," Qwilleran said. "Do you have a baby-sitter?"

"Nick's mother is staying overnight," Lori said. "Thank God for mothers-in-law!"

"How could you be so sure, Qwill, that Yum Yum's kidnapper was the Boulevard Prowler?" Nick asked.

"Just a hunch." Qwilleran pounded his moustache with his fist.

After they had gone, he still had to write a review of the play for the Thursday paper, but the Siamese needed comforting, so he touched a match to the combustibles in the fireplace and made a lap for them. Both cats climbed aboard, Yum Yum sinking like a lead weight with her chin on his wrist. Even Koko, who was not a lap-sitter, huddled close to his ribcage.

Only then could he think objectively. He could visualize the headline in the next day's paper: *Goodwinter Heir Alive and in Jail.* He tried to recall when he had first suspected the Boulevard Prowler to be Dr. Hal's son. Absurd though it might seem, it was Yum Yum's cache of emery boards that steered his mind in that direction. Someone had told him—Carol Lanspeak, he thought—that Melinda's brother was named Emory. Emory spelled with an O was a fairly common name in the Pickax phone book. Every time Qwilleran found a stray emery board on the floor, his mind went to the stray son who was killed in a car crash . . . Then the old gentleman at the Senior Care Facility had talked about the doctor's monthly payments. Emory wasn't Moose County's first remittance man; local historians wrote that wealthy families had often deported undesirable members to areas Down Below to avoid embarrassment to the family name. As for the payments continuing after Emory's death, Qwilleran could invent several explanations but accepted the most credible: Emory was still alive . . . A few days later he met the bearded suspect at the preview of the Goodwinter sale, lingering over a table of family memorabilia: old LP recordings, a much-used piggy bank, the doctor's monogrammed pocketknife, a photo in a silver frame. Upon talking to him, Qwilleran realized that the beard disguised a long narrow face, known in Moose County as the Goodwinter face.

Then, Qwilleran tried to recall, when did I first suspect he had a partner?

The fellow could carry off a solo operation like pilfering a silver pocketknife. And, being a native of Moose County, he would know the best time to break into the Purple Point cottages. But he wasn't smart enough to plot a kidnapping;

that was obvious. Furthermore, having lived Down Below for a decade or so, how would he know about Qwilleran's wealth and his relationship with Polly? How would he know about the renovated barn in the orchard and Qwilleran's obsessive concern for his pets? How did he know that Qwilleran would be attending the play on Wednesday night?

When it had become clear to him that the prowler was the resurrected Emory Goodwinter, all the questions were answered, including, "What was the maroon jalopy doing in the elite Indian Village?" and "Why did Melinda drop in so sociably after the rehearsal Monday night, and why was she working so hard to be sweet?"

She dropped in, Qwilleran now believed, to case the premises, and he had played right into her hands, giving her the T word and demonstrating how it worked. He mentally kicked himself, thinking, God, what a fool I was! He remembered her interest in the Scottish tapes, which she probably instructed Emory to grab—just in case they contained information that might be incriminating.

The blaze in the fireplace burned out, and Qwilleran carried the Siamese to their loft apartment, limp with sleep, and wrote his review of *Macbeth*.

Seventeen

As the Siamese and the rest of Pickax slept, Qwilleran wrote his review of *Macbeth,* praising Larry and being kind to Melinda. Kindness, he had learned, was a large consideration in writing drama criticism for a small town. To maintain some semblance of integrity, however, he expressed his opinion that it was redundant to project the image of a dagger on the back wall of the stage when Macbeth said, *"Is this a dagger which I see before me?"* He wrote, "It distracts audience attention from Shakespeare's great words, although modern grammarians—with their rules about whiches and thats—may be uncomfortable with the famous line."

Convinced that his review was sufficiently charitable, he retired for the night, taking care to set his alarm clock. He had to drive Polly to the library the next morning. Even though the Boulevard Prowler had been apprehended, her car was still at Gippel's garage, awaiting a rebuilt carburetor.

"I was concerned about your sudden exit last night," she said when he called for her, "but Arch said it was a bit of theatricality indulged in by drama critics."

"There's an element of truth in that," he replied evasively. "I'll tell you the whole story when we both have more time. Meanwhile, I'd like you to do me a favor—with no ifs, ands, or buts. Yours not to reason why! Just do it!"

"Well!" she said warily. "Is it so very terrible?"

"Ask your sister-in-law to sneak a look at Irma's medical records in the clinic office. I'm curious about her heart condition and the prescribed medication."

"You're like a dog with a bone, Qwill; you simply won't let go of the matter. I'm not sure it would be ethical, but I'll ask her at church Sunday."

"Ask her today. Phone her and take her to lunch at Lois's. Charge it to me . . . But don't eat too much," he added to lighten the serious aspect of his request.

"I'm overwhelmed by your generosity!"

"Are you going to the women's banquet tonight? I'll take you there and pick you up, and you can tell me her reaction. If it's unethical, ask her to do it anyway. I won't tell."

"Under protest, dear," she sighed as she stepped out of the car.

"Have a nice day. Issue lots of new-reader cards!"

From there he drove to the *Moose County Something* to hand in his breathlessly awaited copy, and Arch Riker beckoned him into his private office. "Man, have we got a story!" said the publisher, waving a galley proof. "It's set up in type and ready to go, and we'll break it as soon as your burglar is arraigned. Is this why you ran out of the theatre last night? You must have some kind of burglar alarm implanted under your skin! Or did Koko alert you via mental wireless?" Riker never missed a chance to make a mocking reference to the cat's remarkable abilities, which were beyond his understanding. He handed over the galley:

BREAK-IN EXPOSES
GOODWINTER HOAX

A suspect has been charged with breaking into the Pickax residence of James Qwilleran Wednesday night, bringing to light a six-year-old hoax. The suspect, Charles Edward Martin of Charlestown, MA, is in fact

Emory Goodwinter, allegedly killed six years ago in a car crash on the New Jersey Turnpike. Records show his name was legally changed at that time. He is the son of the late Dr. Halifax Goodwinter.

Articles stolen from the Qwilleran residence have been retrieved. The cost of damage is not yet known. Stolen articles in the suspect's possession have been identified as those taken from Purple Point cottages in the last week, total value $7,500. Loitering and shoplifting charges also have been brought.

The suspect is a police prisoner at the Pickax Hospital, where he is being held for treatment of injuries incurred during Wednesday night's break-in.

Qwilleran taunted Riker in return by saying scornfully, "Is that all the information you were able to get?"

"Why? Do you know something we don't?"

"Plenty!" he said, looking wise.

Junior appeared in the doorway. "How'd you like my headline, Qwill? I hated to do that to cousin Melinda, but this is the biggest news since VanBrook. We've been trying to reach her for further details. Can't find her. Emory had a police record before he left town, so the burglaries won't surprise her."

Uh-huh, Qwilleran thought.

"He was running with a gang of vandals from Chipmunk while he was still in high school. The big surprise was to find him alive after his father insisted for six years that he was dead. Do you think she was a party to the hoax, or an innocent dupe like the rest of us?"

Riker said, "Do you have something you want to tell your old buddies, Qwill?"

"Not yet." He had no desire to relive the painful moments of Yum Yum's abduction. As for the identity of Emory's partner, that was something for Emory to disclose. "See you later!" he said with a debonair wave intended to confound them. He was eager to talk to the police chief.

Brodie hailed him as soon as he crossed the threshold at headquarters. "I see you're gonna get your name in the paper again!"

"You should be thanking me for doing your work!" Qwilleran retorted.

"How'd you find him?"

"Nick Bamba, who has an eye like an eagle, had tracked the Boulevard Prowler to the Dimsdale area, and I'd already decided he was Emory. When he broke in and kidnapped my female cat—"

"What! You didn't report anything like that!"

"I didn't know it when I gave the report to the officers. As soon as I learned she was missing, Nick and I found Emory in Shantytown, rescued her, and radioed you. Did Emory identify his accomplice?"

The chief looked at him sharply. "You know about that?"

"I knew he had to have an accomplice, and Melinda was the only person who qualified. Her behavior has been irrational ever since she returned from Boston. Some of us suspect drugs."

"I'm glad the good doctor isn't alive to face this mess. It'd kill him!"

"What are you going to do about her?" Qwilleran asked.

"That'll be up to the prosecutor . . . If you ask me, there was bad blood on her mother's side."

"I assume Emory answered questions cooperatively."

"Best damned suspect we've ever had! Answered questions before we asked 'em. His sister knew about the hoax; they were in touch all the time she was in Boston, and after Dr. Hal died, she sent Emory money once a month. He didn't come for his dad's funeral last June; he came expecting to collect his inheritance in instant cash. When that didn't work out, Melinda told him another way to get rich quick: Get rid of Mrs. Duncan."

So that was the plot! Qwilleran realized in horror. Murder, not ransom!

His expression caused Brodie to say, "Sit down. Have a cup of coffee."

Qwilleran took his advice. "Melinda had always wanted to marry into the Klingenschoen fortune. She hounded me all summer and halfway across Scotland. Last Sunday, Emory again failed to grab Polly, as you know. The next night, Melinda showed up at the barn after rehearsal, and she was playing America's Sweetheart, without the curls. I couldn't fathom her motive. Now I know. She was plotting with Emory to kidnap one of my cats! For ransom! That woman needs help!"

After his visit with Brodie he stopped at the drug store to buy a few items and chat with the pharmacist, a young man more congenial than the crabby old pill counter who used to be on duty in the prescription cage. Then he went home to brush the cats. Only then did he realize what it would have been like to lose Yum Yum—not to have her pawing his pant leg, reaching up for his moustache, and croodling—worse still, not to know her whereabouts or her fate. Koko himself had not fully recovered from the trauma of the night before; he prowled incessantly and muttered to himself.

"Shall we listen to some tapes?" Qwilleran asked, and Koko ran to the desk, yowling with anticipation. Either he had added "tape" to his vocabulary or he was reading Qwilleran's mind. Of the tapes recorded before Melinda left Scotland, one segment in particular caught Koko's attention—a brief exchange between Polly and Melinda:

"I didn't know she had a bad heart. She never mentioned her symptoms, and we were the best of friends."

"She was too proud to admit to any frailty—and too independent to take my advice or even medication. It could have saved her."

Qwilleran thought, If Irma refused to take medication, there would be no prescription to foul up; we'll know more about this when Polly's sister-in-law checks Irma's records.

Farther along on the same tape were the voices of, first, the Lanspeaks and then the MacWhannells:

"Do you realize, folks, how lucky we are to have Melinda along on this trip?"

"Irma was coming down with something at the castle today. I told Larry it sounded like laryngitis."

"I knew someone who dropped dead of a sore throat. It's a freak disease—some kind of syndrome."

"Daddy, you suspected something was wrong last night, didn't you?"

"You're right, Mother . . . It so happened we were playing a table game with Polly and Dwight, and I went upstairs to get a sweater for Glenda. We had room No. One, and the girls had Nine and Eleven at the end of the hall. I saw Melinda come out of Eleven and scoot right into her own room. I started to speak to her, but she was preoccupied. I told Glenda right then that Irma must be ill."

Qwilleran thought, Yes, but . . . Irma was out on the moor with Bruce and came in late, according to Polly, so Eleven was empty, because Polly was in the lounge.

"Yow!" said Koko, who seemed to enjoy MacWhannell's chesty voice.

The time came to drive Polly to the Distinguished Women's banquet in the New Pickax Hotel, an event subsidized by XYZ Enterprises with proceeds going to the Pickax Hospital for an intensive care unit. She looked stunning in her blue batwing cape and peacock feather brooch, and he told her so. She wanted to know more about the burglar and the hoax, but he assured her that everything had been reported in the newspaper. The loitering charge, he said, indicated that Emory was the Boulevard Prowler.

After dropping her off, he went to the theatre to have another look at *Macbeth*. He wanted to see if the actors felt more comfortable in their roles and whether Dwight had taken his advice about the dagger. Aware that he could not stay for the entire performance, he slipped into an unsold seat in the back row.

The lights dimmed, and an unwelcome voice came through the speakers—the anonymous voice that announces changes in the cast, usually to everyone's disappointment. "In tonight's performance the role of Lady Macbeth will be played by Jennifer Olson, and the role of Lady Macduff will be played by Carol Lanspeak. Thank you."

There were murmurs in the audience and at least one squeal of delight from some friend of Jennifer's. To Qwilleran the substitution raised an urgent question, and at intermission he went backstage to hunt down Dwight Somers. "Where's Melinda?" he asked.

"I don't know," said the director. "When she didn't report by seven-fifteen, I called her clinic, and the answering machine said they were closed until nine tomorrow morning. Then I called her apartment; no answer. We both live in the Village, you know, and there's an elderly neighbor who knows everything that goes on. I phoned her, and she said that Melinda's car had been in and out of the parking lot all day, but now it was gone again. I even called the police about a possible accident. Nothing! So I decided to go ahead with Jennifer. How's she doing?"

"Not bad, under the circumstances."

"I heard about Melinda's brother. She must be really upset. That's the only reason I can imagine why she wouldn't show, but she should have notified us."

The stage manager was calling "Five minutes," and Qwilleran returned to the auditorium. He stayed through the sleepwalking scene, then slipped out. The banquet would be over.

When he picked up his passenger, she was carrying a large flat box. "I received an award for public service," she said. "It's a very tasteful plaque."

"Congratulations! Recognition is long overdue," he assured her. "What did they serve for dinner? Not chicken cordon bleu, I hope."

"No, some other kind of chicken. It wasn't bad. Of course, the sole topic of conversation was the return of Emory Goodwinter."

"Naturally. How many awards were presented?"

"Ten. It was a tearful moment when Mrs. Hasselrich accepted Irma's posthumous award for volunteerism. Melinda received the health-care award, and a hospital official accepted it, since Melinda had to be at the theatre."

"Correction. She was not at the theatre," Qwilleran said. "Her role was filled by the Olson girl."

"Oh, dear!" Polly said sympathetically. "Melinda must be devastated by the unpleasant publicity!"

"Mmmm," he agreed without conviction. "Who else won a plaque?"

"Oh, let me tell you the sensation of the evening," she said, laughing. "Lori Bamba, as secretary of the auxiliary, was the presenter, and she was wearing a batwing cape just like mine, but in violet. When Fran Brodie went up for the arts award, she had the same thing in green! Mildred Hanstable received the education award, and she was wearing one in royal blue. Finally, Hixie Rice had it in taupe. We stood on the platform in a row looking like a malapropos chorus line—tall, short, plump, thin—but all with batwing capes and peacock brooches! The whole room was in a screaming uproar that simply wouldn't stop until the hotel manager rang the fire bell."

"It just proves," Qwilleran said, "that I know a lot of distinguished women."

Polly invited him up to her apartment for coffee and cake, and they were welcomed by Bootsie, who had the brassy voice of a trumpet.

"How's old Gaspard?" Qwilleran greeted him.

"Really, Qwill, you treat him with such disrespect," she complained.

"He treats me with disrespect. I think he's jealous."

"I think you're jealous, dear." She started the coffee brewing and cut a large wedge of chocolate cake for him and a sliver for herself.

After the first few bites he asked casually, "How did your sister-in-law feel about my request?"

"She said it was highly irregular, but she agreed to bring Irma's records to me at the banquet, provided she could return them early in the morning."

"And?"

"Tonight she informed me that the folder has been removed from the filing cabinet."

"Perhaps they have a special drawer for deceased patients."

"They do, but it was neither there nor in the active file. Why are you interested, Qwill?"

"Just curious . . . Did Mrs. Hasselrich ever mention any disagreement about Irma's funeral?"

"Good heavens, no!"

"She was buried, but Melinda said she wanted to be cremated. How come no one else knew Irma favored cremation?"

"Qwill, dear, I'm afraid to ask what's on your mind."

"Nothing. Just talking off the top of my head. Is there any more cake?"

"Of course. And may I fill your cup?"

After a period of silence, which his hostess attributed to gustatory bliss, he said, "They say vitamin C is good for fighting colds. What kind did you take to Scotland?"

"High-potency capsules, but they were too large for me to swallow comfortably."

"Want me to take them off your hands?"

"I'm afraid I didn't keep them, but you can buy them at the drug store," Polly said. "Irma was complaining of a sore throat, so I offered them to her."

"Did she take them?"

"I don't know. I left them in the bathroom for her and

never saw them again. Do you think you're catching cold, dear?"

"I have a slight cough." He coughed slightly. "This is very good cake. Did you make it?"

"I wish I had time to bake. No, I bought it at Toodle's . . . By the way, you didn't tell me how well the Olson girl performed."

"She was scared stiff, but she knew her lines. She'll be better tomorrow night if Melinda doesn't make it." He noticed Polly glancing at her watch. "Well, I'll pick you up tomorrow morning, same time. . . . *What's that?*"

They heard sirens speeding down the boulevard, and they caught glimpses of flashing lights.

"Sounds like an accident," he said, moving toward the door like the veteran reporter that he was. "I'll go and check . . . See you tomorrow!" He ran down the stairs, jogged the length of the driveway, and found neighbors standing on porches and looking westward. Walking rapidly toward the end of the street, he met a couple standing on the sidewalk—the city attorney and his wife.

"We were just coming home," said the woman, "and this car was speeding down the boulevard. There was a terrible crash."

"Going eighty, at least," her husband added. "The driver must have been crocked. Obviously didn't know this is a dead-end street, although it's posted."

"Here comes the sheriff's wagon," Qwilleran said. "They've got to cut someone out of the wreckage." He hurried toward the scene of the accident. Police floodlights were beamed on the small park, the granite monument, and the car crumpled against it.

Running back to his car, he drove home to call the newspaper. He could hear the phone ringing as he unlocked the door, and he caught it before Riker hung up.

"Qwill, I'm phoning from a gas station. If you can rustle up some Scotch, I'll be right there—with some breaking news."

"Come on over," Qwilleran said. "I've got news, too."

Within minutes, Riker walked in, his ruddy face unusually flushed, and he was beaming. The drink was waiting for him, and the two men took their glasses to the lounge area. "What do you think about Mildred Hanstable?" the publisher asked.

"Nice woman."

"She doesn't like living alone, and neither do I. We get along very well. What do you think?"

"I'd like to see you two get together," Qwilleran said with sincerity. "It would be good for both of you."

"Amanda was only a divertissement."

"That's a good word for her. Mildred is more your type."

"Glad to have your blessing, Qwill . . . Now what's your news?"

"A suicidal car crash!"

"Who?"

"Melinda. I recognized the silver bullet she drives. She raced it down Goodwinter Boulevard and rammed it into the Goodwinter monument at the end of the street. She may have been drinking; she may have been stoned. Whatever, I'm positive it was intentional. She grew up on the boulevard; she knew it's a dead end with a speed limit of thirty-five."

"Let me use your phone." Riker tipped off the night desk in his newsroom, then said, "Any idea of the motive, Qwill? Don't tell me she died for love of you, old chum!"

"I don't kid myself that it was anything like that. No, she had personal problems. Lady Macbeth was a metaphor for what was happening in her own life, in my opinion." He declined to divulge the rest of the story to the press, even though Riker was his best friend. If he discussed it with anyone, it would be with Brodie.

The next morning, the opportunity presented itself. The only person in Moose County who would dare to phone Qwilleran before eight A.M. was the police chief. He seemed to take sadistic pleasure in rousting his slow-starting friend out of bed.

"Rise and shine!" Brodie shouted into the phone. "It's daylight in the mines! I'm on my way over to see you."

Groaning and spluttering a few comments, Qwilleran pulled on some clothes, ran a wet comb through his hair, and started the coffeemaker.

In short order the chief strode into the barn, looking bigger than ever as the importance of his mission added to his stature. "Weel, laddie," he greeted his reluctant host in familiar Scots style, "the dead is risen and the mighty is fallen! Did you hear about Dr. Melinda?"

"I heard, and I saw. I was on the boulevard when the ambulance arrived. How about some coffee?"

"Tell you what, pour half a cup and fill it up with hot water, and I'll be able to drink it without having a stroke . . . Got some more news, too. They picked up your bus driver in London, but the loot was smuggled out of Scotland—gone to chop shops on the continent. He admitted the theft but not the murder. Do you still think he drugged her?"

"No, I think Melinda was responsible for Irma's death. It was guilt that drove her over the edge."

"Hmmm, interesting notion," Brodie mused. "She left a suicide note in her apartment that didn't make much sense—all about the smell of blood and a damned spot she could never wash out."

"Those were her lines in the play. It's a confession of murder."

"What did she have against Irma?"

"It was an accident, but she lied to cover up, saying Irma died of natural causes. She wanted the body cremated to conceal the evidence. Then it appears that she destroyed Irma's medical records. No doubt they'd indicate that Irma did not have a heart condition."

"Did you figure this out yourself? Or did your smart cat stick his nose in the case?"

"Andy, you wouldn't believe what he's been doing!"

"I'll believe anything after what Lieutenant Hames told me Down Below."

"First, Koko let out a bloodcurdling howl at the exact moment Irma died in Scotland, and he wasn't even there! Then he shredded her obituary—another indication that something was wrong—and kept pointing his paw at Melinda. He threw a fit when he heard her voice on tape and also destroyed photographs of her. There's something else remarkable, too. Let me play you a tape if I can find it."

Koko, having heard his name, came ambling out from nowhere and stationed himself between the recorder and the police chief, with an ear cocked in each direction.

Fast-forwarding the tape, Qwilleran picked up fragments of his own voice: "another historic inn. I suspect . . . hundreds of pictures on this trip . . . medical school at Glasgow . . ." He said, "Okay, Andy. Listen to this:

". . . the infamous Dr. Cream was a Glaswegian. He was the nineteenth-century psychopath who became a serial killer in England, Canada, and the United States—not as legendary as Jack the Ripper but noted for pink pills . . ."

Koko interrupted with a stern "Yow-w-w" like a yodel, and Qwilleran snapped off the recorder, saying, "Now let me play another tape recorded on the eve of Irma's death, when Melinda came to my room, uninvited." After a few stops and starts, the following dialogue was heard:

". . . So I'll make you a proposition—since one has to be conventional in Moose County. If you will marry me, you can have your freedom at the end of three years, and our children will resume the name of Goodwinter. We might even have a go-o-od time together."

"You're out of your mind."

"The second reason is . . . I'm broke! All I'm inheriting from my dad is obligations and an obsolete mansion."

"The K Foundation can help you over the rough spots. They're committed to promoting health care in the community."

"I don't want institutional support. I want you!"

"To put it bluntly, Melinda, the answer is *no!*"

"Why don't you think about it? Let the idea gel for a while?"

"Let me tell you something, and this is final. If I marry anyone, it will be Polly. Now, if you'll excuse me . . ."

Qwilleran pressed the stop button, relieving Koko's anguish. He had accompanied the dialogue with a coloratura obbligato particular to Siamese vocal cords.

"On this same evening," Qwilleran told Brodie, "while Polly and Irma were occupied elsewhere, Melinda was seen going into their empty room. It's my theory that she tampered with some vitamin capsules that Polly had taken to Scotland, substituting a drug that would stop the heart. I checked with our pharmacist here, and he said it could be done—in several ways. Melinda didn't realize that Polly had stopped taking the vitamins and had turned them over to Irma, who was catching cold. Inadvertently, Melinda killed one of her best friends."

Brodie grunted a wary acceptance of the story, but Qwilleran had not finished. From a desk drawer he produced a small bottle, uncapped it, and poured a few capsules into the palm of his hand. "These are similar to the vitamins Polly took to Scotland. They're pink, Andy! Pink pills!"

The chief shook his head. "The rest of Koko's shenanigans I'm willing to buy, but this . . . I don't know. It's a little hard to swallow."

"Lieutenant Hames would swallow it."

"That he would! Hook, line, and sinker!" He stood up and groped in his pockets. "I'm forgetting what I came here

for . . . Here! This is for you." He handed over a square
envelope with Qwilleran's name in a familiar handwriting.
"It was in Melinda's apartment along with the suicide note.
I've got to get back to the station."

Glancing at the envelope with a mixture of curiosity and
dread, Qwilleran dropped it on his desk while he accompanied Brodie to the police car parked at the back door,
and after the chief had driven away with a wave of the
hand, he walked around the barn three times before going
indoors. He was in no hurry to read Melinda's last missive.
No matter what the gist of it—remorse, apology, passion-
ate outburst, or bitter accusation—it would be painful
reading.

As he walked he pondered Koko's incredible involvement
in the case. There was no knowing how much of it was
coincidence, how much was serendipity, and how much
was his own imagination. The cat's tactics in revealing clues
ranged from the significant to the purely farcical. Even
Qwilleran had to admit that the pink-pill business was farfetched. So was Koko's sniffing of the spot on the rug, as
if he knew Shakespeare and, more particularly, *Macbeth*.

And then he thought, I owe Irma an apology. She was a
wonderful woman—unapproachable, perhaps, and annoy-
ingly private, but she had her reasons, and she did a tre-
mendous amount of good for the community. She went out
on the moor with Bruce every night to try to straighten him
out, the way Katie wanted her to do. It didn't work.

Suddenly he remembered he had to drive Polly to work.
But first he would read Melinda's farewell note, his curiosity having overcome his apprehension. He let himself in
the front door, and the moment he stepped into the foyer
he sensed complications. He experienced that oh-oh feeling
that always swept over him when bad news was impend-
ing—when a cat had thrown up on the white rug, or had
broken a tray of glasses, or had stolen the shrimp Newburgh. There was a guilty stillness in the place.

Slowly he moved through the foyer, looking to left and

right. In the lounge area his experienced gaze skimmed every surface, every corner, in search of disaster. In the kitchen, scene of many a catly crime, everything was in order. Then he turned toward the area where he had his desk and telephone, his bookshelves and comfortable reading chair. There, on the desktop and the floor beneath, was a shower of confetti. Minute scraps of paper, some of them chewed into tiny wads, were all that remained of Melinda's note.

"Koko!" he shouted. "You did this, dammit! You fiend!" Qwilleran glanced quickly around. "Where the devil are you?"

Yum Yum was on top of the fireplace cube, looking down on the scene like an innocent bystander, sitting on her brisket, her whiskers upturned as if smiling . . . but Koko wasn't there.